D0179049

THE PAINTING

Alison Booth

Red Door

'Trust dies but mistrust blossoms'

Sophocles

Other fiction titles by Alison Booth:

Stillwater Creek
The Indigo Sky
A Distant Land
A Perfect Marriage
The Philosopher's Daughters

Praise for Alison Booth's novels

THE PAINTING

'Deceptively simple, deeply human, *The Painting* lights the shadows of dispossession in Hungarian immigrant lives in Australia through art and romance, meat and menace, totalitarianism, provenance and Pest.' Tom Flood, author of *Oceana Fine*

'An enthralling and intelligently-plotted novel whose lead characters are drawn with such depth they could be sitting on the sofa beside you. Their lives are movingly woven together by the painting that means something quite different to each of them.' Ann McGrath, historian and author of *Illicit Love*

'*The Painting* by Alison Booth offers a compelling and incisive portrait of Anika — a wise and wary exile from an oppressive regime — as she struggles to regain her trust in humanity.' Michelle Wildgen, author of *Bread and Butter*

THE PHILOSOPHER'S DAUGHTERS

'[T]his lively novel… is a page-turner in the best sense: a story that causes us to emotionally invest in and care for the futures of two appealing and interesting protagonists… Booth's rendering of the land… makes this story sing… and many of her descriptions deftly combine a sensual beauty with informative detail.' *Newtown Review of Books*

'Wonderfully evocative... *The Philosopher's Daughters* deals with large issues of race and gender while keeping the focus on the two main characters and their relationships. There is enough drama here to keep the reader engaged to the last page.' *The Canberra Times*

'A delicately handled historical drama with a theme of finding self, both in relationships and art.' Tom Flood, author of *Oceana Fine*

'A lyrical tale of wild frontier Australia. Evocative, insightful, thought-provoking.' Karen Viggers, author of *The Lightkeeper's Wife*

'Booth is superb at the small detail that creates a life, and the large one that gives it meaning.' Marion Halligan, author of *Lovers' Knots: A Hundred-Year Novel*

A PERFECT MARRIAGE

'With crystal-clear prose and an artful warmth, Alison Booth leads us into the heart of contemporary human relationships, exposing tough – and necessary – truths. Very moving.' Nigel Featherstone, author of *Bodies of Men*

'With an intricate plaiting of past and present that both tantalises and beguiles, this novel is a poignant account of a marriage that is not what its title suggests.' Marion Halligan, author of *Lovers' Knots: A Hundred-Year Novel*

'Alison Booth captures the magnificence of female friendships and the tragedy of a disastrous marriage in a narrative that has the most satisfying of conclusions, hope.' Nicole Alexander, best-selling author

'This cleverly structured book begins and ends with the same dead body, starting at the morgue and ending, ten years later, at the cemetery. In between Alison Booth uses the slow reveal to develop and build up her portrait of a young, bad marriage.' *Sydney Morning Herald*

STILLWATER CREEK

A mythical town and its people are brought beautifully to life... a really lovely book.' *Sunday Telegraph*

'A finely observed historical drama... evocative and eminently readable.' *The Age*

'A story that lingers long in the imagination.' Debra Adelaide, author of *The Household Guide to Dying*

'Who could not be charmed by *Stillwater Creek*? I loved the characters, the scenery, the dramas, the gentle humour and the sense of Australia as it once was.' *Good Reading*

THE INDIGO SKY

'A charming, big-hearted tale, told with skill and grace.' *Madison*

'This charming follow-up... captures the heart and soul of a time... you can practically smell the eucalyptus, and picture that titular indigo sky.' *Bookseller & Publisher*

'Alison Booth's distinctive characters live in Jingera, a small fictional town on the coast of NSW... Booth puts steel into the charm by addressing the harsher realities of the times.' *The Age*

A DISTANT LAND

'*A Distant Land* is part thriller, part romance, and... I found myself engrossed in the drama of Zidra's investigation into corruption in internal security and of the aftermath of Jim's South-East Asian ordeal, all the way to the final page.' *The Canberra Times*

'*A Distant Land* is a moving story of love set against the backdrop of the Vietnam War.' *Aussie Reviews*

Published by RedDoor
www.reddoorpress.co.uk

© 2021 Alison Booth

The right of Alison Booth to be identified as author of this Work has
been asserted by her in accordance with sections 77 and 78 of the
Copyright, Designs and Patents Act 1988

ISBN 978-1-913062-65-1

All rights reserved. No part of this publication may be reproduced,
stored in a retrieval system, copied in any form or by any means,
electronic, mechanical, photocopying, recording or otherwise
transmitted without written permission from the author

A CIP catalogue record for this book is available from the British
Library

Cover design: Emily Courdelle

Typesetting: Jen Parker, Fuzzy Flamingo
www.fuzzyflamingo.co.uk

Printed and bound in Denmark by Nørhaven

PART I

Sydney, March 1989

Chapter 1

Aunt Tabilla was banging about downstairs, rattling crockery and crashing saucepan lids like cymbals, an early morning concerto that only Anika could hear. Reluctantly she threw off the bedcovers, stumbled to the bathroom and confronted her green-tinged reflection in the pitiless mirror. After splashing her freckled face with water and finger-combing her sleep-mussed hair, she was ready to greet the day.

'Good morning, Aunt Tabilla.' In the kitchen Anika had to shout over the rat-a-tat-tat of cutlery landing in the drawer. The open back door framed the view of a narrow brick path leading to the disused outhouse. Beyond the paling fence at the end of the yard, terraced houses stepped down the hill like rows of dominoes waiting to be knocked down. In the distance were the curves of the Glebe Island wheat silos and, above it all, the already-brilliant cobalt sky of another hot March day.

'I can hear you,' Tabilla said. 'No need to bellow.' Her face might have been ordinary if it wasn't for her smile that made dimples appear by her mouth and crows' feet radiate out from the corner of each eye. This gave her the lively look of someone who laughed a lot, although she didn't. Yet somehow the rarity of her smiles and the asymmetry of the dimples made her expression irresistible and Anika found herself smiling whenever she did.

And Tabilla was smiling now as she jabbed with her forefinger at the *Sydney Morning Herald* that was spread across the kitchen table. It was open at the arts pages and an advertisement ringed with a black felt-tip pen. Before giving Anika a chance to read it, she explained that on the first Wednesday of every month the Art Gallery of New South Wales invited people to bring in their artworks to learn if they were genuine or forgeries.

'That's next week,' Tabilla said. The date – Wednesday 7th March 1989 – had been twice underlined. 'Now you can find out if the picture you have is something worth taking care of.'

'Of course it's worth taking care of. But it's really your painting.'

'It's yours, Anika,' Tabilla said. 'I gave it to you, remember?'

When Anika's father had said she was to take the portrait with her the day she left Hungary, he'd explained that it belonged to Tabilla, or more precisely, to Tabilla's husband, who'd died years before. After Anika arrived in Sydney, Tabilla had refused to accept it; she said it brought back too many sad memories. Besides – Anika had quickly learned that Tabilla was fond of her 'besides' – she'd been without it since 1956 so she could manage without it now, and anyway, she'd never liked it much. Mawkish pictures of women with badly fitting dresses falling off their shoulders weren't her thing, she was a dressmaker after all. But she was happy that Anika loved it.

Her aunt was ever magnanimous, Anika knew, but if the portrait of the auburn-haired woman turned out to be worth something, maybe she would talk to Tabilla about selling it. Even with Anika's study-allowance and cheap board at Tabilla's house, she found it a struggle to make ends meet. It had been a struggle ever since she'd given up hairdressing and become a part-time university student with a part-time draughting job that could go belly-up at any time, interest rates were that high.

Yet there was so much emotional baggage attached, limpet-like, to that portrait of the auburn-haired woman.

Anika loved having her on the wall at the foot of her bed; she loved waking up to see her reflecting the morning light and her own radiance – that glow that the artist had captured with so many small brushstrokes laden with colour. The woman in the portrait reminded Anika of home; that particular afternoon when she'd left Budapest. That afternoon when her father, watched closely by her grandmother Nyenye, had thrust the painting into her hands, and later into the bottom of her suitcase where it had fitted perfectly. Now it was her legacy from Tabilla, and she couldn't ever think of getting rid of it, could she? Still, she would love to learn who the artist was; the signature at the bottom of the picture was nothing more than an illegible scribble.

Tabilla ripped out the advertisement from the paper and handed it to Anika. 'I'd love to know more about it too,' she said.

'I'm happy to go,' Anika said. And she was, although she knew from Tabilla's expression that she had no choice in the matter.

* * *

In the city centre, Anika alighted from the bus and walked towards Macquarie Street. It was already hot and her shirt was beginning to stick to her back, and even her parcel containing the portrait felt warm. She hurried on to the green oasis of the Domain and the dense shade of the Moreton Bay fig trees.

On the far side of the park was the art gallery. Its entrance was a classical Greek temple stuck on to high sandstone walls so blank they might have hidden a prison. Bronze men on horseback stood guard at the front. Too early, Anika perched in some shade on the sandstone steps, still deliciously cool, and waited for the gallery to open.

5

'Assessments are downstairs,' the cloakroom attendant told her when she was finally admitted. A wafer-thin man, he had trouble understanding her, though she enunciated impeccably, sounding out every consonant and paying attention to her vowels. He told her to unwrap her package and leave the paper and cardboard with him. When she bent over to pick up the string that had fallen on to the floor, she caught him peering down the front of her shirt.

The escalator led to a basement, where there was an empty space and a long counter with nobody behind it. After a couple of seconds, a large man strode across from the bottom of the escalator. He was built like an athlete, the sort who lifts weights and swims competitively. Standing next to her, he said, 'Are you the queue?'

'A queue of one.'

'Of two now.' While the skin under his eyes was like crumpled tissue paper, the overall impression was of boyishness. 'What are you here for?'

'Same as you, probably,' she said, smiling. 'Is that a painting?'

'My mother persuaded me to bring it in for her.' The bright blue shirt he was wearing exactly matched his eyes. 'She's convinced it's by Elioth Gruner. My name's Jonno, by the way.'

Anika was about to ask who Elioth Gruner was when a kind-faced, elderly woman joined them. Although out of breath, she immediately began to talk but it was impossible for Anika to make out any of the words. Closely watching her lips didn't help. It could have been another language she was speaking, though Jonno seemed to understand what she was saying.

Anika drifted into a reverie, broken only by the appearance of a curator behind the counter. Apart from his golden skin, he was all in black. Black shirt and black trousers, black hair, and eyes so dark it was impossible to distinguish iris from pupil. Of medium height, he was so even-featured he might have been formed on an assembly line. The expression on his face was far from welcoming, she thought: his nose was raised in the air the better to look down on her.

Suddenly nervous, or perhaps it was his unfriendliness that upset her, she said, 'I'm sorry I interrupted your tea break. There's a crumb or something on your top lip.'

This disconcerted him; this removed the supercilious expression from his face. From his trouser pocket, he pulled out a red handkerchief neatly ironed into a small square. When he shook it, the creases took a moment or two to unfold. In the meantime, he rubbed at his mouth with the back of his other hand.

'It's gone now,' Anika told him when the hanky was unfurled. She switched on her best smile as she carefully lifted the picture on to the surface of the counter. The painting looked small. Its forty six by thirty-eight centimetres were dwarfed by the expanse of counter – or perhaps desk better described the furniture on which so posh a person was about to rest his elbows.

'Do you have any idea of who painted it?' The curator's voice was baritone, and as smooth as velvet.

'No.'

'Where are you from?' He might have been addressing the glowing woman of the portrait, with her abundant auburn hair and pale skin, and the blue dress slipping off one luminous shoulder.

'I'm Australian. Like you.'

When he grinned, he seemed like a different person but he kept his eyes on the painting. He lifted it up and held it so close to his face that he might have been counting the brushstrokes. 'Remarkable.' He was now muttering more to himself than to her. 'I think I know who did this but I want to get my colleague to take a look. Wait here, I'll be back in a minute.'

He returned with a woman whose shiny silver hair was held back from her face with a couple of tortoiseshell combs. Her black linen shift dress looked expensive and the silver choker too heavy for her slender neck. When she saw the painting, she peered at it for a bit through orange-rimmed, half-moon spectacles, before beaming at Anika. 'This is a beauty,' she said. 'You were right, Daniel. It's by Antoine Rocheteau, a French Impressionist.'

Anika felt her face flushing with pride, and the room seemed to grow bigger, as if it were expanding to contain all the new prospects that were opening up. 'French?' In times of stress her accent tended to falter. She heard herself saying, 'Painting is Hungarian. Dat's vat I believe.'

'It's not Hungarian.' The woman's tone was emphatic. 'Rocheteau has a very distinctive style. Just look at the blue of the woman's dress. It's reflecting the tiniest brushstrokes of colours from adjacent areas. And look at the white of her shoulder, it's hardly white at all but many different hues.'

'The hair too,' Mr Black Eyes said.

They were right, Anika thought. From a distance the woman's hair did indeed look red but close up you could see that its colour came from tiny strokes of crimson and orange and yellow ochre, with undertones of brown. Around the hairline, there were contrasting shadings of blue and green that were borrowed from the dress and the way the light fell.

'Probably it was painted in the early 1900s,' the woman curator told Anika. 'Where did you get it from?'

'It was my uncle's.'

'Do you know its provenance?' When the curator saw

Anika's blank face, she added, 'Any details about where it came from and its ownership history. You'll need that, as proof of ownership and to prove it's not a forgery.'

'My grandmother said that a friend gave it to my Uncle Tomas.' Anika struggled to remember what Nyenye had told her that afternoon in Budapest. At the time, she'd been more preoccupied with wondering if she might be stopped at passport control with a painting in her suitcase than trying to commit to memory her grandmother's words. After a brief pause, she added, 'Apparently the friend didn't like it much but Tomas loved it.'

'Do you know where the friend got it from?'

'I think my grandmother said he bought it from the Hungarian state auction house. I'm not sure when though. My uncle died in 1956 so it must have been sometime before that.'

'Does your grandmother know any more than that?'

'Not that I'm aware of.' The picture had been one of the many hanging in Nyenye's flat. Anika's euphoria shrank a bit, for her family didn't speak about the paintings and no one apart from family ever saw any of them. The room in which they hung was dark and gloomy, though when the lights were switched on the pictures glowed and Anika could never see enough of them. But Nyenye didn't let anyone who wasn't family beyond the entrance hall. Families kept to themselves, everyone in Budapest knew that, and Anika and her brother Miklos had grown up avoiding questions. But Anika thought that her father didn't much like Nyenye's collection. Probably he preferred still-life artworks and she had none of those. Or maybe he thought that all the paintings would be better off in a museum. Anika was guessing though, for she never really knew what he was thinking.

The elegant curator scrutinised Anika over the top of her

spectacles. 'Make sure you keep it out of direct sunlight,' she said. 'And do try to track down its provenance. If it belonged to your uncle, someone in your family must know where it came from.'

'I'll try to find out. Do you know its worth?' Anika coughed to clear her throat.

'I can't comment on that. We don't do valuations.'

'I know a few art dealers,' said Mr Black Eyes. 'I could introduce you.'

'Don't let him race off with you,' the silver-haired woman said, smiling to show that she thought this was unlikely.

After Anika thanked her for her help, she said, 'Not a problem.' Anika filed this away for Aunt Tabilla, who hated this expression. Once she learned that gallery curators used the term she might become a convert. *Not a problem, Tabilla. Not a problem.*

'Perhaps you'll give me your phone number.' Mr Black Eyes was Anika's best buddy now he'd learned she was related to a discerning art collector. She was happy with this transformation; he was very handsome in his even-featured sort of way and she wouldn't mind seeing him again, especially now he'd shown he could be useful as well as decorative. He handed her a pen and notepad, and she wrote down Tabilla's number. When she gave it back, he asked for her name.

'Anika Molnar.' She watched him form the letters. His fingers were long and the nails square-cut and very clean. His hands looked younger than his face, as if he had never done with them anything more arduous than turning pages of books and making notes in his elegant slanting script.

'I'm Daniel Rubinstein,' he said, fixing her with his dark eyes. 'We've got lots of Impressionist paintings in our collection. I especially love the Sydney School ones. Those beach scenes and views of Mosman Bay.'

Suddenly she warmed to him. She loved those paintings too: all that golden light and the undeveloped foreshore and those brilliant colours that made your soul sing.

'They're a bit earlier than your Antoine Rocheteau though. I'll be in touch, Anika.'

There was now a string of people waiting behind Jonno and the kind-faced woman. As Anika headed towards the escalator, Jonno winked at her and the woman smiled. The perving attendant had gone from the cloakroom; Anika collected her wrapping materials from a beaming woman who wished her a good day as she handed over the tatty bundle. A good day? This was an understatement. So far it couldn't have been better. Anika was feeling as light as a balloon and as fortunate as if she'd just won the lottery.

Outside, she sat to one side of the top step to rewrap the parcel. The sunlight was too bright and the glare hurt her eyes but she barely noticed as she grappled with the bubble wrap and brown paper. A party of school girls, in green-and-white checked uniforms and panama hats, chattered past her, oblivious of their shushing teachers.

Tenderly Anika refastened the string around the wrapping paper and thought of her family in Budapest. They still didn't know that Tabilla had insisted she keep the painting, and she wondered what they would think about her taking it to the gallery. If only she could phone to let them know the painting was a Rocheteau.

But that was not possible, and of course it was her fault their line was tapped. Four years since she'd jumped Hungary after that trouble about the Danube Bend, and still the secret police were listening to their phone calls.

Chapter 2

'I thought you'd gone.' Jonno was standing on the gallery steps next to where she was sitting. 'Let me buy you a coffee to celebrate.'

'To celebrate? Did you have good news?'

'Not really. The painting I brought in is just a copy. My mother will be disappointed. She'd hoped it might be valuable.'

He didn't look as if he came from a background where money was scarce. It was in the way he spoke, the way he looked. There were some tiny golden hairs below one cheekbone that he'd missed when shaving and they glinted in the sunlight. At that precise moment Anika remembered the name of the man Nyenye told her had given the painting to her uncle: it was Sebestyén Tinódi, who'd got it from the consignment store or auction house. Anika secured the string around her package with a double bow and decided it was too late to go back into the gallery and let the curators know and anyway, there was no reason why it would mean anything to them.

'There's a café over the road that's open.' Jonno gestured to the low building in the Domain opposite. Surrounded by a canopy of Moreton Bay fig trees, it looked cool and inviting.

'I didn't get a chance to see your painting,' he said, when they were sitting on the café terrace, with the Rocheteau on the spare chair.

She thought of her mother's advice. View life like a game of cards; always put on a mask before you begin to play and never let anyone know what's going on behind it.

Jonno continued, 'The lady behind me was absorbing most of my attention. But I did hear that it was by a French Impressionist.'

Surreptitiously Anika felt for the picture, secure in its wrapping. What was the English phrase for an unexpected positive outcome? A windfall. She looped the fingers of one hand through the string of her package and decided that Jonno's comment didn't need a response.

After a brief pause, he said, 'Do you have any more paintings like that?'

'This is all I've got.'

'Did someone give you the painting?'

'Yes, my parents.' This was easier than explaining that it had belonged to her uncle whose widow didn't want it.

'They're generous people.'

'Yes, they are.' Anika's words emerged in a sad tone that she hadn't intended. 'They're wonderful people.'

'I'm sorry. I didn't mean to upset you.'

'You didn't. I just miss them a lot sometimes. They live in Budapest.'

'Behind the Iron Curtain.'

'We write quite often. And sometimes we talk.'

'Speaking on the phone isn't the same as seeing someone,' Jonno said.

'That's true. You miss out on all those other messages.'

'Those things that the face and the eyes show. Do you know that saying about the eyes being the windows into the soul? You know, when you look at someone and feel you've made a connection.'

'I haven't heard that expression before but I know what you mean.' Anika stared at the grass rather than meet his eyes.

'Where do you live?'

'Rozelle.'

'I live in Kings Cross but I've got a friend in Rozelle, a mate I went to uni with. He lives in Reynolds Street.'

'Rozelle's a nice suburb. A little like a village, with good transport too. I live not far from Victoria Road so there are lots of buses to hop on to.'

'Must be a bit noisy there though.'

'It's not too bad. It's a terraced house with thick stone walls.'

'There aren't that many stone houses there.' He smiled as if to show he was teasing her. 'What street?'

Anika chose to ignore this question. She said, 'It's my aunt's house.' Over the time she'd been living with Tabilla she'd discovered this was a useful turnoff for men who were trying to chat her up.

'You're living with your aunt? I put you down as the independent type sharing with a bunch of friends.' His tone was flirtatious.

'I'm a student.' For some reason she added that she was mature age, and he laughed. Her cheeks began to feel hot; she blushed too easily. The abrupt movement of her hand knocked her water glass over and water spilled out on to the table top. They each made a grab for their paintings first and the paper napkins afterwards.

'Take these.'

It was Mr Black Eyes – Daniel, she should say – standing next to their table and holding in one hand a bunch of paper napkins and in the other hand a takeaway coffee.

'We don't need them,' Jonno said at the same moment that Anika thanked Daniel and used the napkins to mop up the last of the water.

Daniel pulled out his wallet as if he were going to shout them both another coffee to celebrate his timely arrival. It turned out not to be bank notes that he was removing but a business card. When Anika took it, Jonno glowered, miffed for some reason that she did not understand.

Daniel looked pleased with himself though. 'Ring me,' he said. 'The home number's best. I wrote it on the back of the card.'

After nodding to them both, he strode off towards the gallery. He was taller than he'd looked when he was standing behind the curator's counter.

The business card was in a tasteful font, Garamond perhaps, and Anika ran her fingers over the embossed lettering: *Daniel Rubinstein, Curator, Art Gallery of New South Wales.* It showed his office telephone number but no home number. She turned over the card and found that her fingers, still damp from the mop-up, had smudged the writing and she couldn't make out the digits. The regret she felt was irrational; she had his office number after all.

'Are you going to call him?'

'Probably.'

'About a valuation?'

'He knows some art dealers.'

'What about me, will you call me if I give you my number?'

'Why would I do that?' Her answer sounded rather rude, so she added, 'You don't have anyone doing valuations in your family, do you?'

'I can evaluate essays,' he said, laughing. 'And beautiful women too.'

This statement made Anika cringe. Then he did that staring-into-her-eyes thing, as if trying to use her eyes as a portal to her soul when she suspected it was really her body that he'd like to get his hands on.

The waitress brought the bill. Jonno squinted at it before taking out a pair of glasses with tortoiseshell frames. Anika preferred the new look, it was much more intellectual than

15

that blonde-headed surfer-boy appearance. But he took them off again once he'd read the bill and they stood up together.

'Would you like to meet up for a drink or dinner next Friday?'

'Possibly but I haven't got my diary with me.' Anika sometimes spent Friday evenings with fellow-architecture students at the Hero of Waterloo, an old sandstone pub in The Rocks area. But if she declined right away Jonno might suggest another day and she wanted to have time to think. 'Give me your phone number,' she said.

'*Don't call me, I'll call you*. I get it.' But he found a scrap of paper in his jacket pocket and scribbled a number on it.

After stowing it in a pocket, she thanked him for the coffee and headed off along the path bordering the gallery side of the Domain. Jonno asked too many questions, she thought, and it was a relief to get away.

Before she had reached the bus stop, Jonno had been driven out of her head by thoughts of the portrait of the beautiful auburn-haired lady. The day seemed to expand around her and she started to feel lighter, as if she were shedding weight, losing density, and filling with buoyant gas – helium perhaps – that lifted her above the pavement of this sun-drenched city, which began to vibrate with possibilities. Passing a council bin, she pulled out the scrap of paper Jonno had given her and dropped it into the bin.

Chapter 3

Anika got home that evening to find that her aunt had cooked chicken paprikash for dinner. The smell of it made Anika feel slightly homesick, for it was a dish her mother was passionate about and one that she made for special occasions – and today had been a special occasion – always with paprika from the Kalocsa region of Hungary. Anika could almost hear her mother saying, in her low and husky voice, how incomparable those paprika were, how rich their flavour and colour.

Tabilla was surprised when Anika told her, over the chicken paprikash, that the picture was by a well-known French Impressionist. 'Who could have guessed?' she said. 'It meant a lot to Tomas but I always thought the painting wasn't up to much.'

Interrupted by her aunt's frequent questions, Anika explained what had happened at the gallery. When she'd finished, Tabilla said, 'I wonder what it's worth.'

That was one of the things Anika had been thinking about ever since her visit to the gallery. She said, 'It hasn't been valued yet. If it's valuable I'll give it back to you.'

'I don't want it. How many times do I have to tell you? It's yours.' Tabilla lightly smacked Anika's hand.

Anika smiled with what she knew was relief. The painting felt like a part of her. Now she noticed that a gentle breeze was wafting through the open doorway, making the heat more tolerable, and carrying with it the faint sweet scent from some vine that Tabilla was cultivating. She said slowly, 'I'm not altogether sure I want to know its value. I'm never going to sell it. Never ever.'

'Paintings are lovely but they're only things,' Tabilla said. 'Only stuff.'

On the table in front of Anika now was a plate of chocolate pudding; Tabilla wanted to fatten her up and Anika wanted to thin herself down. She said, 'This painting's more than that.'

'I'm glad you feel like that, Anika.'

'The painting stands for home. And you gave it to me.'

'It's your little bit of Europe,' Tabilla said.

Her little bit of Europe? Anika thought it was more a connection to her family, and to the uncle whom she'd never met, a man whom she guessed had loved this painting at least as much as she did.

'Your little bit of Europe,' Tabilla repeated, smiling.

Perhaps she was right. The painting was a symbol of the place Anika still thought of as home, a place whose absence hurt, sometimes viscerally. Her memories snaked back through the years, some fading, some growing in prominence. Family and friends and more than this: the quality of the light, softer than here, smoothing the edges of things. Or was she misremembering? If she were to go back now, she might find that everything was distorted, that the gap between her memories and the present reality had been widening all the time she'd been away. Yet nothing would alter the turning of the four seasons that she loved so much: the smells of chestnuts roasting in winter, of leaves decaying in autumn, the hot humid summers and the freshness of spring.

'Are you making tea?' Tabilla said. 'I'd like the Clarice Cliff mug please.'

She said this every time they had dinner together. Her friend Magda had given her the mug years ago. Me, Anika thought, smiling to herself, I'm not fussy about mugs; I'll have whatever is going provided it's plain white.

Afterwards, Tabilla carefully washed the Clarice Cliff

mug and dried it with the tea towel patterned with red and blue parrots, before putting it away.

'If I were to go back to Hungary after all these years,' she said, finding a cover to put over the remaining chocolate pudding, 'I'd see a very different country to the place I left. I understand that, Anika, but I'll never go back.'

Tabilla knew a lot about Hungary from all her listening to the BBC World Service and other radio programmes. She was right on top of current affairs in Central and Eastern Europe.

She might have fled Budapest decades ago, Anika decided, but Hungary still had her in its maw.

* * *

A few days later, Tabilla asked Anika over breakfast what progress she'd made in getting a valuation.

'I'm waiting to hear from Daniel,' Anika said.

'Daniel gave you his business card,' Tabilla said. 'He's probably wondering why you haven't contacted him. But if you don't want to get a valuer through him, maybe you could get in touch with one yourself. There are plenty of galleries around and plenty of valuers too.'

'I'll try calling Daniel first. He might have lost my number.'

The truth was that Anika was starting to feel ambivalent about getting the painting valued. If it were worth a lot, it would become more than a memento. It would become a liability that had to be looked after properly instead of a lovely picture that she saw each morning when she woke up. Yet with another part of her mind she wanted it to be worth a lot. A couple of thousand dollars, maybe. If it was, she could consider selling it. She began to fantasise about what she could do with the money. Not worry any more about whether she was going to lose her part-time job with Barry

Oreopoulous and Associates. Or better still, give up the job altogether; those Mondays, Wednesdays and Fridays would be better spent studying full-time. But perhaps it would be worth more than that – 10000 dollars even. If so, she could qualify as an architect years earlier and not have to watch every dollar. Maybe she could help Tabilla a bit more. Buy some nice clothes. Perhaps even set up her own practice in a few years' time.

'You could always try Sotheby's or Christies',' Tabilla said. 'They do valuations.'

'I don't want to go to a big auction house.'

'There's a man I know slightly with a gallery in Paddington. He might be able to help. I expect Magda knows someone too.'

Magda was Tabilla's oldest friend in Sydney, and she knew all the diaspora, not only the Hungarians but people from all those other waves of refugees who'd washed up in Australia escaping from some war or other. Magda was kind but Anika didn't want to get caught up in her vast network that criss-crossed Sydney, she didn't have the time for it. And she did want to see Daniel again.

'I'll be late for work,' she said, kissing Tabilla's cheek. 'Love you.' And she was out the door before her aunt could come up with any more bright ideas.

* * *

At the office, the morning sped by while Anika engrossed herself in the drawings she was working on. Barry, her boss, had done the design, a series of sketch plans and beautifully executed perspectives of a brick and concrete house that was to be constructed on a steep hillside out Mosman way. Her task was to translate his design – all horizontal planes and split levels stepping down the hill – into 1:100 working drawings on sheets of tracing paper. The builders would work from these.

She was about to have a break and try phoning Daniel when Barry appeared at her draughting table, and began to go on and on about the floorplan pinned on the board in front of her. Usually she was glad that he kept her under close supervision but it was now almost three-thirty and if she missed Daniel she'd have to wait till next week to try again. Barry was starting to repeat himself, though she'd understood what he meant the first time he told her. But she held her tongue: he was a lovely man and she was lucky to have this job with him.

'Yes,' she told him when he'd talked himself out. 'I'll do what you suggest.'

He headed for his office, bursting into a few bars of a song from *La Traviata* that he'd been practising in his spare time – he was playing the lead baritone role in an amateur production of that opera. He had a beautiful voice but it was so loud that the office partition shook and she feared for the glass. The other two draughtsmen, Tim and Greg, looked up from their draughting tables and grinned.

Once Barry had shut his office door, she dialled Daniel's work number. Someone else answered, a man with a light voice and a lisp, who told her that Daniel was out of the office. She left a message and at five o'clock she packed up and headed out of the office into the hot streets of Woolloomooloo.

Outside there was a strong stink of car exhaust and the air still felt heavy with humidity. That was what she could never get used to about Sydney in summer: the humidity that she felt was almost tropical. Inlets and bays fragmented the harbour-side suburbs, and that mass of water saturated the air, so that her clothes always felt slightly damp, her hair developed a will of its own and frizzed this way and that, and mildew appeared in the grouting between the tiles in the bathroom.

* * *

The Hero of Waterloo pub had been too hot and Anika wondered if she'd had too much to drink, or perhaps it was more that she'd had too little to eat. A sausage roll and a handful or two of peanuts didn't take you far, especially when washed down with a few middies. Woozy was the way to describe how she felt, and she was glad to go out into the fresh air.

Some of Anika's friends stood chatting on the pavement outside the pub. The Hero was on a corner, a sandstone building with its original Georgian character little altered, which was one reason it was loved by architecture students. The cooling breeze was a welcome relief after the heat of the pub and Anika could feel the sweat on her face evaporating.

'Anika!'

She jumped. The voice from behind her was unmistakably Daniel's.

'I'm so pleased to see you,' he said.

'Small world.' Anika tried to speak slowly, wanting to give herself time to breathe, wanting to still the ridiculous knocking of her heart against her ribcage. 'It's pronounced *Uh-nee-ka*.' Daniel was about a metre away, but the street was sloping down and she could look straight into those dark eyes from which the streetlamp was reflected.

'Not *arnica* then,' he said. As if guessing her lack of comprehension, he added, 'Arnica's an ointment used to soothe bruises.'

'Balm for the body, is that what you mean?' She regretted these words as soon as they flew from her lips; they could easily be misinterpreted. Quickly she added, 'It's good to see you. I hoped you'd ring back.'

'I got your message after a meeting this afternoon. I would have called you but I've been so busy.'

'So have I,' she said, grinning. 'A hard night at the Hero.'

He laughed. 'And I've had a tough evening at the pub at the bottom of George Street. You're a student, right?'

'Part-time.'

'What are you studying?'

'Architecture.'

'Really?' He couldn't keep the astonishment out of his voice. When he'd recovered – to his credit it didn't take him long – he said, 'So you've studied art history?'

'That's next year.'

Now they had that established, they carried on chit-chatting for a while. The others had moved away and Anika could see, further up Lower Fort Street, Sally and another friend, Peter, standing next to Sally's car while they waited for Anika. Sally lived in Gladesville a few suburbs west of Rozelle and had offered Anika a lift home.

Daniel began to tell Anika about the fine arts degree he'd finished a few years ago and his wonderful lecturers and he couldn't resist mentioning his high distinctions. Most men were full of themselves, she told herself before realisation dawned that he was trying to impress her, and she found this thought touching.

When he drew breath, she said, 'How can I get my painting valued?'

'Would Wednesday fortnight suit you? I made a tentative appointment at five o'clock with this really great guy who's an expert in Impressionism. I'll drive you there if you like.'

After thanking him, Anika gave him her address. Her accent sounded even to her ears more Hungarian than usual, the way it always did when she was feeling emotion – of any kind. 'This is very kind of you.'

'It's quite a long time to wait, Anika, but it was the earliest appointment I could get.'

There was a silence while she struggled to think of how to answer. *No worries* might be the appropriate response, or even *not a problem*. She was about to try this out when he said, 'Have you been to any of the Northern Beaches?'

It had been months since she'd been out of the inner city and his invitation conjured up images of sunlight and the Sydney School Impressionist paintings that Daniel had mentioned the day they met. 'I've been to Manly, does that count?'

'That's certainly on the northern side of the harbour,' he said, smiling. 'I'm heading north on Sunday for a surf and wondered if you'd like to come.'

Her stomach squirmed with what might be excitement but could be apprehension too. And then there was the thought of her shabby old swimsuit; she could really do with a new one. She said, 'I've never been anywhere further north than Manly.'

'Time for an adventure then.'

Once they'd made the arrangements, he headed down the side street, while she danced up the hill to where Sally and Peter were waiting. Even she recognised that her elation was not solely to do with getting her Rocheteau valued. Her excitement was only a little bit to do with Daniel, she told herself; it was mostly about the prospect of visiting a beach on the northern side of the harbour, where there'd be bushland, and hardly any people in the surf, and the sand wouldn't be marked out with footprints like Bondi.

* * *

Goodnight, darling family, she told the photograph on her bookshelves later that evening, as she did most nights when she was preparing for bed. She picked up the photo and examined her family. Lined up outside Molnars' Butchers, they were graded by size like beasts at a market. Anika as a ten-year-old, her brother Miklos three years older, her paternal grandmother Nyenye, and her parents. Miklos's face was angelic and Anika's grimacing. His hand, casually resting on her shoulder, was secretly yanking her hair that had been styled into loose curls for the photograph. Anika's lovely mother and Nyenye were smiling in their frumpy overcoats and headscarfs. Her father might have been waiting for a firing squad rather than the click of a camera. Above their heads, slightly out of focus, was a large mural of a cow with all its body parts labelled as cuts of meat. The family shop looked like something from the 1950s, although the photo had been taken in 1975.

Anika felt a pang of homesickness. It was frustrating not being able to talk properly to her family – not in disguised sentences or about banal topics but to really talk about the things that mattered. It was Friday night here, Friday early afternoon there, and she wondered what they were doing right now. Her parents would be at work, that was easy to predict. Miklos could be up to anything, and so could Nyenye. And at this moment it was her mother and grandmother whom she missed most. The being-able-to-hold-them, to hug them, to talk about everything that was happening in her life. Her work, the trip to the gallery, the news about the portrait, and maybe even about Daniel. She put the photograph back and glanced up at the portrait. It made her smile: it really was a magnificent work of art. 'Goodnight, beautiful auburn-haired woman,' she said aloud. 'Thank you for all the good things you're bringing into my life.' The new opportunities, the opening of new doors, a way of meeting new people. Nothing but good could come from this picture.

After switching off the lamp, she pushed aside the curtains for a moment. Apart from the street lights, the road was in darkness. Skeins of cloud trailed across the indigo sky, veiling the half-moon, and she could feel the temperature drop degree by degree, second by second, as the breeze metamorphosed into something stronger. Shivering, she climbed into bed and snuggled under the blankets. Shortly afterwards, she was lulled into sleep by soothing fantasies of waves that rolled endlessly on to the shoreline. Outside, the wind rattled Mr and Mrs Opposite's front gate and fingered the loose corrugated iron of someone's roof, and a couple of cats down the road fought over something – a fish head perhaps – but tonight nothing was to disturb Anika's sleep.

* * *

The next morning she awoke late. The southerly change had blown away the dust and pollution, and the fresh-washed day was so brilliant it made you glad to be alive. On her way to the corner shop for the newspaper and some groceries, she bumped into Mrs Thornton, the old lady next door, who was sweeping her front verandah as she did every Saturday morning and most other mornings besides. The perfect excuse to monitor the street and catch up on people's news.

'Have you had a good week, dear? Glad to hear it. Not working too hard then. You're only young once, that's what I always say, make the most of it. Heard you getting home last night.'

'Sorry. Was I noisy?'

'I was awake anyway. I'd just gone upstairs. It was only the car door slamming, and then there was the wind. By the way, there was a man looking for you yesterday. He didn't know which house you lived in but knew it was a stone terraced house. As soon as he gave me your name I was able to tell him which. Must have been early evening after your aunt went out. I told him you weren't at home but he knocked on the door anyway.'

'What did he look like?'

'Tall with thick fair hair, and on the wrong side of thirty. He said his name was Jonno.'

The Jonno who'd taken Anika for coffee at the café opposite the art gallery, Anika thought, and wondered what he wanted. 'I'd better get going,' she said. 'Would you like me to get you anything from the shop?'

'I've already been, love. But ta anyway.'

Further up the street, outside the rundown terraced house that the landlord refused to spend any money on, Ty Nguyen was cleaning the ute that he'd had for a couple of months. Every Saturday morning the ute got washed and polished. It was his third job that gave him enough cash to buy it. Moonlighting, such a graphic word. Though the black economy thrived here, it was tiny compared to Hungary, where everyone was struggling to make ends meet, the success of *gulyás* communism nothing more than a chimera.

Just before the dogleg in the street that led to the corner shop, Anika passed the house that two women her age were renovating. This morning there was a heap of bricks in their front yard. Penny was mixing sand and cement on a sheet of plywood while Jane was laying bricks to raise the height of the low wall in front of the house. While Anika watched, Jane plunged a brick into the big bucket of water on the path next to her, before smearing cement on to it and slapping it on to the top of the wall. She did it neatly, so the brick lay square and level, and then she tamped it down with the handle of her trowel.

A sundried elderly man Anika hadn't seen before stopped next to her and critically examined what Jane was doing. 'You need a spirit level for that love,' he said. 'And a plumb bob. You hang that from a bit of string and it gives you a vertical reference line.'

Jane looked up. 'Don't need that, mate,' she said pleasantly. 'I've got a good eye.'

Penny, who was continuing to combine sand with cement, cut into the mixture harder than necessary with her trowel. On the ground next to her were a spirit level and a plumb bob. She looked up, caught Anika's eye and winked. As Anika moved on, Mr Know-it-all started offering more advice. Soon after, another couple joined him and a lively conversation was beginning.

Outside the corner shop, a woman in a T-shirt and pants that were a size too small was fingering the oranges displayed in a rack. She picked up each one and squeezed it, before putting it into her plastic shopping basket next to a couple of rolls of toilet paper. They never had oranges when Anika was growing up in Budapest. They often didn't have toilet paper either. People cut up newspapers into squares and threaded these through a piece of string suspended from a hook next to the toilet.

Community spirit, Anika thought as she paid for her purchases; it was almost like a village here in Boggabri Street on a Saturday morning. Everyone knew what their neighbours were up to. That had made it easy for Jonno to figure out where she lived. She hoped he wasn't going to become a nuisance. She'd liked him but there was something threatening about him. Perhaps it was his size, perhaps it was his persistence. She couldn't quite put her finger on what it was.

Chapter 4

On Sunday morning Anika was ready much too early. Wearing a loose green dress that would be easy to pull on and off for swimming, she dumped her swimming things in a canvas tote by the front door and went into the downstairs front room to wait for Daniel. She could hear Mrs Thornton sweeping her front verandah again.

The curtains in the front room were still drawn and the room was gloomy. The sight of a woman in front of the folding modesty screen made Anika jump until she realised it was only Flossie. A fully adjustable dressmaking dummy, Flossie was modelling Mrs Barling's bridal dress – it would be Mrs Barling's second marriage – a bright blue confection tightly fitted over the bust and hips, with a matching bolero bolstered out with shoulder pads. Flossie had twelve dials for Tabilla to play with, so that Flossie could range from a sylph-like build to a tall buxom shape. At the moment, she was somewhere in the middle, just like Mrs Barling.

Occasionally Anika glanced through the window. Mrs Thornton had now finished sweeping and Anika heard her front door slam. Maybe Daniel was running late. She checked her watch but it was not even ten o'clock yet. After straightening her dress, she examined her reflection in the cheval mirror and smoothed down her recalcitrant hair. Closer to the time Daniel said he would collect her, she watched the street closely; her aim was to get away promptly without running into Mrs Thornton or having to introduce Daniel to Tabilla. After the end of her relationship with Frank, Tabilla liked to inspect the men she went out with. 'It's not that you've got really bad judgement,' she said. 'It's just that I can ask the sort of question that you mightn't think of and that gives you more information.'

The street was one-way, and as soon as Anika saw a vehicle she didn't recognise – it was a yellow VW Beetle – passing slowly by the house, she collected her bag and opened the front door while Daniel parked his car further up the street.

She'd locked the door before he had time even to open the gate of Tabilla's tiny front yard. He was wearing brown sandals, shorts the colour of white coffee and an orange and white flowered Hawaiian T-shirt hanging loose. He raised his sunglasses as she opened the gate, the better to fix her with his dark eyes.

'You look lovely,' he said. 'That green dress suits you.'

You look pretty good yourself, she was about to say, before caution got the better of her and she coughed instead. Daniel relieved her of her swimming bag but not without a little tussle, their bodies so close she could smell the faintly spiced deodorant he used and the scent of freshly laundered cotton. As she got into the car, the net curtain twitched: Tabilla – and Flossie – were witnessing their departure, and she'd bet that, next door, Mrs Thornton was as well.

Daniel certainly could talk. You might have called him a *windbag* if he hadn't been so interesting. Their journey over the bridge and up to Roseville Chase and French's Forest was a voyage through the Australian Impressionist School and Early Modern and on to Abstract Expressionism. Her head was reeling by the time she glimpsed the ocean. They descended through bushland to the coast, before winding their way further north. Beach after beach, until they stopped, nose into the kerb, and saw, beyond a row of Norfolk pines, lines of breakers rolling in. There was a cluster of sun umbrellas towards the south end of the beach, near the tidal pool and the Surf Life Saving Club, and in the ocean a few body surfers in the area between the flags.

When Anika came out of the change room, Daniel was waiting for her. His dark blue swimming shorts reached almost to his knees and he had an orange and white striped beach towel draped over his shoulders: the casual look – he might have been modelling for a fashion shoot. She felt underdressed, the way she always did when visiting a beach. But Daniel looked only at her face; not a glance did he cast at her body, encased in the new black one-piece swimsuit that she thought was probably too revealing and had certainly been too expensive.

After they'd marked out a bit of the beach between the flags as their territory, with their bags and towels defining the borders, Daniel asked Anika if she could swim. She told him about the baths of Budapest, the heated and unheated ones. The heated ones were too hot, you'd step out of those looking boiled, and they were filled with people playing chess, now wasn't that an odd thing, you couldn't do that in the surf, could you? But where she'd been taught to swim, the water was unheated so you had to keep moving, and moving fast or you'd freeze, and that's why her father had taken her and Miklos there when they were young and had more-or-less thrown them in and told them to keep moving or they'd die. Daniel looked at her curiously, as if he knew from all her burbling against the background thudding of waves that she was prevaricating. As if he guessed she wanted to delay the moment when she entered the surf.

The beach was without shade and the relentless sun beat down. The heat reflected back from the golden sand burned Anika's feet. It was a relief to get into a few centimetres of water and feel it so cold, water eddying around her ankles. She loved that the coolness was just the contrast; that it was not cold really, not at the fag-end of summer after the coastline had been basking in heat all summer long. When you thought about it, there was little land between Sydney and South America all those thousands of kilometres away. To the east only tiny New Zealand stood between them and that land mass, and to the south they were exposed to the icy continent of Antarctica. Just thinking of all that emptiness made her halt.

Sensing her reluctance, Daniel grabbed hold of her hand and led her into the shallows; he released her only when they were standing waist-deep in the water. Though it felt silky against her skin, around her feet it was more abrasive, like being exfoliated with a pumice stone, as grains of sand pushed and pulled around her ankles. Daniel dived under a wave. She was too late to follow and the water broke over her, knocking her off her feet. It was impossible to fight against the drag that pulled her under and she began to panic as her body was tossed around as if it weighed nothing. Fighting for breath, she resurfaced only when the wave was ready to let her go, only when it was ready to dump her in the shallows, along with a few shells and skeins of seaweed and a lot of sand.

'I've never been surfing before,' she spluttered.

'Now you tell me.' Daniel hauled her to her feet. His hair, plastered darkly over his forehead, dripped beads of water down his neck. 'I would have stayed with you if I'd known.' At once he began a lecture on how to body surf, while seizing her hand again. He led her further out beyond the line of breakers.

She held hard to Daniel's hand till realising that she was more likely to be dragged inshore than offshore. That gave her the confidence to let go. He swam further out and she followed him. Here the ocean rose and fell like the breathing of a living creature.

'Catch this one,' he said, as a bigger wave rolled towards them.

She started stroking to shore. The wave lifted her up and carried her forward in a rush of water and adrenaline before gently dropping her near the beach. Here was Daniel again, his hand outstretched. 'You're a natural,' he said. She laughed and flicked hair off her face. She knew she would never forget this day.

After they got out of the water and had showered and changed, they bought fish and chips from the little shop opposite that Daniel referred to as a greasy spoon. They ate them while sauntering along the deserted northern arc of beach almost as far as the sandstone headland. There they sat in the shade, on sand still warm from the sun, and watched the waves rolling in from the Pacific. This is freedom, Anika decided; this is safety. On this beach there was no one watching them, no one reporting on them.

'Once I'd hoped to be an artist,' Daniel said, staring at the surf. 'That was a long time ago. Then I realised that I'm not much good at it. The funny thing is that I can paint a pretty good copy of something but there's no inspiration in it. Anyone with an analytical mind can parse a view into patches of light and shade and put those on to canvas. And the rules of perspective are easy once you swot them up. But brilliant paintings are a lot more than that.' He looked at her and smiled, before adding, 'What I can do though is appreciate the difference between competent and brilliant works of art.'

'That's a big positive, isn't it?'

'I guess it makes me good at what I do.' He picked up a handful of sand, letting it sift through his fingers. 'Why did you choose architecture, Anika?'

'I love the way buildings create space and the space can make you happy,' she said slowly. 'And I love knowing how to put things together.'

She'd been lucky to get into architecture in Australia, she knew. After her arrest in Budapest, the authorities had withdrawn their formal offer of a university place. She'd spent two days with the secret police, a memory that even now, five years later, made her heart thud and her palms grow sticky. When they'd let her go, she'd worked in the hairdressing salon where she'd had a weekend job for the last two years of secondary school.

Daniel was looking at her, waiting for her to say more. She took a deep breath before saying, 'One of our design tutors told us about good architecture offering gifts and surprises. When he said that I knew right away what he meant.'

'Maybe that's analytical too?' Daniel said.

'I suppose it is, in the sense that you have to figure out what works and what doesn't and then you have to imagine what it's like to move through the space and how to construct it.' A breeze had sprung up and she tried not to shiver. She didn't want to suggest moving yet.

'Is anyone in your family an architect?'

'My family's business is a butchers' shop.' Carefully she checked out his reaction. His expression was unchanged. She added, 'Budapest is a beautiful city, very inspiring.'

'I'd love to visit. I had a few months off after graduation and hitched around Western Europe. I had a terrific time but to be honest, I couldn't wait to get home to all this. There's something about the light here that I love. You're shivering, Anika.'

'I'm freezing. I didn't bring a jumper.'

'I didn't either.' He looked concerned and for an instant she wondered if he were about to put an arm around her shoulders. Instead he said, 'Should we head back?'

Their footprints had been washed away, and there was a new line of detritus being deposited by the incoming tide.

Shadows were starting to form in the small depressions above the high tide mark where the surface of the beach hadn't been flattened by the previous tide. The Norfolk pines cast jagged patterns over the low dunes and on to the beach, and the waves were breaking over the edge of the swimming pool below the southern headland.

On the drive home, they sat in a companionable silence until Daniel asked her to pick a tape out of the box. She pulled one out at random: Vivaldi's *Four Seasons*. It wasn't any old version but one that had been *reimagined* – and that seemed to summarise who Daniel was. She put the tape into the machine and shut her eyes as soothing sound washed over them.

When they reached Rozelle it was twilight and the street lights were on. Tabilla was in her front yard talking to Mrs Thornton. They had their backs to the road and, in spite of the poor light, Anika's aunt was showing their neighbour the new bloom on her beloved grevillea. It was a spidery red flower too large for the shrub. Neither woman looked up as they puttered past.

'Can you drop me just there?' Anika asked Daniel, pointing to the house with the new brick wall. 'I'll introduce you to my aunt another time.'

The last thing she wanted him to undergo was Mrs Thornton's inspection and possibly her interrogation. Quite why, she didn't understand. Perhaps it was the legacy of keeping oneself to oneself when it was common knowledge that anybody could be an informer. She wondered how many years it would take for her to abandon that distrust.

'Thank you for a lovely day, Daniel.'

'It was a pleasure.'

'I'll see you on Wednesday week for the valuation.'

'Would you like to do something else before then? There's a terrific pub at Watson's Bay we could go to. The beer garden looks out over the harbour.'

'I'd like that.'

This was an understatement. What she would have really liked to do was throw her arms around his neck and hug him, and she might have too – if it had been later in the evening and the street was deserted and she'd had a few glasses of wine to rid herself of her ghastly reserve. Or if she'd been a different person – the overtly warm and affectionate person that she longed to be.

'I'll collect you at five o'clock.'

'Thanks. See you next Saturday.' She jumped out of the car before he had time to turn the engine off, and waved as he carried along the one-way street and turned into the dogleg that would lead him into the two-way street system and back on to Victoria Road.

It was only later that she wished she'd invited him in. For four years she'd lived in Australia. Perhaps it was time to move on from her past, time to ditch her suspicions. Mrs Thornton and her ilk were not her enemies but her friends. *Neighbourhood Watch*, they called themselves. They were a *Neighbourhood Watch* street.

Then she thought of their neighbour in Budapest: the widow Balog who used to give Anika sweets and a pat on the head whenever she saw her. Mrs Balog was taken away one night when Anika was very young, no more than four or five; Miklos overheard their parents whispering together the next morning that she'd been taken by the secret police. Some weeks later she was returned. Her front teeth had gone and her face looked as if half of it had slid sideways. Even her gait was different, more a shuffle than a walk, and she had developed a nervous tic in one eye. Anika didn't see much of her after that. She stayed in her apartment all day and came out only to buy food. If they met on the walkway Mrs Balog would nod at Anika but would never meet her eye. This made

Anika frightened. 'Am I a good girl?' she began to ask her mother and Nyenye. They always said yes. But a kernel of fear had been planted in Anika's mind. If Mrs Balog could be taken, maybe the secret police could one day take her mother or father or Miklos or her, or her beloved Nyenye or Nagyapa. And return them broken. Broken in spirit and in body, like Mrs Balog.

The paranoia that was everywhere when Anika was growing up was justified. Though you couldn't see the surveillance, people knew it was there. In a war, soldiers wore uniforms and the enemy could be easily identified. But in a totalitarian regime like theirs, the enemy could have been anyone. It was necessary always to be careful and always to trust no one.

Maybe distrust like hers was a scar that she would never be rid of.

Chapter 5

Late Monday afternoon, not long after Anika got home from work hot and tired, there was a knock on the front door. Anika opened it to a late-middle-aged woman she hadn't seen before. The woman's face was asymmetrical, the nose twisted slightly to one side, and she had beautiful deep-set brown eyes and that fine olive skin that aged well even in this climate. At the sight of Anika, her mouth formed an O, like a goldfish gaping in a fishbowl.

'Are you looking for Tabilla?'

The woman's mouth now formed a straight line and her face puckered as if she'd sucked at a sour lemon.

'I'm her niece.' Anika sugared her smile to take that sour expression off the woman's face. 'Do you have an appointment?'

'No appointment. I was just driving by and thought I'd drop in. It's been years since I saw her last. I wondered if she's still dressmaking.'

'She still makes clothes. Are you looking to have something made? You can come in and wait. She should be back soon.'

The woman shook her head. 'Thanks, but I'd better get on. It was just an impulse thing. I thought she might make me a dress.'

'Who shall I say called?'

'I'm Sarah. Your aunt will know who I am. I saw a lot of her at one time.'

'Were you a client?'

'Yes, you could say that. She used to make all of my clothes.'

Anika glanced at what she was wearing. A black knitted top over a pair of black pants whose dark colour concealed to some extent her enormous hips. Built for child bearing, Anika's mother would have said, and not for wearing trousers. Around her neck was a heavy gold chain and from her earlobes dangled gold earrings so long they would rattle against the chain if she leaned forward.

'You are from Hungary?' She didn't wait for an answer. 'I'm originally from Middle Europe.'

Anika found this odd. No one she knew ever said they were Middle European. They would give a country or say Central Europe. But then she remembered this was a German way of saying Central Europe. She too might be thought as from Mitteleuropa. Perhaps this woman was from more than one country; one of those people who stayed in one place while the boundaries around them shifted, countries and empires expanding and contracting. Like Anika's distant cousins: in Hungary one day and Transylvania the next. Or maybe Sarah was one of the diasporas who moved from place to place as wars raged around them.

'Which part of Middle Europe?'

'Austria.' Sarah's expression became defensive and at once Anika regretted her probing.

There was such a fine line between genuine interest that made a person feel valued, and voyeuristic curiosity that might easily be construed as prying. Anika knew from Sarah's expression that she'd overstepped the mark and it was easy to guess why. Sarah would have come here from a concentration camp or a displaced persons camp or both. Anika's heart went out to her but words were hard to find. 'Are you sure you won't come in? I was just about to make some tea but I can make coffee if you prefer.'

'Perhaps I will pop in after all. Just for a couple of minutes to use your bathroom – would you mind? I've been driving around half the afternoon and I've got to make it home through all that heavy traffic.'

'Of course, do come in. It's at the top of the stairs. I'll be in the kitchen if you need anything.'

The woman was a while upstairs and when she came down again Anika asked if she'd changed her mind about a cup of tea.

'Thanks, but I've got to dash.'

She preceded Anika down the hall towards the front door, and paused to peer into Tabilla's sewing room. Flossie was modelling Mrs Barling's going-away outfit, an orange linen dress with exaggerated square shoulders.

Sarah took a deep breath before saying, 'Do give your aunt my regards. By the way, I've changed my mind about getting a dress made. I seem to live in trousers these days.'

Anika opened the front door and for several seconds they stood on the path outside. Sarah looked as if she was about to say something more but at that moment Mrs Thornton's front door opened and there she was attacking her spotless verandah with a broom. 'Good evening, love,' she said. 'Didn't see you at first. I don't want to cover you and your visitor with dust.'

'I must go.' Sarah was out the front gate so quickly that neither Mrs Thornton nor Anika had time to draw breath.

Ten minutes after Mrs Thornton ran out of small talk and Anika had managed to get inside to the kitchen, Tabilla burst through the front door, her hair mussed up by the breeze and her cheeks flushed.

'Someone dropped by to see you,' Anika said, after her aunt had put down her things. 'You've only just missed her.'

'What was her name?'

'Sarah. She said you used to make a lot of her clothes.'

'Ah, yes. I hope she doesn't want any sewing done.'

'I don't think so. She said she was just passing by. She sends you her regards.'

'What was she wearing?'

'Separates. Non-iron.'

Tabilla turned, grinning. 'Did you notice her waist?'

'Not really.'

'It's hard to get off-the-peg pants for a small waist and big beam. Someone else must be sewing for her. Doing alterations if she's buying off-the-peg. She used to look gorgeous in dresses gathered into that slender waist.'

'I didn't notice the slender waist.'

'I wouldn't want to sew for her again. She's quite a difficult woman.'

After dinner Anika went upstairs to her room. The portrait of the auburn-haired lady was bathed in moonlight that washed out most of the colours. When Anika turned on the overhead light and drew the curtains, the vibrant colours in the painting reappeared. *Your little bit of Europe,* was how Tabilla had described the portrait. And perhaps she was right.

Chapter 6

It was midweek in the office of Barry Oreopoulous and Associates and unusually there was no whistling or singing. Barry arrived late and in a bad mood. He meandered around, looking over people's shoulders at what they had on their drawing boards but seeing – and saying – nothing. His bowtie had migrated sideways, giving him a dissolute air. The tail of his shirt had come out of his trousers and his curly hair was standing on end as if it wanted to distance itself from whatever was going on inside his large domed skull.

When it was Anika's turn for a stop on his tour, she hardly dared breathe. Recently he'd been guiding her through a 1:20 detailed drawing for the Mosman house. Now she waited for an outburst. Only two days ago he'd told her off for her draughtsmanship: she wasn't holding the draughting pencil correctly and really, she should have been taught better. It was all very well having a few design skills and a bit of training with computers, he'd said, but between the idea and the reality fell the shadow. It was the quality of the draughtsmanship that mattered when you were working for an architect like him. And now that he was breathing down her neck again, she noticed that one of the measurements of the cross-sectional drawing was wrong by some millimetres. The individual dimensions didn't add up to the total dimensions, a hanging offence. Yet even this didn't register with Barry and he wandered wordlessly into his office, a glassed-in enclosure at one end of the space.

For the rest of the morning, when it was necessary to

speak, the other two draughtsmen and Anika whispered to one another. She carefully rechecked all the dimensions on her drawing and made several corrections. At lunchtime it was a relief to get out of the office and into the liveliness of the day, a breeze shifting the leaves around, the sky an enamelled cobalt blue, and the streets crowded with office workers, everyone laughing except for them. They went to the corner shop for their sandwiches and hazarded guesses as to what was wrong with Barry.

'A prospective job must have fallen through.' Tim, who was a few years older than Anika, had a wife and a six-week-old baby with colic. There were bags under his eyes from sleepless nights yet he'd found time to gel his hair so that there were little spikes on the top that made him look even taller.

'Barry was hoping to get that contract for the new synagogue,' Greg said, while managing at the same time to make eyes at the pretty blonde waitress at the far end of the counter. She was serving three sundried men in Visiglo tops, tiny shorts and dusty work-boots.

'No, he got that,' Tim said. 'If he hadn't, we'd have all been laid off before now.'

'Not necessarily. He's too soft hearted.'

'Not that soft hearted,' Anika said. 'He's got to eat. And eat well.'

'And to keep his kid at that posh girls' school.'

'She won a music scholarship. He told me that the day I had my interview.'

'Maybe his wife's leaving him.'

'Or he's lost the lead role in *La Traviata*.' Greg thought opera was a joke.

'It's only an amateur production. He'd be far and away the best. Years ago he had a role in Sydney Opera's production of *Aida*.'

'Maybe he just had a quarrel with his wife.'

'He must be hard to live with. A prima donna at work and at play.'

After lunch, as Anika was passing by Barry's office, she heard him pick up the phone and tap in a number. When he asked for Howard Meyer, her design tutor, her feet stopped still. Howard had given her a reference for this job with Barry and it suddenly hit her that Barry might be calling to complain about her. Her mouth became as dry as a dam in a drought and she had trouble swallowing.

Without any preamble, Barry barked into the receiver, 'You're an arsehole, Howard. You're a prize fuckwit.' And then he slammed down the receiver.

Hurriedly Anika returned to her drawing board. Her heart knocked against her ribcage. How would she manage without this job? What would she tell Tabilla? She hadn't got much. Only what her dressmaking business brought in and the small amount of board money Anika paid her. And part-time jobs like Anika's didn't come easy. Barry would never lay off Tim and Greg. They were both good designers and draughtsmen and had been with him for years. Tim had a young family to support and a mortgage to pay off. She was the marginal one, the one who could be easily dispensed with. She'd have to get work as a waitress. Or maybe go back to hairdressing. There was always a shortage of hairdressers. Hair just kept on growing regardless of the state of the economy, unlike jobs in the design and construction industries.

All afternoon, anxieties swarmed in her brain. Maybe she'd have to sell the Rocheteau. At this thought, her concentration went to pot and she began to feel the thump-thump-thump of a headache. She rummaged in her bag for the wonder-tablet the doctor had given her that stopped a migraine in its tracks if you took it early enough. In the kitchenette she swilled down the tablet with a glug of water and drank two more glasses in quick succession. The contents of her stomach sloshed as she returned to her drawing board but neither Tim nor Greg raised their heads. She'd have liked to go home and sleep off the headache but she couldn't afford to ask for the rest of the afternoon off. Barry had been so generous already with giving her time off and with her job on the line she shouldn't give him further reason to sack her.

The hours crawled by. Barry stayed in his office all afternoon with the door shut and refused to come out even when it was time for afternoon tea. Anika took him a mug of his favourite: Assam with a slice of lemon. He barely glanced up when she placed it on his desk. A curt nod was the only acknowledgement she got. At five o'clock she left. Her migraine had gone, leaving behind only exhaustion. Tomorrow Barry would be driving to Queanbeyan to supervise the renovation of a bank and would be away for a few days, so that was a few more days that she'd have a job. But who could guess what might happen after that.

* * *

That evening Tabilla and Anika shared a pot of tea at the kitchen table. Anika's chair looked down the backyard, and suddenly she noticed that there was something about the clarity and angle of the light that hinted at autumn. This made her restless, like she wanted to rush out and seize the day before the season changed and the day was gone.

'After I'd gone to bed last night, I had an idea.' Tabilla was smiling. 'Someone I used to know runs an art gallery. I think I mentioned him to you before… I haven't seen him for years but he's a darling man, his name's Julius Singer, and he's very successful. He might be just the person to value your painting. I'll phone him, shall I?'

'Thanks. I'd love to find out what it's worth. The sooner the better really. I can still go with Daniel next week to see his contact.' Anika didn't mention her anxieties about her job.

'Of course,' Tabilla said. 'Two valuations are better than one, don't you think? If Julius gives you an idea of how much it's worth I can immediately add it to the house contents insurance.' Her face was beaming. 'It's been ages since I last spoke to him. I'll ring him at work, Wednesday's his late opening. He'll have his diary there.'

After Tabilla had found the phone directory, Anika gave her some times when she'd be free. Tabilla said, 'There are your lectures to consider, Anika, and also Barry Oreopoulous and Associates. Though Julius's gallery isn't so far from Barry's office.'

She jotted down notes on a scrap of paper and then keyed in the number. When Anika got up to go, Tabilla motioned her back. 'You can listen too,' she said. 'In case those times you gave me don't work out.'

When the phone was picked up, she said, 'Hello, Julius! It's Tabilla Molnar here.'

'Tabilla, is it really you? How lovely to hear from you.' Julius's surprise was unmistakable, and his voice so loud that Anika could hear his words even from a few metres away. She conjured up an image of him that would fit the sound. He would be tall like her boss Barry, with a long body and deep chest from which that powerful voice resonated.

'I hope this isn't a bad time to call.'

'Not at all,' he said. 'It must be years since we last spoke… Can I help you with anything?'

'I hope so. It's my niece Anika, you see. She's got an oil painting you might like to take a look at.'

There was a pause. Anika tried to imagine what Julius might be thinking. Probably that it would be some gaudy thing that the niece had painted and he'd have to pretend to like it. He'd be drumming his fingers on the desktop and wondering how he could weasel out of this.

'It's not to buy,' Tabilla said. 'It's to value. Anika got it from a distant relative.'

Since when had Tabilla been a distant relative? She was Anika's aunt, if only by marriage. And the painting had belonged to Anika's uncle. If you asked her, that was pretty close as families go. She wondered what game Tabilla was playing. Probably she didn't want to influence Julius.

'Would you mind?' Tabilla said. 'It's for insurance purposes. You'd be doing my niece a great favour.'

'Who painted it?' Julius said.

'Someone called Antoine Rocheteau.'

'It would be a pleasure,' Julius said, his tone more enthusiastic now. 'What about tomorrow afternoon? Or Friday, if she prefers?'

'Friday's good. Anika works not far from you on Fridays. Would two o'clock suit you? You'll love the painting. It's so nice of you to agree to see my niece. I've always known you to be kind.'

After Tabilla put down the receiver, she sighed. 'Poor Julius is run around by his wife,' she said. 'But she won't be at the gallery. Julius will do anything for her but she doesn't appreciate it.'

When Anika went upstairs that night, she began to wonder if it would be possible to borrow some money using the Rocheteau as collateral. She'd have to see a bank and she had no idea of the procedure. Maybe Daniel would be able to give her some advice. But she was getting a bit ahead of herself. Sometimes it was best just to wait and see.

Chapter 7

Friday was like any other day in late March. Hot and humid mostly, with only the barest hint of autumn in the morning before the sun fully rose and again in that coolness at the end of the day. Clutching her securely wrapped painting under one arm, Anika stood outside the 137 Gallery in Paddington and peered through the plate glass window. Inside would be air-conditioned; a man in a black and unseasonable turtleneck sweater and black trousers was standing in front of the reception desk.

Mr Turtleneck, a sturdy man in his mid-thirties, had a round oversized face and steel-rimmed glasses perched halfway down his nose. Opposite him, towards one side of the gallery space, were a couple of black leather chairs. Five or six patrons were viewing the exhibition. Two were looking closely at a very large canvas. With its vibrant colours – yellow, orange, crimson – it gave the impression of glowing from within, like a fireball or the sun in a bushfire. The other visitors were meandering around the space as if it were a promenade and they were there to see and be seen. Anika's arm holding the painting was going to sleep; she shifted it to the other hip and pushed open the door.

'My name is Anika Molnar,' she told Mr Turtleneck. 'And I would like to see Mr Julius Singer.'

'Mr Singer is very busy.' The slight displeasure in this man's voice was almost certainly because he didn't like the look of her. For the niece of a dressmaker, she was rather shabbily dressed. She wished she'd picked her outfit more carefully but she'd been in such a rush that morning, focusing more on wrapping the painting than on what to wear. Though her cotton shirt was neat, it was tucked into the waistband of dark blue jeans that were frayed around the ankle, and on her feet were canvas sandals of the versatile sort that could be worn hiking as well as tramping around the upper reaches of Paddington. The man took off his glasses, as if seeing her blurred might improve her appearance, and checked in the mirror behind her that the strands of his thinning hair were arranged neatly across his scalp.

'My aunt Tabilla Molnar sent me.'

At this moment a man in his sixties stepped out of the back office. He said, in a deep and resonant voice that she recognised from Tabilla's phone conversation with him, 'I'm expecting you. Your aunt called me.'

His appearance didn't accord with the volume of his voice and the image Anika had constructed from listening to Tabilla talk with him on the phone. He was short and slightly stooped and you wondered where the reverberation in his speech could come from. 'Mr Singer?'

He nodded, his smile illuminating his face, and held out his hand to shake her hot and clammy one. 'Would you like a tea or coffee? My assistant James could get you one.'

'Thank you, I won't. My aunt told me you're very busy and anyway I have to get back to work. Thanks for agreeing to look at my picture.'

'Let's view it, shall we?' His tone was hearty. He might have been a kindergarten teacher at a show-and-tell morning. As they walked across the gallery to a table at the side, the soles of her ugly sandals flapped on the timber floor: if you were unable to see how slender she was, you might have thought a heavyweight had marched into his gallery.

Carefully Anika unpicked the string, before peeling back

multiple layers of brown paper and bubble wrap.

When Mr Singer saw the woman in the blue dress, he gasped and took several steps back, before sinking into one of the black leather chairs. After a few deep breaths, he looked at Anika in a befuddled way, as if expecting someone else to be standing in front of him. His perplexity lasted only a few seconds, before excitement, and an expression that you could only describe as aversion, danced across his face like scraps of paper tossed hither and thither by a strong breeze. And he'd gone such a funny colour, she thought, his face a mottled maroon and white. Maybe she should get him a glass of water. Only now did she notice that the gallery had emptied, apart from the assistant Mr Turtleneck, who was busy doing something at the front desk. Schubert's 'Death and the Maiden' began to play, the notes reverberating through the gallery.

Mr Singer croaked out some words that Anika could barely hear. She had to ask him to repeat them.

'This is not possible,' he said. 'It can't be yours.'

It was a couple of heartbeats before she understood what he was implying. 'Yes, it is mine.' Her voice sounded too loud in her ears.

Through clenched teeth he hissed something that she couldn't understand. There was now no mistaking the antipathy in his expression. Her breathing became ragged and she began to feel lightheaded. Julius must have heard that the picture belonged to her aunt, although Tabilla certainly hadn't said that when she phoned him. A distant relative, that's what she said. Anika was about to explain how Tabilla gave her the painting when a tiny worm of distrust squirmed into her brain. Quickly she shut her mouth and watched Julius's curling lips as he hissed, 'Can't be yours.'

'It is mine,' she told Julius, hastily fastening the wrapping paper round the painting. Perhaps he was suffering from the early stages of dementia. Keeping her tone as cool as possible, she said, 'It was given to me.'

'Do you have the provenance?' Julius looked almost pleased when she winced at the sarcasm in his voice. The skin under her left eye began to twitch. 'That's the ownership history. The painting's worth nothing without that.' He stood and took a few steps towards her. He wasn't much taller than she was but she felt frightened. 'In other words,' he said, as slowly as if she were an obtuse child who had trouble understanding English, 'where did it come from?'

After this reaction she didn't want to tell him it was Tomas's, the uncle whom she never knew, nor did she even know how he'd acquired the painting.

'You heard what Mr Singer said, where did the painting come from?'

She looked around. The assistant was standing right behind her. Her warning system was revving up. Tell them nothing, it was saying. Protect yourself. Protect Tabilla. Losing her husband was bad enough without having to face these questions. Get the hell out of here and don't tell these ghastly people any more.

'Don't you know where it came from?' Julius's brows were lowered, the forehead scowling, the mouth thin-lipped and grim.

The assistant moved from behind Anika and stood next to Julius. His expression was more than unfriendly; she could almost be facing the security police again. As her alarm intensified, her heart started to thump too hard. She wanted to take the painting and run. Julius asked the question once more and, although she didn't have a clue, in her panic she improvised, words bubbling from her mouth. 'My father said the painting had been bought from the consignment store or a state auction, I can't remember which.' Afterwards, she paused, rationalising what she'd just said, rationalising what she'd just made up.

She didn't see why she should tell Julius that it had been Nyenye who'd said it came from an old friend, Sebestyén Tinódi and that he'd got it from a state auction. Her grandmother was old and needed protecting. And what she'd said about the consignment store or the state auction was probably right, though she didn't know for sure because they'd only briefly spoken of Tomas's picture.

'Is your father alive?'

'Yes. He's in Budapest.' Beads of perspiration gathered on Anika's upper lip. The armholes of her shirt felt too tight and sweat was beginning to pool in her armpits.

'Is he a collector or a dealer?'

'He's a butcher.'

'A butcher who likes paintings?' The assistant looked as if he might laugh.

Anika began to hate the snobbery of this man. Suddenly he lunged towards her and seized hold of one corner of the picture, tearing the brown paper. 'Let me have a look,' he said.

Shaking him off – he was a big man but not agile – Anika turned tail and raced out of the gallery. For a moment she was blinded by the harsh sunlight, before adrenaline kicked in and she took off along the street.

Somehow, she made her way back to the office, confused and with her head reeling. She spent the afternoon bent over her draughting table. But the working drawing engaged only part of her brain and the scene with Mr Singer just wouldn't let her alone. It didn't help that he was Tabilla's acquaintance and Anika didn't know how she was going to tell her aunt about his reaction and his words. Could he have known that legally speaking the painting was Tabilla's? Not possible,

Tabilla hadn't said that, and Anika had heard every word of their phone conversation.

Julius was obviously unstable and she was certainly not going to contact him again. She needed to forget about him but that proved to be impossible. Her thoughts continued churning around. All she'd told him was that her father reckoned it had been bought from a state auction or from the consignment store. A sentence that implied her father knew a bit about its provenance but not that he or any close relative had purchased it.

Yet savings weren't allowed in Hungary; her grandparents must have gone against the Communist Party in acquiring their collection, and Sebestyén Tinódi might have too. Of course, they wouldn't have been alone. There was a thriving black market in Hungary, a concealed network of contacts and exchanges. The last thing Anika wanted was for her family to get into trouble.

Chapter 8

Tabilla was in the kitchen when Anika got home. The door to her sewing room was open and Anika saw that Flossie was modelling one of the bridesmaids' dresses. It was made of light pink silk, the fabric gathered in tiny pleats from the padded shoulders down to the bosom, where it was caught into a narrow band before cascading down to just below the knee. The style would suit someone very slim but Flossie was adjusted to her most buxom setting.

'How did you get on?' Tabilla said.

She looked exhausted and the last thing Anika wanted was to upset her. There was no need for her to know what Julius had said about the painting. She had surely suffered enough in her life, and Anika didn't really need to add this to her woes or raise doubts in her mind about how her husband had acquired it.

'Not very well.' Anika leaned against the kitchen door jamb. 'Did Julius call you?'

'No. Should he have?'

'Of course not.'

It was as Anika had hoped. Since Tabilla hadn't told Julius the portrait belonged to Tabilla's husband and neither had she, as long as Julius didn't phone Tabilla it was unlikely that he would ever learn about her husband's involvement.

'Did he give you an idea of how much the painting's worth?' Tabilla peered at Anika short-sightedly. With the strong arch of the bone above her eye sockets and the dark semicircles under them, she looked almost like that picture of a raccoon that Anika had seen in the *National Geographic*.

'He didn't. It wasn't a very successful meeting. Mr Singer got distracted.'

'That's too bad. I'm sorry about that. I know he's a very busy man. Did he suggest you go again?'

'No.'

'Perhaps I should ring him again though I don't really want to.'

'Please don't do that, there's no need. I'll wait till next week and see the place Daniel recommended. He's going to drive me there.'

'You told me that. And you're seeing him again next Saturday.'

Tabilla had a knowing expression on her face that Anika ignored.

'So the trip to Julius's gallery was a bit of a wild goose chase,' Tabilla said.

'You could call it that.'

'I'm sorry I sent you.'

'It doesn't matter. Let me get you some wine.'

Anika poured two glasses from the wine box of Sauvignon Blanc that was kept in the refrigerator. The box was almost empty and she had to angle it to fill the second glass. She waited until they were sitting in chairs on the little area of brick paving immediately outside the back door that Tabilla termed the terrace before posing her question. 'Do you mind if I ask you something, Tabilla?'

'Ask away.'

'Why don't you want the painting?'

'Didn't you ask me that before? I don't like it much. It's not quite chocolate-boxy but it's heading that way. Besides, it brings back sad memories. About the last time I saw it. The day Tomas died. I really don't want to go through all that again.'

'Yet you don't mind me having it here in your house?'

'Not in the least.'

This seemed inconsistent. If it brought back sad memories, Anika couldn't see what difference it would make having it hanging in her bedroom rather than the lounge room. Either place she'd see it every day.

Tabilla said, 'I've always thought that when you decide to move on you should. You shouldn't be trammelled with things around you from the past. So the point is that I don't want stuff from that old life. But I don't mind if other people have it.'

'But what if I don't want it either?'

'I know you do. I see the way you look at it. I heard you when you said it symbolises home. That makes me very happy.'

'And if I were to change my mind?'

'That's entirely up to you. That's the thing about a present. When you give it away, you give up all responsibility for it. And the act of giving means you forgo the right to stipulate what it should be used for. You look puzzled again.'

'I'm just thinking about what you said. No strings attached, that's what you mean.'

'Exactly,' Tabilla said, smiling.

For once Anika didn't want to smile back. She felt unsettled. Beyond the back fence, the rows of terraced houses – and beyond them the Glebe Island wheat silos – were catching the late afternoon sun and glowing golden. Yet she was relieved that Tabilla hadn't asked any more about Mr Singer. They sat in silence for a while, until Anika heard Tabilla's stomach rumble and remembered it was her turn to cook. Perhaps pasta with a tomato and ham sauce and lots of fresh oregano from the garden, and a small salad.

She swigged down her glass of wine and got up to start

cooking. When the pasta was on, she checked the wine box: there was a small amount of liquid sloshing about inside. After managing to break open the cardboard box with the kitchen scissors, she cut out a corner of the bladder inside and topped up Tabilla's glass and then her own.

When they were sitting with their tea after dinner – as usual Tabilla wanted hers in the Clarice Cliff mug – Tabilla asked Anika how she was going to track down the Rocheteau's provenance.

'Nyenye told me who gave it to Tomas so I thought I'd try there.'

'Did she? That's more than I ever knew. Who was it?'

'Sebestyén Tinódi.'

'Are you sure she said Sebestyén Tinódi?'

'Positive. She said that he got it from a dealer who got it from the state auction house.'

'That's impossible, Anika. I knew Sebestyén. He was a very good friend of ours. He had no money and absolutely no interest in art. His only passions were politics and tinkering with motorbikes. And besides, Tomas had that painting since he was a boy, and Sebestyén was much the same age as Tomas, or maybe a bit younger. So I think she got that wrong.

'Perhaps I could ask him about it anyway. Is he still in Hungary?'

'No, Anika. Maybe your Nyenye meant another Sebestyén.'

Anika didn't much like the way Tabilla said your Nyenye. It was almost as if she didn't have much respect for her and this upset her. Struggling to keep her voice calm, she said, 'Nyenye definitely told me it was Sebestyén Tinódi.'

'Well, it couldn't have been him, I would have known. And you certainly can't ask him. He was one of the people trying to get over the Austrian border the night I left. He was shot dead in the middle of the swamp near Andau.'

Anika felt shocked by this. She hadn't known Tabilla's crossing was dangerous and didn't know what to say.

'Why don't you ask Nyenye if maybe she meant someone else?' Tabilla said. Her face had gone paler than that Daz whiter-than-white advertisement and Anika guessed hers had too. 'You could do that next time you talk on the phone.'

'Nyenye doesn't have a phone.'

'You can ask her in one of your letters.'

'Nyenye's convinced her letters are checked by the censor. She'll only write about little things.'

'Ask your father then.' Tabilla's voice was subdued. She was staring out towards the wheat silos with unseeing eyes.

Anika collected the tea things and turned on the sink tap to rinse out the dregs. With her back to Tabilla, she said, 'What did my grandparents do in the war?'

'Your paternal ones? I don't really know. I didn't meet Tomas until we started university and it was a year later that I met your father György. Tomas was only ten when the Germans occupied Hungary in 1944 and eleven when the Russians kicked them out in 1945 and occupied Hungary themselves. Hasn't your grandmother told you what they did in the occupation?'

'No.'

'Perhaps you haven't asked. I've noticed young people aren't much interested in that sort of thing until it's too late.'

Anika sat down at the table again.

After a pause, Tabilla said, 'When Tomas died, I decided I was going to leave Hungary.' Her voice was so low Anika had to lean forward to hear her words. 'At once, that evening. When I got home after telling Tomas's parents, I looked around our flat. We had just a few belongings scattered around the room. *They are only things*, I told myself. *With Tomas gone there's nothing to keep me here.*'

Tabilla picked up her water glass and absently swirled the liquid around before putting it down again. 'I knew there'd be photos of me circulating. People were taking pictures of the demonstrators and we'd thrown a few Molotov cocktails at the Russian tanks. Some of the photographers were bound to be AVO. I was in no state for interrogation. So I picked up my overcoat and handbag and headed for the Austrian border.'

Anika took her aunt's hand. It was icy cold. 'No looking back?'

'No looking back. That's always been my way.'

Anika kept hold of her hand and waited. After a few seconds Tabilla continued, 'I met up with a couple of friends who were also trying to get to the border. One of them was Sebestyén. On the way we bumped into someone else we knew, Sandor. Have I ever mentioned him to you?' When Anika shook her head, she said, 'He was a student with Tomas. His family was from eastern Hungary, from the marshy area near the border with Austria. He was guiding people across the border. That's how some of us got away. Not Sebestyén though. And now I think I'll go to bed, Anika. It's been a long day.'

She went upstairs and shut her bedroom door, and not long afterwards Anika heard the strains of classical music. She'd got to know her aunt well enough to understand that her choice of music was a barometer to her emotions. What she was playing now was one of Shostakovich's piano trios, the part that made you want to weep. It sounded manic and tragic at the same time.

* * *

Tabilla's information about Sebestyén Tinódi had blown away any hope Anika had of verifying Tomas's ownership of the

Rocheteau through contacting Tinódi. That evening she called the international operator and gave him her parents' number in Budapest. When the connection went through, her mother picked up the phone. Immediately afterwards there was a little click, barely discernible but once you'd learned to recognise that sound you never forgot it. Anika heard that little click every time she called home, every time her parents called her; the barely noticeable sound that indicated somebody was listening in.

Anika's mother's voice was thick, she had a sore throat that she couldn't seem to get rid of, *but that's the way it is, Anika*. She talked on and on and Anika let her lovely voice, huskier than usual with her cold, wrap her in that warm feeling of security it always induced, overlaid with an intense desire to be sitting in the same room as her mother. She felt tears fill her eyes and wiped them away before beginning to answer her mother's questions about what she'd been doing and how the studies were going and her trip to the beach.

'Daniel is a nice boy, I hope,' her mother said.

'He's no boy, Mum, he's probably late twenties.'

'Time he was married then.' She must have noticed Anika's ostentatious sigh but she carried on talking without a break. 'And how lucky you are to be young and by the ocean, I should love to have some sunshine to help me to get rid of this infernal cold.'

Anika's father interjected a word from time to time. He had been listening to this conversation. Her parents had some semaphore system to let the other know that Anika had called, though it wouldn't have needed to be all that sophisticated. They were never far apart. In the butchers' shop or out of it, they were nearly always within a coo-ee of each other.

When it was Anika's father's turn to hold the receiver, her mother backed out of the conversation. Anika had prepared what she wanted to ask him, the vague words to use so that he could understand her meaning but no one else but her mother could.

'Remember that thing you gave me when I left?' Anika asked him.

'That thing?' There was a pause. 'Oh yes, that thing, what about it?'

'Where did it come from?'

'I think you know that.'

'But beforehand.'

'It came from the bakers,' he said, deliberately obfuscating. 'We knew how much you love those poppy seed cakes.'

Anika understood then she was not going to be able to get anything out of him in a phone conversation. They chatted on for a little while, not too long, for her father was a man of anxieties and silences. Yet when they had talked themselves out, she hung up feeling a little more grounded, as she always did after calling home, although none the wiser about where Tomas got his auburn-haired lady from.

Upstairs in her bedroom she inspected the painting. 'If only you could tell me your history,' she told the portrait. 'I wouldn't need the provenance. And I certainly wouldn't ever need to visit that Julius Singer again.'

Chapter 9

Sydney folk who lived in a *Neighbourhood Watch* street thought it made them feel safe, Anika reflected, as she turned off Victoria Road and into Boggabri Street. It had the reverse effect on her, making her feel uncomfortable; were curtains twitching as she walked by, or was she imagining that? When she was almost home, she saw that Mrs Thornton was standing just inside her picket fence, so still she might have been a part of the council furniture, a sculpture like the one that appeared overnight a few weeks back in the pocket-handkerchief park beyond the corner shop.

Anika checked the letterbox while Mrs Thornton embarked on one of her monologues. Something about Penny and Jane, the women Anika's age who lived down the street and were building a brick wall around the little garden in front of their house.

Anika stopped listening when she saw that there was a letter for her from Nyenye. It had been weeks since she'd last heard from her grandmother. They never spoke on the phone though Nyenye could have used Anika's parents' one. But she wouldn't talk on it, nor would she have a phone in her flat, in spite of the pleas of Anika's parents. They were worried that something might happen to her, she was an old woman after all, in her mid-seventies and living alone.

With undisguised curiosity, Mrs Thornton stared at the airmail envelope Anika was now holding. 'Is it from your family?'

'Yes.'

'Sad when you leave your loved ones behind.' This thought stimulated a new stream of consciousness, and off she went. She could talk with the ease of a prayer wheel spinning its mantras.

Anika broke into the flow with a mantra of her own. 'Must dash,' she told her, and repeated the words twice, before sticking her key into the front door lock and shutting it firmly behind her.

There was a murmur of voices from the front room where Tabilla must have been doing a fitting. In the kitchen Anika found a knife and carefully slit the flap of the envelope. It never did to open a letter too quickly. It was better to prolong the experience, to enjoy the anticipation. Then to unfold the pages and slowly read the cramped handwriting. And here was a surprise: the first page was written in Miklos's hand; Miklos her brother who was so busy completing his PhD at the University of Szeged that he rarely had time to write letters.

Anika took the sheets of paper into the garden. Sitting on the step of the little terrace – where the scents of rosemary and roses mingled with the star jasmine that Tabilla was training over the side fence – she began to read.

Dear Anika,

I am in Budapest for the weekend and Nyenye is standing over me with a whip in her hand. She said I don't write enough letters and she is right, of course, but what's a man to do when there's too many other things demanding attention? Wine is wonderful, women are wonderful, song is wonderful. And the trouble is that I'm better at maths than at writing. But you'll be pleased to know that I'm over halfway through my thesis now. I've read your letters to Mama and Papa and I'm glad to hear that all is well with you.

Love you, little sister!
Miklos

Miklos's few words made Anika laugh. She visualised him struggling with a pen at Nyenye's kitchen table. Miklos with his ovoid head, high cheekbones, sandy colouring and the green eyes flecked with yellow, writing his exquisite calligraphy in large letters, while Nyenye hovered behind him to make sure he filled an entire sheet of paper. Wine, women and song; how typical that sentence was of him. He was the only member of Anika's immediate family who managed his life with joy, who was unfailingly demonstrative. And who saw only what he wanted to see.

Nyenye wrote about domestic things, about the herbs she'd bought from the market that were flourishing on her kitchen windowsill and the spring cleaning she'd begun. Her letters brought her to Anika as if she were sitting by her side.

Darling Anika,

Spring has officially started; the newspaper has announced it. And I can see with my own eyes that the daffodils are emerging, I even have one in a pot on my kitchen windowsill, the bloom is the palest yellow with a deeper yellow trumpet, and it brings me such pleasure. The birds are building nests and the days are getting longer and even I am feeling that my joints are easing, and perhaps all the scrubbing is good for me. The flat will soon be sparkling and maybe I'll even wash the net curtains once the days get warmer, though I fear they will disintegrate, so perhaps I should begin with just one, from a window that doesn't matter.

Nyenye wrote that Anika must find her letters boring but she never did. The day-to-day domestic details bound them together in a way that other topics wouldn't. Politics, world events, these could be found in other sources. But Anika could see that single daffodil on her windowsill and know how important that was after a long winter. Nyenye had an eye for beauty. And from no one else could Anika get the minutiae of Nyenye's life, the little details that connected them.

When Anika was young, Nyenye would laugh at things Anika's parents would disapprove of. 'We are complicit, little Anika. Speaking across a generation gives us such licence,' she told her once. It took her years to understand what her grandmother meant, that they were an alliance against the limits set by Anika's parents, that Nyenye would always provide a sympathetic ear when Anika needed one. And that, although she never undermined Anika's parents, she could interpret how and why they behaved as they did, so Anika could better understand them.

By the time Anika had read the letter twice, Tabilla had finished with her client and joined her on the terrace. A cooling breeze had arisen and the fading sky was streaked with a few lavender clouds, brushstrokes dashed across a pale blue canvas. It was nice having Tabilla sit beside her, Anika thought; she felt like proper family, as if she'd known her all her life rather than the few years since she'd reached Sydney.

'Do you think Mrs Thornton has ever heard of the lady of Lesbos?' Anika said.

'Probably not, but why do you ask?'

'Just now she said that Penny and Jane hang about together too much, and the other day she told me it's strange for two young women like them to be doing up a house together.'

'She might have meant that it's unusual for women to do

building work. She would have seen the Gay Mardi Gras on television so she must know about lesbians.'

'But there's a leap from seeing lesbians in fancy dress on TV and making the connection to Penny and Jane.'

'That's true. And she's lived in this street all her life so she's probably had quite a sheltered life.'

'What did Mr Thornton do?'

'He was a wharfie. Died on the job. They had two children, both grown up now and living in Queensland, so she hardly ever sees them. She's very lonely, I think, and that's why she likes to make the street her family. She's a great asset except when you're in a hurry.'

At once Anika started to feel sorry for Mrs Thornton, a solitary old woman forever looking out of her house for someone who would never come home to her. This was followed by regret: too often she let impatience get the better of her and surely she could sometimes let Mrs Thornton ramble on. All that was needed to make her feel connected was the occasional nod and smile while she talked. It was not as if that time was wasted. Anika could always think of something else to dam that river of fatigue that threatened to overwhelm her once Mrs Thornton opened her mouth.

'I've been living in this house for exactly fifteen years,' Tabilla said pensively. 'I would never have been able to afford it if it hadn't been for Mrs Barraclough.'

'Who was she?'

'My very first customer after I started dressmaking.'

'Did she drop the price?'

'No, this house wasn't hers. She left me some money in her will. She had terrible arthritis and couldn't get about easily, so every time she needed something made I went to her little flat just off Darling Street with my pins and fabric swatches and a tape measure. After she died I was amazed to discover that she was actually quite comfortably off and she'd left me some money so I used it to buy this place. It was cheap and needed a lot of work, and when that was done I began to consolidate my business.'

'And you haven't looked back.'

'Anika, I've told you that I never look back unless I have to.' She hesitated, her face thoughtful. 'But if I did look back,' she continued, her voice so quiet that Anika had to lean forward to make out the words, 'I would see a woman who was training to be an engineer when Tomas and I thought, like all the others, that we could throw the Russians out of Hungary. How naïve we were.'

This was the first time Tabilla had mentioned that she'd been an engineering student. Anika's family in Budapest had never referred to it either. Although her mother had never met Tabilla, her father certainly had, and he seemed fond of her. Had Nyenye not spoken of Tabilla much because she'd survived the Revolution and Tomas hadn't? Now Anika thought about it, Nyenye's face had taken on an odd expression whenever her name came up, and maybe she hadn't liked her much. Yet all Anika's life Tabilla had kept in touch with her and Miklos. She had sent them postcards throughout their childhood. Of landmarks like the Opera House and the Harbour Bridge, of extraordinary marsupials and those brilliant lorikeets that Anika had never tired of looking at, with their technicolour bodies that looked like something an imaginative child had coloured in.

'Anika, don't look sad,' Tabilla said. 'I am not in the least bit sorry to be dressmaking instead of designing concrete beams. It is much more colourful and sometimes it is even rather satisfying.'

Peering down the garden, Anika wondered how much you ever knew of one person. Probably not much. An orange cat appeared from the back of the outhouse, caught her eye and then withdrew quickly. Mrs Thornton in her kitchen began to sing a few bars and then lapsed into what might have been silence if you couldn't hear the distant hum of traffic from Victoria.

You learn a bit about someone, Anika thought, from observation and what they choose to tell you, but you could live side-by-side with them for years and never know who they really were. She herself kept so much concealed, and so too did her parents and her grandmother. Amazing that when she was living at home she hadn't thought to ask what sort of war they'd had. Tabilla was right when she'd said earlier that young people often never thought to discover more about their families until it was too late. Too late. There were so many questions she wanted to ask her family before it was too late.

Chapter 10

Late on Saturday afternoon Daniel collected Anika for their date. Drinks and dinner in the beer garden of a pub overlooking Watson's Bay, somewhere to the east of the city, somewhere she'd never been before. They chose a table close to the water, where the air smelled salty and a light breeze, twisting the leaves of a eucalyptus tree, tempered the heat and filled the sails of a dozen or so yachts that danced across the harbour. Small waves slapped against the sandstone shelf below them, the wake from a ship that was being towed towards the heads by a fussy little tug.

Daniel asked what Anika would like to drink and returned with a bottle of dry Riesling – in an ice bucket that looked like a length of clay drainage pipe – rather than the glass she'd expected. This gesture touched her; they were to be here for the evening and were not to be caught up in that 'your shout, my shout' business that drinking in pubs entailed.

Sitting opposite her, he poured the wine. He was unusually quiet this evening. After handing her the glass, he scrutinised her closely with those dark intelligent eyes. She drank too quickly: the wine loosened her tongue and she began to talk, releasing all those words that had been bottled up inside her. She told him how, as a teenager, she'd often fantasised about going to Sydney for reasons she still didn't understand. Maybe it was because Australia was one of the countries that had absorbed Hungarian refugees after the Second World War and the 1956 Revolution, maybe it was because she had family here, maybe it was because of the colour and sunshine of the postcards Tabilla had sent that acted like a magnet to someone who'd grown up in a cold and drab communist country.

When Anika explained to Daniel that the migrant points system gave extra points for hairdressing, he looked surprised. 'There was a shortage,' she said. 'There still is. So what with my hairdressing qualifications and my English language skills and an Australian relative, I was able to get into Australia.'

He glanced at his watch, and Anika wondered if he was finding her conversation tedious. But when she faltered, he smiled and prompted her, so she carried on talking. He refilled her glass and still he was watching her closely. Watching her face, watching her hands as she raised them to express something she was struggling to tell him, as if the motion of her hands would reveal more than her words. When she was attracted to someone, something happened to her eyes, and she felt it now and had to use her willpower to stop her eyelids batting. How embarrassing that would be, a real giveaway. You would think that after all these years of concealing feelings it would have become easier to keep those eyelashes under control but it had not. It was a distraction too, having to concentrate on her eyelids, and it diverted her attention from what she was trying to express.

It was easier to look away, to gaze over Daniel's shoulder at a point on the eucalyptus tree behind him, where the slanting sunlight made the smooth salmon-pink trunk glow, it was almost incandescent, as if it were about to burst into flames. But after a while she sensed that this made him uncomfortable, and he didn't deserve this, him being so helpful to her. When their eyes met again, a blush began in her neck and moved inexorably up to her face. Cheeks hot, she turned away again from the intensity of those dark eyes. He barely touched his second glass but sat observing her as she babbled on.

The light slowly faded and a crescent moon rose and glided

across the darkening sky. They ordered and ate their fish and chips, and she drank too much and talked a lot, and it was late by the time they left. The beer garden had become raucous, words spilling out over the harbour water, and laughter too. She felt unburdened for reasons she couldn't quite fathom. Maybe the act of telling someone about yourself was an act of trust and her subconscious had decided that Daniel was worthy of it. It had been a long time since she'd opened up to someone in this way; even Tabilla had not heard as much as she had told Daniel. She wondered if he felt the same about the evening; that receiving her history had moved them closer together.

Daniel struggled to start the yellow Beetle and eventually the engine ticked over. He smiled and Anika knew where that smile was directed. His affection for his Beetle was palpable; strange how people could fall in love with a car. She told him how the splutter of a two-stroke engine made her homesick for Budapest and the belching blue smoke that stank up the streets with fumes. Right away he understood what she meant, without her even mentioning the word Trabant, and she liked that he was clearly not in the least bit tempted to explain the workings of the two-stroke engine.

On the journey back to Rozelle, they drove along Old South Head Road. Past the rows of shops, a string of villages by the foreshore, and bay after bay glittering in the moonlight, and on through the city centre towards the inner west. Daniel drove slowly the better to talk; he had a lot to say after listening to her all evening. He told her about his family. He had two brothers who were older than he, both of them lawyers. His parents were immigrants who'd left Germany in the mid-1930s, lucky to get out while they could.

When they reached Tabilla's house he opened the car door for her from the outside, like a doorman at a posh hotel or someone in an old movie.

'Thank you for everything, Daniel.' Though the streetlight behind him lent a glow to his hair, his face was in shadow.

'It's been a wonderful evening, Anika.' He rested his hands gently on her shoulders and leaned towards her. She raised her face and wished she could see his eyes. She felt they'd been moving towards a kiss all evening and felt unexpectedly nervous. When there was a sudden blast of gunfire she jumped away, heart fluttering like a bird in a trap.

'It's just a car backfiring from Victoria Road,' Daniel said, his voice calm. 'Or a truck.'

At this moment Anika heard a squeaking from behind her. Cursing inwardly, she turned and saw that Mrs Thornton's front door, with the hinges that needed oiling, was shifting in the breeze. Once her eyes adjusted, she spotted her neighbour standing in the shadows on her verandah. She was wearing a floral dressing gown over a pink nightdress that was too long and almost dragging on the ground. When she lifted the hem slightly you might have thought she was about to curtsy, but instead she took a couple of steps along the path to her gate to inspect Daniel more closely.

'Nice evening, isn't it?' she said. 'A bit of a wind sprang up just now and it's cooling things down nicely. I didn't mean to make you jump, Anika. It's just that I heard a strange noise and thought I should investigate. Must have been a car backfiring. We're normally a quiet street,' she said to Daniel. 'In spite of being near Victoria Road. It's the one-way system, you see. A real blessing.'

'I'm sure it is.' Daniel was nodding and smiling at the same time. 'I hope we didn't disturb you.'

'No,' said Mrs Thornton. 'Anyway, I won't hold you up any longer. Goodnight.' She hauled up her nightie again and was shutting the door behind her before they had time to reply.

'It's been a lovely evening, Anika.' That moment when they might have kissed had gone and Daniel's tone had become formal. He shifted and the shadows cast by the street lighting now defined his face. His head might almost have been one of those Greek busts you see in museums, so sculpted did it appear.

'Thanks for taking me out, Daniel.' Anika's words, heartfelt when she first spoke them, sounded stilted on repetition.

'Let's do it again soon.'

'I'd love to.' She opened the front gate, put her key in the front door lock and heard it click open before turning her head. Daniel was still watching her but his face was again in shadow and his expression unreadable. She wondered if she had imagined that almost-kiss. When she stepped inside, the door slammed shut behind her.

A moment later she heard Daniel's car engine revving up – that characteristic putter-putter noise – and then he was gone.

Chapter 11

Only at this moment did Anika become aware that there was a gale blowing down the hall. The television was turned up so loudly that Tabilla didn't notice Anika entering the lounge room. With her back to the door, Tabilla was leaning forward in her chair the better to peer at the images on the television screen. When she saw Anika, she waved her over to the sofa. Immediately Anika recognised the streets all those people were marching along, she recognised those buildings. The camera shifted to Kossuth Square, a place very familiar to her, no more than a kilometre or two from the apartment block where her parents lived. A vast crowd filled the square, thousands upon thousands of people gathered in front of the Parliament Building.

Eyes brilliant, Tabilla turned to her. 'They reckon there's over a hundred thousand people there. And look, not a policeman or uniform in sight!'

'What's happening?'

'Can you credit it, Anika, they've just announced that free elections are to be held within a year! Gorbachev doesn't care what the Eastern European satellites get up to now. The Soviet Union is fed up with subsidising them.'

Anika wondered if her parents were among the crowd in Kossuth Square, and Miklos and his friends too. 'So Prime Minister Németh's trip to Moscow's paid off.'

The pictures of Kossuth Square were replaced by an ABC commentator talking about momentous changes in Central and Eastern Europe. When the piece finished, Tabilla said, her face luminous with excitement, 'This morning I didn't have time to tell you what I heard on the BBC World Service. Németh wants that fence dismantled.'

'Which fence?'

'That electrified one along the border with Austria. The one with the flares that Hungary can't afford to maintain. Németh spoke to Gorbachev about that too.'

This was the border over which Tabilla had escaped over three decades before; no wonder her face was glowing. Anika felt as if a burden was shifting from her shoulders and in its place that lightest of feelings, hope, fluttered by. Brushing her with its wings, it left behind the thought that before too long – perhaps next year or the year after – she might be able to visit her family in Budapest.

When the news from Hungary was replaced by the smiling image of Australian Prime Minister Bob Hawke, she skipped down the hall to shut the back door. In the kitchen she slid on fragments of something hard that were scattered across the floor.

Grabbing hold of the bench, she turned on the light and her delight dissipated. Shards of glass littered the vinyl-covered floor. The back door was wide open and all that remained of its once-glazed top panel were jagged edges. Edges as sharp as sharks' teeth.

My painting, she thought, and the breeze through the doorway suddenly felt icy. She dashed back to the lounge room, where her aunt was smiling to herself as she absently watched the cricketing highlights. 'Tabilla, come into the kitchen, quickly!' Anika had to shout to make herself heard. 'Careful, there's glass all over the place.'

'It's odd that I didn't hear anything.' Hands on hips, Tabilla contemplated the mess. 'When I got home from the concert everything was fine.' She turned on the outside light that illuminated the herbs and the roses.

'The garden's deserted.' Anika's voice cracked as she spoke. 'You can see that from here. Unless there's someone really thin hiding in the old dunny with the gardening stuff.'

'There's no need to be sarcastic. I'd like to see if the gate's locked.'

'I'll look upstairs while you do that.' Although Anika wanted to race up the stairs right away, she was frightened of what she might find.

'Don't go up,' Tabilla said, seizing hold of Anika's arm. 'Someone might still be up there, with a gun or a knife or something. I'll phone the police. We'll let them do the checking.'

Tabilla dialled the emergency number and in a few seconds was connected to Balmain Police Station. After she put down the receiver, she said, 'They want us to wait out the front until the police get here, in case there's someone upstairs still.'

The two policemen, who arrived almost immediately, might have been pensioned-off rugby players. Ryan and Warburton, they were called, thick-necked burly men at least six feet tall, and wide too. One of them reeked of tobacco smoke and they seemed to take up all the space in the hallway. While they searched the house, Ryan said, Tabilla and Anika were to wait out the front under the streetlight.

Anika and her aunt stood next to the police car. They didn't wait alone; in next to no time Mrs Thornton was on the scene. While Tabilla explained what was happening, Anika leaned against the car, nerves stretched taut while her thoughts skittered around. The police presence in the house made her feel even more nervous than she already was. The past and the present, in her heightened emotional state, seemed jumbled up together. She began to think of the day five years ago when the police had ransacked the *samizdat* boutique in Laszlo's Budapest apartment. She'd been right there, browsing the illegal literature. After the police had burst through the front door, she'd managed to get out the back door unnoticed. On the way, she'd tucked into her trouser pocket the leaflet she'd wanted, the one about the protest march near the Danube Bend, the march against the construction of the Nagymaros Dam. Afterwards, she'd heard from her brother Miklos – who'd got it from a friend – that the police had seized all the dissident literature and the duplicating machines and shifted Laszlo into a flat on the outskirts of Budapest. 'And didn't that raid give you a clue that the Communist Party is cracking down on protesters?' Nyenye had raged days later, after Anika had been released.

Yet the Sydney police weren't like the Budapest secret police, Anika reminded herself now, as she twisted a strand of her hair, tighter and tighter until it pulled at her scalp. And maybe even the secret police were changing, just think of that march in Kossuth Square she and Tabilla had witnessed on television. Her thoughts shifted again to her painting, and her worries gathered around it like moths beating against a lamp. Keep calm, she told herself. Art thieves didn't hit on a suburb like Rozelle. Not when there were rich pickings in the Eastern Suburbs or the North Shore.

The neighbours were appearing in the street one by one. As soon as Tabilla finished telling Mrs Thornton her tale, they were joined by the neighbour from their other side, an old man who had trouble hearing; it must have been the flashing blue light that disturbed him. Anika felt disengaged from the scene. Detachment was one way of staying calm. Hiding your nagging little fears from others helped to conceal them from yourself. This remoteness didn't stop her observing things though, clocking Mr and Mrs Opposite coming out of their terrace in their matching navy-blue terry towelling bath robes, and then Ty Nguyen from down the road. Again, Tabilla told the story of what had happened, with Mrs Thornton nodding her head all the while, as if she'd been present in the kitchen with them. And none of them had seen anything.

When the policemen had finished their search, they called Tabilla and Anika inside. The taller one said, 'All's clear. There's no one here and the place looks OK. You'll need to see if anything's been taken, but we want to ask you a few questions first.'

'What about the back yard?' Tabilla said.

'We've checked that. The gate wasn't fastened. You might want to get a padlock for that bolt. We reckon that they got out through your gate but they got in via next-door's yard, the one that's a bit closer to Victoria Road. Then they took down a few palings from the side fence to squeeze into your place. You'll want to find a handyman to fix that. The palings look rather old and that whole fence probably wants replacing.'

At this moment there was a knock on the front door. It was Mrs Thornton. Stepping into the hall, she said, 'I've just remembered something. You know the dunny lane that runs along the back of our houses? Penny – that's the girl who lives down the road,' she explained to the police, 'told me she was looking out of their upstairs rear window a few days ago. Late afternoon, it was, and she saw someone walking along it.'

'Is that so unusual?' the taller policeman said.

'He was walking up and down it like he was looking for something.'

'Maybe he'd dropped something.'

'Furtive-like,' Mrs Thornton added.

'What did he look like?' Tabilla said.

'Penny said it wasn't light enough like to see, and anyway he was wearing a hat. But he seemed to be shaking the back gate of each yard. Maybe he was figuring out how to get into your place.'

'We'll interview Penny afterwards,' the taller policeman said. 'What number house?' He wrote down this information in his notebook. 'Thanks for letting us know,' he said. 'If there's nothing else you can tell us, you can leave now. You're next door, right? If we need a statement we'll know where to come.'

He shut the door after Mrs Thornton, and turned to Tabilla. 'Were you in all evening, Mrs Molnar?'

'No, I was at a concert with a friend.'

'Who's the friend? We need a name.'

'Julius Singer.'

Anika clutched at the stair rail. It was clammy. Even its thick varnish couldn't block out the humidity. There was silence apart from the scratching of the taller policeman's pen on paper. 'Julius?' she said. 'But Tabilla, I thought you never saw him.'

'I hardly ever do but he called me on Thursday night. They'd been given some concert tickets and his wife was unwell. Your visit must have reminded him that years ago we used to go to concerts together.'

'Did Julius mention me?'

'No, not a word. It's been ages since I last saw him. And as soon as the concert ended he had to rush home to see his wife. She's not been well, as I said, and he was worried about her. I came straight home and started watching the news.'

'Can I go upstairs now?' Anika asked the taller policeman, her voice cracking. Her aunt never went out with Julius. Why tonight, the same night that there'd been a break-in?

'Once we've finished with the statements,' the taller policeman told her, before asking Tabilla what time she got back, and jotting down some more notes.

After filling a couple more pages of his notebook, he turned to Anika, and wanted to know where she'd been that evening. Meticulously – and slowly, oh so slowly, if only he'd get a move on – he wrote down the time she'd got home and where she'd been and who with. When he snapped his notebook shut, she noticed that his fingers were stained with nicotine. He must be a heavy smoker, she decided, and began to feel even more jittery, as if she'd drunk too many cups of coffee. 'I've got to go upstairs,' she muttered, taking the steps two at a time, the policemen and Tabilla not far behind.

Her bedroom was in darkness and the door was wide open. She counted to seven, her favourite number, before flicking the switch. The room blazed with light.

It looked different. Somehow bigger. There was a gap on the far wall. A gap ringed with a faint mark. A mark framing nothing.

The painting had gone.

PART II

Sydney, March 1989

Chapter 12

It was as if Anika were floating out of her body, as if she were hovering above it, looking down on the two policemen and her aunt and what must be her exoskeleton. She could hear no sounds, apart from the clock on her bookshelf that was counting out the seconds, but their passage was distorted, not the usual regular tick-tock. The interval between each sound was longer than usual, and indeed it seemed to vary. This made her feel suddenly dizzy, even vertiginous. Yet it was impossible to halt the strange elevation she was experiencing. Up and up she went. Now she seemed to be outside the house, and floating above it. Glancing down at the roof, she saw that some of the slates were sliding and there was nothing she could do to stop them. Alarmingly, Rozelle was getting smaller and smaller. The Rocheteau was floating just ahead of her, like a magic carpet that she needed to reach to take her safely back home. As she floated higher and higher, she began to feel queasy. The sky started to pulse with waves of darkness and she felt herself falling falling falling.

'She's fainted,' Anika heard Tabilla saying. 'It's a terrible shock.'

Anika was lying on her bed under a rug, with her feet propped up on two pillows. Her face felt cold and clammy, and her legs surprisingly heavy. Again, she could hear the clock's tick-tock tick-tock, it was a regular beat now.

And at that moment she remembered what she'd lost.

Anger would come, she knew it would. It was just hanging around the edges of this numbness, waiting for a chance to burst out. Breathe, breathe; it was necessary to be on your guard. With a setback you had to be careful, you had to stop your feelings showing. Revealing any emotion would give them information, these two police officers, here in her room and too close for comfort.

Suddenly her anger was replaced by terror. She shut her eyes. A moment later, she was in a cold and windowless cell that reeked of cigarettes. There was a grey man sitting opposite her. Ashen-faced, ashen-haired, charcoal-uniformed, this man fired questions at her. He grinned as she stumbled through responses that were always the wrong ones. Grinned as she struggled against something that was holding her down. Grinned as he lit another cigarette. Panicking, she opened her eyes. Tabilla's concerned face was looking down at her.

'They are detectives,' Tabilla murmured to Anika in Hungarian. She was holding Anika's left wrist, smoothing the scar, soothing the skin around it. 'You are in Sydney, dearest Anika. Everything is fine. Painting is only stuff. People are what matter. Everything is OK.'

'What's it a picture of?' one of the policemen asked Tabilla.

'A woman in a blue dress,' Tabilla said. 'A portrait in blue.'

Anika had to focus, she had to get that dreadful memory out of her head. 'A portrait of a woman with auburn hair,' she muttered.

One of the policemen scribbled some words in his notebook while the other man told her that nothing had been taken from Tabilla's room and did she have anything else missing.

She sat up. Her room looked tidy, nothing appeared to have been rearranged. Then she noticed that the photograph of her family outside Molnars' Butchers had been moved a few centimetres. Someone had been in here, going through her things and checking her stuff and choosing the painting to steal. How she hated the thought of someone she didn't know rummaging through her belongings. It felt like a violation. She got up and with trembling hands opened the drawers and the cupboard. Nothing else had gone.

The policemen began to talk about photographs, did they have any that might help them recover the painting. Tabilla led them out of the room. Anika could hear them talking on the landing. Words like measurements and police report and getting the back door fixed.

Her room seemed sullied. She was feeling increasingly disturbed by the fact that someone had known to go straight for the painting. Someone with information. Someone who was able to distinguish between her picture and all the others that Tabilla had on her walls, modern prints mostly. John Olsen and Fred Williams were her favourites. Again, Anika looked at the blank wall where the painting used to hang: the portrait was home, it was family, it was the uncle she'd never met, it had become a part of who she was. Frantically she struggled to fight down the rising waves of panic.

The taller policeman stuck his head back into her room to ask if they could take away a photo of the painting. She had only one picture of it and, after a bit of rummaging, she found it in the top drawer of her bedside table. As she held it out, stupid little fears flooded into her mind, flushing out rationality. Fears that her only photo would blow out of the police car window, or that one of the men would use it as a coaster once he got it back to the police station and would return it with an ugly brown ring on it from a mug of coffee. Or maybe he'd just bin it, and later tell her it had been lost. As the officer took hold of the photo, she said, unable to hide her anxiety, 'Can I have a receipt please?'

For an instant the man looked at her strangely. That was when hysteria hit her and she burst into tears, great sobs that wrenched their way painfully out of her chest. It was as if a part of her family, part of her, had been torn away. And at the same time, she felt humiliated by this weakness, this inability to contain her emotions. The two policemen began to shuffle awkwardly.

Tabilla took her arm and said to the men, 'The painting means a lot to her and this photo is her only record. I tell you what, I'll photograph it with my Instamatic.'

After Anika had recovered a bit and blown her nose several times on a wad of tissues, they trooped downstairs and Tabilla got her camera out of the drawer in the sideboard. The surface of Anika's photo was so shiny that when Tabilla used the flash the picture would come up with reflections glaring back at the viewer. Tabilla seemed to understand this and took several photos from different vantage points with different lighting. 'I'm a wizard at photography,' she said, as if to reassure her niece.

The taller policeman looked at Anika appraisingly. 'Your painting was upstairs. Nobody would see it from the window. Who knew about it?'

'The curators at the art gallery. I took it in two weeks ago.' Daniel knew about it. Julius did too, though he had an alibi in Tabilla. Jonno also knew of it. Yet he didn't seem to have a clue about art, that much was clear from their conversation. And it couldn't have been Daniel because Anika had just spent the whole evening with him and he'd been by her side all the time.

Yet Daniel did look at his watch when the wine had loosened Anika's tongue. She'd thought at the time she might be boring him with all her talk about the points system for immigrants, and maybe she was. Yet he could also have been wondering how long he had to wait before he could take her home. It was possible that he was the robber's accomplice, someone charged with keeping her out of her bedroom while the house was broken into and the painting stolen. He could even have been working with Julius Singer, who had managed to get Tabilla out of the house at the same time.

Of course, the other curators would know about the painting too. For instance, that elegant and beautifully dressed woman who'd identified the picture as being by Antoine Rocheteau. And you could bet they would have all been discussing it afterwards. Maybe one of them could have arranged to have it stolen. Yet these were reputable people with reputable jobs and Anika could hardly accuse them. Anyway, they wouldn't have known where she lived, unless Daniel had told them.

'The only people who knew where the painting was are Julius Singer and the curators of the art gallery,' she told the policemen. 'They're hardly going to steal it.'

'Which gallery?' The police had become more interested and Tabilla gave them a detailed account of why Anika took the painting to the Art Gallery of New South Wales and how Tabilla had suggested it, after she'd seen the advertisement in the *Sydney Morning Herald*.

Then they asked Anika for the names and addresses of everyone who knew about the painting. And one thing led to another and they wanted to know where the painting came from. Tabilla shut up at this, so Anika burbled on, explaining how it was in her family, that it had belonged to her deceased uncle. The taller policeman gave her his odd look again but it was probably just because of the way she said deceased. That was a word she'd picked up from the cop shows on television, the ones who spoke in their own police jargon, and maybe normal people didn't talk about deceased relatives, but what else could she have said? She could hardly have said dead uncle. Then she had a lightbulb moment: she should have said, 'my uncle who passed away'. She began explaining this but the taller policeman, the one called Tom Warburton, interrupted her. 'Calm down, young lady,' he said.

His tone was avuncular but Anika disliked being told to calm down and hated being called young lady. Those words were so patronising although she didn't want to tell him that. They'd been sympathetic, these men, unlike the security police where she'd come from.

'Julius Singer knows about the painting,' she said to the policeman, her voice pitched too high. 'That's the man Tabilla went to the concert with tonight.'

'But he was with me all evening,' Tabilla said gently. 'And anyway, they've already taken down his details.'

The second policeman looked at his watch and Anika realised they probably had other more urgent jobs on, like domestic violence and road accidents, and that their break-in was one of many calls.

Once the police had gone and the emergency glazier had patched up the broken pane in the back door, it was nearly three o'clock in the morning. Too tired even to draw the curtains, it was all Anika could do to drag herself to bed where she fell deep into an all-embracing unconsciousness. Before too long, cocooning sleep became a vivid nightmare; she was caught up with her brother Miklos at the Danube Bend near Visegrád, in a peaceful demonstration that morphed into a riot. Faceless figures wielding truncheons seized hold of her and dragged her to a vehicle. Only when the doors slammed shut did she realise she'd been thrown into the back of a hearse. Peering through the back window, she saw Miklos – together with the other demonstrators – receding into the distance. Abruptly she wrenched herself awake, her muscles tensed for flight and her body slick with sweat. Trapped between nightmare and wakefulness, she was pulled into the moment by the screaming of an ambulance from Victoria Road.

Tick-tock, went the clock, a metronome counting out

time, pushing the present into the past. In the background was the faint hum of late-night traffic from Victoria Road. Anika sat up: a lozenge of moonlight illuminated the wall at the end of her bed and the faint dirty mark of a rectangle that framed nothing.

She doubted if they were ever going to get the Rocheteau back again.

Chapter 13

Anika dozed until late morning, with periodic memories of that nightmare flickering through her brain, the police of her dreams occasionally replaced by distorted images of Ryan and Warburton blundering around Rozelle and Balmain. When the downstairs clock chimed eleven, she sat up in bed. Automatically she peered at the wall at the foot of her bed and registered that the painting was no longer there. Maybe she'd never get used to that void. All that remained was that smudged rectangle defining where it used to be, a rectangle that for the barest instant conveyed the hope that the picture might be returned one day.

It took only seconds to leap out of bed and throw on yesterday's clothes that lay crumpled on her draughting stool. Then she shouted a greeting to Tabilla through the bathroom door and burst out through the front gate and on to the street.

Mrs Thornton was nowhere to be seen – she was probably still at church, she went every Sunday – and Anika headed down the footpath to the house that Penny and Jane were renovating, the last in the terrace immediately before the road swung to the right. She pushed open their gate. Really, she shouldn't have been doing this. It was Sunday morning after all and Penny and Jane would want to sleep in on a Sunday when they worked hard all week and set themselves construction jobs on the weekend. Just looking at the freshly painted wall around their front yard made her feel guilty, but she had to find out and for all she knew they might be going out shortly.

Now she noticed that there was a radio on somewhere inside the house, so they were definitely at home and awake. She banged on the front door. Guilt fighting with her desire to track down the painting made her rap harder than she might otherwise have done; she sounded as urgent as a debt collector. When Penny opened the door, Anika blurted out an apology. Penny was wearing two towels – an orange one as a turban around her head and a yellow one in sarong-fashion – but in spite of all that cotton she was dripping on to the floorboards. Somehow the dribbling water made Anika feel out of control and she might have wept if it hadn't been for the self-discipline that she'd learned growing up in Budapest.

'It's OK,' Penny said, her smile a little forced. 'It's time I got out of the bath anyway.'

Anika asked her if she could remember what the man she saw in the dunny lane the other day looked like, the one that Mrs Thornton had said was rattling the gates.

'It wasn't really light enough to see and anyway he was wearing a hat so I couldn't see his face. He was shortish, I think, though that lane is lower than the bottom of our yard so maybe he wasn't all that short.'

'Would you recognise him if you saw him again?'

'I doubt it, Anika. I told the detectives all that last night. They were very thorough. I'm really sorry you got broken-into.'

* * *

That afternoon Anika realised that something else was bothering her, a little thread of bewilderment about what Tabilla was doing last night, a little thread that was becoming rope-like as the hours passed by. But she needed to handle this with diplomacy and neither she nor Tabilla were at their best when hungry. She waited until after dinner when Tabilla was sitting at the table sipping her mug of tea. Wanting to get this awkward conversation out of the way, Anika swilled hers down too fast, so hot it burned the roof of her mouth.

'Tabilla, did Julius Singer talk to you about meeting me?' She took a sip of cold water and held it in her mouth for a second or two to cool the burning sensation on her palate.

'No. Should he have? I thought you'd already told me what happened when you visited his gallery.'

'He was very interested in my painting.' Anika watched Tabilla carefully.

'You said he wasn't.' Tabilla gazed back, with wide-open eyes and a baffled expression.

'That's because he was rather rude. He said it couldn't be mine.'

'You didn't tell me that. How could he possibly say that?' Tabilla's face grew even more puzzled.

'He seemed very confused.'

'You mean, like dementia?'

'Not really. Just muddled.'

'He was fine when I saw him last night. And he certainly didn't mention your painting.'

'Did you talk to him for long?'

'We met at the Opera House and chatted for a few minutes before the performance and in the interval. That was all.'

'I'm wondering if he arranged to have it stolen.'

'He'd never do a thing like that.' Tabilla began to jiggle her leg so the table shook. 'He's one of the most honourable men I know.'

Anika kept to herself her view that Tabilla was biased and that anyway she didn't know many men. 'He knows where you live.'

'So what? He was with me all the time. While we were at

the performance, that is. Anyway, lots of people know where I live but that doesn't mean they'd break into my house and steal something.'

'But it's odd that only the painting was taken and nothing else.'

Tabilla frowned at the kitchen sink. 'Well, here's another theory that's got nothing to do with Julius – suppose that your new curator friend told people about it. Isn't Daniel supposed to be taking you to an auction house this Wednesday for a valuation? He would have told them about it. And who knows how many other places he might have called up.'

'I'll have to cancel the appointment.'

'Leave it. The picture might turn up before then.'

'Get bloody real,' Anika snapped. 'It will never turn up.'

Tabilla's face was pained and at once Anika wished she'd kept her mouth shut. Her aunt didn't deserve such rudeness, her kindness and generosity repaid with ingratitude. She was probably feeling at least as upset as Anika was. After all, it was her Tomas's painting – a bit of her old life that had gone as well as a bit of Anika's.

'I'm sorry, Tabilla, I really am. I don't know what possessed me.' Filled with remorse, Anika bent down to hug her and without the slightest hesitation Tabilla hugged her back.

'We mustn't let this upset things between us,' she said. 'We're family, after all.'

'Yes, we're family.'

Anika sat opposite her. Smiling in a forced sort of way, Tabilla nudged the Clarice Cliff mug towards her. 'I wouldn't mind another cup of tea if there's one going, Anika,' she said.

Chapter 14

The mellow voice of Anika's design tutor, Howard Meyer, reverberated off the towering stone wall to one side of Butler's Stairs. Howard was standing halfway down the long stair, so far below that Anika had a bird's eye view of him, his face foreshortened so that only his chin was visible and the narrow-brimmed homburg covering his bald pate. He was pointing to the escarpment at right angles to the steps, the sandstone quarried away or eroded by millennia, the brick arches set forward to support the dunnies and the backs of the terraced houses above. When all the students in the group caught up with him, the stragglers too, those who had trouble finding parking spots, he began all over again, gesticulating as he talked. Anika's friends Sally and Peter smiled at each other, including her in their exchange.

Their tutor had already given his students the dimensions of the arches; he didn't want them trampling all over the yards of the houses below them. Now that everyone was gathered around him, some on higher steps, some lower, he gave them a pep talk. 'Be inspired by this glorious structure,' he bellowed. A couple of students sniggered but Howard ignored them. 'Think of the person who conceived this idea! These brick arches are a wonder of nineteenth-century design.' He explained that the design project this semester was for clients – imaginary of course – who wanted to use the space behind the arches for an apartment. The students' mission was to provide them with the floor space they needed.

They took out their pads and knocked out a few sketches.

This was one of the things Anika loved most about this course: summarising what she saw, in a few lines drawn with a 6B pencil on a sheet of blank paper. She augmented her drawings with photos – she'd borrowed Tabilla's Instamatic for the excursion – and what the camera revealed and what her sketches exposed were not the same. Her eyes looked at the arches but somehow her brain altered what she saw, and her drawings came out different – all strong verticals. And who was to say what was reality? These were complementary views and both the sketches and the photographs would be useful when it came to designing the apartment. Already she knew it was going to be all about internal design. The integrity of the strong and soaring arches could be maintained only by setting the apartment back a bit. The colonnade would remain and the apartment would be recessed, illuminated by a wall of glazing.

After putting away the camera and her sketches, Anika found Howard Meyer by her side. 'I heard you've had a painting stolen. I was sorry to learn that.'

'Thank you.' With unsteady hands she folded down the top of her satchel and fastened the straps. Sally and Peter were heading up the steps, arguing about the arches, whether the apartment should be in modern idiom or in character with the 1870s.

'An Antoine Rocheteau, the newspaper said.'

'The newspaper?'

'Yes. There was a piece in today's *Gazette*. The painting must be worth a fortune.'

'It hasn't been valued.' Though it was hardly Meyer's fault the papers took up the story of the theft, Anika's annoyance transferred itself straight to him, and she feared that her words sounded like a snarl.

'That doesn't matter. All Rocheteau's pictures are worth a fortune, even the small ones. Did you know?'

'No.' She stared at Meyer's polka-dotted bow tie while a little worm of anxiety began to wriggle in her stomach.

'My wife said Sotheby's just sold a Rocheteau for half a million. Half a million sterling, that is. You'll be rolling.'

Anika's palms had begun to sweat. She lunged for the railing and clutched it tightly. 'It wasn't insured,' she said. A couple of thousand dollars, that's what she'd thought the Rocheteau might be worth. OK, she'd fantasised that it might be worth more, but that was just a daydream and one that she'd dismissed almost at once. If she'd thought the portrait was really valuable she would have hidden it, not left it hanging on her bedroom wall. What a fool she'd been.

Meyer's lips curled with what looked like a suppressed smile. It was that old human reaction of smiling at another's misfortune. Trying to restore emotional equilibrium, Anika's mother used to say: you heard bad news and it was instinctive for some people to smirk. Yet this didn't stop her wanting to punch him.

And she wanted to punch herself too. When you were born and bred under communism, you didn't think of insurance. Communism provided for all, didn't it? Panic began to expand in her chest and her throat closed up. If she'd been thinking like a true Australian, she would have acted quickly after her trip to the gallery. She would have hidden the painting somewhere safe and insured it herself, even though she had no idea of its true value. The person who stole it knew its worth – its monetary worth. But they didn't know its psychological value, all those family memories encapsulated in a canvas that she would never get back.

'Did you see the report, Anika?'

'No. I haven't read the paper today.'

'I tore it out of the *Gazette*. You can have it, if you like.' Meyer pulled out of his top pocket a crumpled piece of paper and passed it to her.

Nodding her thanks, Anika peered up at the arches, as if they required her attention rather than the tatty piece of newsprint in her hand. She couldn't bring herself to look at it right away. Seeing the theft reported in the *Gazette* would make its loss more real. The police must have notified the media, or their neighbours had. Neither she nor Tabilla had spoken to any journalists.

'Like a lift somewhere?' Meyer said.

'No, thanks.' Anika's breathing was ragged and her voice no more than a croak. 'Sally's driving me.'

After he'd gone, she unfolded the paper.

Art thief steals valuable painting from Rozelle home
In a brazen suburban art heist, a thief has stolen an expensive portrait painting from a Rozelle home.

The Impressionist painting *Lady in a Blue Dress* by renowned French artist Antoine Rocheteau was stolen on Saturday night while the owners were watching television.

Lady in a Blue Dress is a portrait of a young woman with dark red hair, and is forty-six centimetres high by thirty-eight centimetres, Miss Anita Molnar aged 24 explained.

Balmain crime manager, Detective Inspector McIntyre said the theft was reported on Saturday night by the owners, believed to be mother and daughter.

Police were appealing for information, especially from anyone in the art world.

Anyone with information can call Crime Stoppers on 1800 333 000.

Sloppy reporting and she'd never spoken to a journalist; the reporter must have got garbled details from the police or a neighbour. But at least they'd got right the description of the painting and its size. Anika found it an effort to plod up the steps, there was litter everywhere and the sun beat down relentlessly on her head. Sally and Peter were waiting at the top; Sally's face was concerned when she saw Anika's expression. Anika told her and Peter about her conversation with Howard Meyer and showed them the article.

'This makes everything worse.' Anika climbed into the back seat of Sally's car. Sally would drop her off at the Rozelle traffic lights on Victoria Road.

'But why should it?' Sally pulled out in front of their tutor's car. Meyer had banked-up traffic behind him. Like a traffic cop he waved out the cars of his design group. Sally gave him a mock salute and a tiny toot of her horn and slipped into second gear with a crunching sound.

Peter's sharp intake of breath showed his sympathy lay with the engine. 'It's going to be harder for the thief to get rid of it if it's that well known,' he said.

Anika kept her thoughts to herself for the journey home through the busy peak-hour traffic that claimed most of Sally's attention. Tonight, she was going to have to phone Daniel to cancel the valuation meeting and she really didn't want to. Cancelling the meeting was equivalent to abandoning all hope that she'd get the painting back and she wasn't ready for that yet.

The painting had hung in Nyenye's flat for as long as Anika could remember. Maybe Nyenye knew something else about its provenance. Something more than the wrong name of the man who'd given it to Tomas. Anika and Miklos had spent hours playing in Nyenye's living room when they were very young. A room full of contrasts, darkness and dinginess until you looked closely at the walls through the dim lighting and saw the beauty of the paintings hanging there; the backdrop to the games that the children played, when Nyenye gave them ancient curtains from her rag bag and a free rein to push around the furniture to make a cubby house. The Rocheteau had hung to the right of the chimney breast – the fireplace that was never used – and immediately above it was a painting of women in brightly coloured hoop dresses proceeding through a gloomy landscape. Anika had grown up with those paintings, she'd grown up with the Rocheteau. Losing it was losing a bit of her past.

Tabilla clearly had no idea of its value or its origins. Maybe knowledge of its provenance had vanished with Tomas. They were almost at Pyrmont Bridge when – mouth suddenly dust-dry and hands clutching at the edge of the seat – Anika was blindsided by a question. How did her parents come to give her such a valuable painting to carry out of Hungary – could they really have had no idea of its worth? Surely if they'd known it was so valuable they would have told her to be careful. Yet they hadn't said a word about that and they'd never mentioned it since, apart from asking in their indirect way if it had cleared customs OK.

Chapter 15

After dinner, Daniel phoned Anika before she had a chance to ring him.

'I saw that article in the *Gazette*,' he said, once the courtesies were out of the way. 'Why didn't you tell me your painting's been stolen?'

'I was just about to. I didn't want to call you any earlier because I'm still hoping it'll turn up.'

'I'll put off our meeting with the dealer.' There was a pause during which she heard the phone's static and then Daniel's sigh, before he said, 'It might turn up yet.'

'I doubt it.'

'You must be feeling awful. I'm so sorry, Anika.'

'It's a terrible shock.'

'I bet it is. How did it happen?'

While she explained he made sympathetic noises, and from time to time asked a question. When she'd finished, he said, 'You need cheering up. Would you like to have dinner with me next Friday night?'

'I can't on Friday. What about Saturday night instead?'

'I can't on Saturday.'

Anika imagined a girlfriend. Maybe that was why their kiss last Saturday night was aborted. It was as if the car back-firing and Mrs Thornton's arrival had given him a chance to have second thoughts about that almost-kiss. The girlfriend would be artistic and pretty, with a confident manner to match his. Or perhaps it was a boyfriend. Arty and devastatingly handsome, like those men in the advertisements for impossible clothes that you see sometimes in the colour supplements of the weekend newspapers.

There was a short pause, before he said, 'What about a walk on Sunday afternoon?'

'I'd like that.'

'I'll collect you at two. I know a great track from Taronga Park to Clifton Gardens and on to the old quarantine station.' After a brief goodbye, he put down the receiver.

For a second or two Anika listened to the dial tone. The conversation left her confused, not knowing where she stood with Daniel. His feelings towards her were unclear, and her own were equally ambiguous.

That night, sleep would not come. Anika was chasing it too hard and it slipped away. Soon she was caught up in the bedding and her hip began to ache, a reminder of the beating she'd received from the police when they'd scooped her up at the Danube Bend. She got up to smooth out the tangled sheets and start all over again. If only she could empty her head but thoughts kept crowding in, as if there was a party going on that they simply had to attend.

It wasn't only losing the painting that was so awful, though that was bad enough. But added to this was the fact that it was so valuable, if Howard Meyer's wife was to be believed. Once more Anika rolled over. Her parents surely couldn't have known what the painting was worth. Her father had told her that in communist Hungary there wasn't a well-established market for paintings. Nyenye had misinformed her when she said Sebestyén Tinódi had given the picture to Uncle Tomas. Maybe Tomas had bought it himself. Anika imagined him heading to the consignment store to buy the painting. Not with a wallet stuffed with forints but with a wheelbarrow full, like those pictures of what hyperinflation looked like in 1946. Scarred by galloping inflation, he might have thought it was better to keep any savings in a painting rather than under the mattress. Yet how could he have afforded a painting? He was only a boy after the war and still a student when he died a decade later, no doubt penniless as students always were.

She tossed and turned. Her head was spinning and sleep more elusive than ever. To calm herself, she tried deep breathing. Learn to concentrate on the moment, that's what Sally advised. But it didn't work; her thoughts kept turning back home, to the expressions on her parents' faces – and Nyenye's too – before she'd left Budapest and her father had placed the painting in her suitcase. Could they have known they were handing over something valuable but she wasn't smart enough to realise it? No, they were simple people, honourable people. More likely was that their faces were clouded by her imminent departure. As was hers. It was a big step she was about to take.

On the afternoon she'd left Budapest it had been so cold. She'd felt chilled through and through, not only by the weather but by what she was embarking on. The dear faces of her family – her parents and Nyenye and Miklos too – were pinched with anxiety and blanched by the icy wind. They had all known that they might never see one another again. And Anika was convinced that her family had no idea that the painting they'd put in her luggage was valuable.

Through the open window now she heard the distant drone of late-night traffic from Victoria Street. A drunk passed by, singing raucously. After he was out of earshot she got up. Flinging open the curtains, she watched wisps of cloud pass across the marbled moon, blurring its edges.

Tomas was in his early twenties when he died. Her father was ten years younger, so he'd never had much of a chance to get to know his brother well. It was clear to Anika that he'd loved him and idolised him, yet some of that might have been because Tomas died like a martyr and was kind to his little brother. And her father wouldn't have been Tomas' confidant, would he? He was too young. Anyway, even if Tomas had told her father or Nyenye where the painting had come from, they hadn't passed on that information to her. So where had Tomas got it from? He must have got lucky picking up a work of art on the cheap.

Now it was too late to find out.

* * *

On Sunday morning Anika dressed carefully, in cream cotton trousers and the multicoloured floral silk shirt that she'd found a few months back in the Gladesville opshop and bought for only five dollars. When she was tying up the laces of her sneakers, she heard the front gate squeak. Much too early for Daniel. Leaning out of the window she saw a blonde head that she recognised right away. Before Jonno had a chance to ring the bell, she was downstairs and opening the door.

'I was just passing by and thought I'd drop in.' Jonno was bigger than she remembered and seemed to dwarf the narrow verandah. 'You know, on my way to see that mate of mine. The one I told you about when we met at the gallery. He lives in Reynolds Street.' He held out a business card: *Jonno Jamison, Freelance Journalist*.

'How did you find out where I live?'

'Easy. You said you lived in a stone terraced house not all that far from Victoria Street and there aren't all that many of those. It's not for nothing I'm a journalist.'

Anika rolled his card back and forth in her hand. It looked

very new. 'For some reason I thought you were a teacher not a journalist,' she said.

'Once upon a time I did some tutoring. But I didn't tell you that when we had coffee that time.'

'You sort of implied it. *Evaluating essays*, isn't that what you said?'

'You've got a good memory.'

'For some things.'

'I'm sorry you had your painting stolen.'

'How did you know about it?'

'From the newspaper reports.'

'I didn't expect those.'

'That's not why I'm here though. I've been thinking for a while about doing a story about what it's like for a new arrival in Australia. I want to interview a few people, five or six maybe. Would you be interested?'

'Thanks, but I don't think so.'

'Mine would be a human-interest story.' His hair glinted in the sunlight and, when he smiled, his entire face lit up.

'I don't think so.' Anika had no desire to let him know too much about her background.

'It would only be a very *simple* human-interest story,' Jonno's eyes were now on her hands holding his card. 'I just want to know about *you*, Anika.'

Sometimes it was better not to decline outright. 'Let me think about it.' If Jonno hadn't stolen the painting – and he wouldn't be here if he had – maybe he could help find it.

'OK.' Jonno's voice was patient and the friendly expression still on his face. 'How long do you need?'

'I'll call you.' The patch of sunlight he was standing in was so bright he might have been under a spotlight: she shut her eyes for an instant against the glare.

'That'd be good. But why don't I drop by on my way back from seeing my mate?'

'What time will that be?' Anika opened her eyes and saw that he was staring hard at her.

'Right after lunch.'

'I've got a friend collecting me at two.'

'I'll drop by before that. One-thirty, let's say.'

'See you then.'

She watched him concertina himself into a red Mini that was far too small for him. There was information and disinformation, she reminded herself, and she knew that you should find things out for yourself even if that did involve reinventing the wheel. If Jonno really was a freelance journalist, his articles would be in the newspaper archives under his name. Checking up on him was something she should do and soon.

The brilliant sapphire blue of the sky hurt her eyes and she didn't understand why she felt a sudden sharp stab of loneliness. Part of her wanted to welcome Jonno's friendship – if that was what he was offering. Another part was urging her to be cautious and have nothing to do with this journalist and what he was suggesting. If you let someone have too much information you could lose control of your life. Keep yourself to yourself. Keep your head down. That's the way she was brought up. And that's what she had learned. Consenting to a human-interest interview with Jonno could cause trouble back home. Even now.

'Who was that?' Tabilla was behind her, framed in the open front door, and wearing the rather smart blue dress that she put on when she was going out somewhere special. It had dark-blue embroidery round the neck and around the hem.

'Just a man I met at the gallery.'

'Which gallery?'

'The Art Gallery of New South Wales.'

'When you took the painting in to be identified?'

'Yes.'

'You met a lot of men that day.'

'Only two.'

'And he knows you had a painting and where you live.'

'Yes.'

'He could have taken the painting.'

'I know. I've thought about that. But if he had, why would he turn up here again? That just doesn't make sense.'

Tabilla stared into the distance for a few seconds. When she looked at Anika again she frowned and leaned forward to turn down her collar. 'You should check the mirror before you answer the door. And both those young men have invited you out?'

'No. This one's a journalist. He wants to interview me for a human-interest story. *How Sydney treats new migrants*, that sort of thing.'

'That's one way of getting to know someone.'

'I'm going to think about it.'

'He's a nice-looking man, though maybe a bit too old for you.'

A honeyeater swooped down from next door's gutter. It perched on a branch of the shrub that was flourishing in Tabilla's pocket-handkerchief front yard, only a metre away from where she stood. The branch swung to and fro while the bird sipped at the nectar of one of the spidery red flowers.

'You were peeping out of the upstairs window, weren't you?'

'I like to know who comes calling. Especially after the break-in.'

Anika didn't reply but kept her eyes on the bird in Tabilla's grevillea.

'Sometimes it's almost as if you're not alive,' Tabilla said, her voice low. 'Your face becomes expressionless. It cuts you off, it makes you seem unapproachable.'

She was awaiting a reaction from Anika, who kept her face unreadable. It was not difficult.

'I know you were brought up to never show your feelings, Anika, but I think you've carried it too far. And I know that dreadful ex-boyfriend of yours, that Frank, was a pain. But don't let that experience change you, or he will have won.'

Anika kept quiet while she watched the bird and thought about what Tabilla had said. She had begun to trust again, she'd begun to trust Daniel. But how could she trust people now, after having the Rocheteau stolen?

'By the way, you don't think it could have been Frank who took your painting?' Tabilla said.

'No, never.'

'He knows about it though.'

'He thought it was a worthless piece of junk. He's not into art.'

'He might have found out somehow that it was worth something.'

'Only after it was stolen and only if he'd read the newspaper reports. It would have been too late by then for him to nick it. Anyway, he's gone away.'

'Oh, yes, I'd forgotten. But he might have come back.'

'I doubt it. His family's from Perth and he went back there.'

'That's a nice long way away.'

'He went there soon after we split up.'

'You didn't tell me that's where he'd gone.'

'You didn't ask. And I know you don't like hearing about him. I don't either. I don't like talking about him or hearing about him or thinking about him.'

He had called Anika a couple of weeks after she'd broken

off with him to say he was moving to Perth. He'd been offered a great job there, he said. She had wished him well and was glad that he was going. When something was over, you couldn't have regrets or dwell on the past.

Yet the past was not always so willing to let you go. Even though you did all you could to kick it behind you, it could bounce back when you least expected it and knock you hard.

Chapter 16

Jonno didn't return until two o'clock, just after Daniel had rung the front doorbell. Ignored, Anika stood watching as he and Daniel sized each other up like two dogs, and not much liking what they saw. Daniel's expression was unwelcoming, Jonno's face was thinly veneered with an artificial-looking smile.

'I've seen you before somewhere,' Daniel said to Jonno.

'It was at the art gallery when I brought in a fake Gruner.'

'Before that.'

'I don't think so, unless you were on duty the time I brought in my uncle's Lister Lister. But I don't believe you were. I've got a good memory for faces.'

Anika noticed Daniel's annoyance. It was disproportionate to Jonno's presence. She wondered if there was something more than simple jealousy going on here. 'Anika and I are just about to go out.' Daniel took a step in Jonno's direction, as if to chivvy him out the front gate.

Jonno ignored him and turned to face her. 'Have you thought about that interview, Anika?'

'Not yet.'

'No rush. Call me when you get a chance.'

'What interview?' Daniel said.

'Jonno's a journalist. Thanks for dropping by, Jonno. I'll give you a ring once I've decided.'

'Looking forward to it.' Jonno gave a jaunty wave before striding down the street to his Mini.

Unlike Anika's trip to the beach with Daniel, today's

excursion over the Harbour Bridge was not an entrée into the world of Australian Impressionists. Instead it was an inquisition about Jonno. Daniel had taken a strong dislike to him; Anika could tell from the way he wouldn't abandon the theme, whatever tempting red herrings she threw in his path. Like a cat off its food, he stepped fastidiously over them. She looked at his exquisite profile, all features in perfect proportion, and was moved against her better judgement by the fine lines around his eyes as he squinted against the dazzling light.

He said, 'Had you met Jonno before that morning you brought the Rocheteau into the gallery?'

'No.' His use of the definite article 'the' rather than the demonstrative 'your' unsettled her but she kept this to herself. She asked, 'Didn't you bring your sunglasses? You seem to be having trouble with the glare.'

Ignoring her question, Daniel said, 'Why were you and Jonno having coffee afterwards?'

Wretched man; had he really asked her out only to interrogate her? Time to throw him another red herring. 'I've heard that going to Taronga Park by ferry is best. That way you avoid all the traffic.'

'That may well be the case but I'm taking you by car. You haven't answered my question.'

'I just bumped into him on my way out of the art gallery and he invited me. I suppose he liked the look of me.' Her laughter was forced and elicited none from Daniel.

'You didn't think it was a bit suspicious? You'd just had your painting identified as a Rocheteau and then this man turns up and takes you for coffee and asks where you live. I'm guessing that's what happened, otherwise he wouldn't have turned up at your door today. I'd be really suspicious if that happened to me.'

'He didn't know it was a Rocheteau. He couldn't have heard what you and the other curator said about it because there was another woman behind him in the queue waiting to see you. She was a big talker, surely you remember. All Jonno learned that day was that my painting was by a French Impressionist.' Anika's heart had started pumping too fast, an uncomfortable pitter-patter. Maybe Daniel was right, she should have been a bit more careful. Knowing the painting was by a French Impressionist might well have been enough to make Jonno think it was valuable.

'You didn't mention it was by Rocheteau afterwards?'

'I'm pretty sure I didn't.'

'I've seen Jonno before.'

'That's what you said when you picked me up.'

'And I've just remembered exactly when the first time was. It was at the gallery, months ago. He brought in an oil painting by Alfred Sutton and wanted to know who Sutton was. Odd that he comes in so often.'

'Does he?'

'We know that he brought in the painting he'd hoped was a Gruner, that was the morning you met him. And before that there was the Lister Lister that he mentioned just now, remember? And before that there was the Alfred Sutton.'

'What's odd about that?' Although Anika's pulses were still beating too fast, her voice was calm. 'Maybe he's just hoping he's got something valuable.'

'Maybe he's hoping to get some other information by chatting up everyone in the queue. And once he knew your painting was by a well-known artist he started hanging around you.'

It would be tactless to mention that Daniel was doing the same. Instead she said, 'Jonno's not exactly hanging around me. He invited me to coffee that first day we met at the gallery and I haven't seen him since, not until late this morning.'

After a brief pause, during which Daniel seemed to be thinking deeply, he said, 'Perhaps Jonno stole your painting.'

'I doubt it. If he had, why would he come back again? Anyway, he doesn't seem to know much about art.'

'I'd be very careful what you tell him, if I were you.'

'Oh, I will, don't you worry.'

Daniel looked at her sceptically, or perhaps it was the glaring sun that was giving him that squinty look.

She said, 'You'd better keep your eyes on the road.'

'And you, Anika, might want to check that he really is what his business card said he is.'

'You mean, ask for his CV?'

'I mean find some of his articles.'

'I've already thought of that.'

'Maybe asking for Jonno's résumé *is* a good idea. He wants something from you, why shouldn't you get something from him first?'

'Is that what life is, a series of exchanges?'

'Of course. Sometimes it's an exchange of gifts. Good conversations and laughter. Sometimes of punishments.'

'An eye for an eye, that sort of thing?'

He grinned and she was ninety-five per cent disarmed. But he knew the power of his smile and was using it, and she was not going to fall completely for it. It was on the tip of her tongue to ask him what he wanted from her. He was taking her out: what did he expect in return? But she decided against it. She might not like his answer.

'I'm going to have to pick up my sunglasses. It's only a small detour.'

'Good,' she said. 'Now I'll see where you live. What suburb?'

'Neutral Bay.'

112

'So you drove all the way to Rozelle only to drive all the way back again?'

'It's lucky I like driving.'

'Lucky indeed.' She grinned at him. 'That's very sweet of you.'

She loved seeing inside other people's houses. It was the budding architect in her, she told herself, not any inbuilt voyeurism. Daniel would be sharing with three or four others, all artistic, and there would be paintings everywhere that she could have a good look at to make sure that none was her Rocheteau, although he was hardly likely to suggest going to his place if he did have the Rocheteau tucked away somewhere.

After a few twists and turns, he pulled up in front of an old house in the Californian-bungalow style. She congratulated herself on her uncanny ability to place people. OK, she'd thought he'd live in a similar building in the Eastern Suburbs, but this was not all that far out, just a bridge away. Yet he strode off, down a weed-choked drive at the side of the house, towards a dilapidated-looking brick garage, with a blocked-up front wall and a faded blue door in the middle.

He warned her to be careful as he unlocked the door. 'This used to be a garage over a storage area, but the floor gave way so the owner rebuilt it as a studio apartment.'

Immediately inside were a few steps that probably contravened the building regulations, and a narrow ladder leading up to a mezzanine level. She followed him down the steps to the living and kitchen area. The overall impression was of a space that was light and bright and very white. The wall at the far end was glass, with a view over a dense hedge and descending layers of red-tiled roofs. Below that was the glittering blue of the harbour. On the wall to her right were three black-and-white photographs, stark scenes with strong contrasts, images spanning that fine line between minimalist realism and abstract expressionism. Skeletons of trees illuminated by moonlight, defining a dark hillside against a darker sky. A dark road zigzagging towards the horizon and cutting through a pale landscape. A jetty reaching so far out into a mist-softened lake that it seemed to illustrate the principle of the vanishing point.

She said, 'Who took these photos?'

'I did.'

'They're very beautiful.'

'Thank you.' He had become distracted, scrabbling around the books on the kitchen bench and coffee table, trying to find his sunglasses.

'No paintings?'

'No. The place isn't big enough. Or not big enough for the abstract expressionist stuff that I like.'

'Is the bathroom upstairs?'

'Yes, at the far end of the loft. It's a bit messy.'

She climbed up the ladder. The cover on the bed was black-and-white striped and there were art history books piled up on the bedside tables, but there was nothing on the walls apart from a white towelling robe hanging from a nail in the wall. At the back of the loft was a narrow door into a poky en suite and next to this a built-in wardrobe whose doors were gaping open. Naturally she took the liberty of peering inside. No women's clothes, only what she guessed were Daniel's: black and white at one end and at the other end vivid colours. No paintings either.

'I found my sunnies,' Daniel called out as she was descending the steps. 'They were in the cutlery drawer.'

'That's a great place to keep them. Guaranteed to protect the lenses from scratches.'

Daniel's absent-mindedness – and the untidiness of his

kitchen bench and his lovely black-and-white photographs – made Anika feel quite tender towards him. It helped that the detour had distracted him from his obsession with Jonno. For the rest of the journey they talked of other things.

* * *

Daniel parked above Taronga Park Zoo. The road below the car park passed by one side of the zoo and down to a jetty. A bus disgorged passengers not far from where they stood. Over their chatter Anika heard a distant roaring that she thought could have been a lion. She and Daniel walked slowly behind a young couple with their arms entwined until, as of one mind, they forged past them, and Anika felt a pang of regret for their innocence. First love: such trust, and so much heartache in store.

Daniel knew where they were going: they headed along a path through bushland, walking in an easterly direction. At first, they didn't talk; there were too many other walkers, tramping in both directions, but after a kilometre or so they had the path to themselves. Through dense trees that Daniel identified as pittosporum, Anika caught glimpses of the sparkling harbour water below. The cloud of gulls circling about reminded her of being with her brother Miklos and watching the birds forever wheeling above the chain link bridge spanning the Danube. A *murmuration*, Miklos called them in English, liking to impress, for they appreciated long words in her family.

When they reached an open area with a kiosk, Daniel suggested stopping for afternoon tea. As if choreographed, a couple rose from a table near the serving hatch and Anika and Daniel took seats that were still warm from their bodies. In front of them, the grass was dotted with groups of people and there were small children running everywhere, their cries and laughter punctuating the quieter murmuring of their families.

Waiting for service, they talked of nothing much, desultory conversation that had no focus. After the waitress took their order, Daniel leaned across the table towards Anika, and for a heartbeat she imagined he was about to take her hand. Instead he clasped his own, fingers over knuckles, and said, 'My Uncle Jake knows a man called Julius Singer. I hear he knows your aunt, Tabilla Molnar.'

Only now did Anika notice that clouds had appeared and the afternoon had become cooler. She tried to speak but her words came out strangled. At the second attempt, she managed to say, 'It's a shame Tabilla was out this afternoon, otherwise you could have met her. She suggested I take the Rocheteau to Mr Singer to see what he thought of it.'

'You didn't tell me that when you asked me to make the appointment to see a dealer.'

'I didn't know then. And anyway, why should I have told you beforehand? I'm telling you now.'

'Only because I confronted you.'

His use of the verb *to confront* irritated her. 'Is that what this is all about?' she asked, and was surprised to hear how well she'd controlled her touchiness. 'I'm sorry I didn't mention it. It was thoughtless, I know, especially after you'd gone to such trouble to be kind. But two evaluations are better than one, don't you think? If one was high and the other low, I could have taken the average and that would be what my painting was worth. But all this is academic with the picture gone.'

He said, 'We had a family dinner last night and my Uncle Jake was there.' He paused to stare at his fingernails as if sizing them up before manicure. When he'd finished inspecting his nails, he directed his attention to the tabletop. 'Jake said Julius told him he'd had a visit from a young woman who'd brought in a Rocheteau painting to be valued. I knew it had to be you from the description of the painting.'

Daniel was now watching Anika closely; she felt it was as if he were trying to catch her out. She seized the initiative and blurted out an account of what happened the afternoon of her visit to Singer's gallery.

When she'd finished, Daniel said slowly, 'That's interesting. So Julius thought the painting wasn't yours. Uncle Jake didn't tell me that.'

These words sowed a seed of doubt in Anika's mind. Surely Julius would have told Jake that he thought the Rocheteau couldn't be hers, especially seeing they were supposed to be friends, or at least acquaintances. Could Daniel have lied about his uncle to get her to reveal more? That was an interrogation technique she'd heard a lot about growing up in Budapest. Fabricate a story that would get the prisoner riled. In attempting to refute it, the prisoner might divulge the truth or something else that could be used against them.

'Mr Singer could have arranged to steal my painting,' she said. 'Or to have it stolen.' She watched Daniel's face closely but it remained inscrutable.

'I doubt it. Why would a man like Julius arrange a break-in? He's a respected figure running an excellent business. He wouldn't want to jeopardise that.'

'But he thinks the painting wasn't mine. So what does he do? He decides to have it stolen. He couldn't take it himself because he was at a concert with my aunt that night. A last-minute arrangement, I might add. He called her up saying he had a spare ticket. That could have been to get her out of the house.'

At this moment the waitress brought out their pot of tea and cups and saucers. Daniel became distracted, as if he'd taken himself somewhere far away. After pouring the tea,

Anika asked if he took milk and he pulled himself back with a start. 'Did Julius say who he thought owned the painting?'

'No. All he said was that it couldn't possibly be mine.'

'And you still don't have the provenance?'

'No.'

'Maybe you'll have to find out more about its history. You must want to know how Tomas came to have it.'

'Of course I do. But I'm going to have to get back to Budapest to find that out, and that's out of the question now.'

A tennis ball rolled under their table and soon after was followed by a laughing toddler and her apologetic father. When they had gone, Daniel said, 'The Nazis stored lots of looted paintings in disused mines or caves or whatever. Secret places. And then after the war ended they were gradually removed, one by one, to be sold. Often on the black market. And they're still turning up, even now.'

'Are you implying my Uncle Tomas was a Nazi? He was barely ten when the Nazis were driven out of Hungary.'

'I wasn't saying that.'

Anika's heart was a trapped bird in her throat. 'What are you saying then? That my Uncle Tomas bought a looted painting after the war ended?' Her palms were so sweaty that the teaspoon slipped from her grasp and clattered on to the wooden tabletop.

'It's possible.'

'What do you expect me to do about it?'

'There's nothing you can do about it. Not at this stage.'

'Not when it's been twice stolen, is that what you're getting at?'

'I just thought you should be aware that it's a possibility.'

'Well, you should know that Tomas was in his early twenties when he died. It was in 1956 when he was an engineering student. He was hardly likely to have had enough money to spend on paintings. So he wouldn't have bought it at that time.'

'Where did he get it from then?'

'I don't know.'

'There must be ways to find out without going back to Budapest. You could try asking your father, for instance. He might have proof that you don't know about.'

'How can I ask him? Everything's censored.'

'Everything? I thought Hungary had relaxed its restrictions.'

'They open my letters to my parents. I got into trouble with the authorities before I left. Do you know what the Danube Bend is?' When Daniel shook his head, she continued, 'I thought you mightn't. There was a big dam planned for the Danube north of Budapest that would wipe out historic towns. I got involved in protests about that. The police caught me. That's one reason I wanted to get out of Hungary after they let me go.' She didn't mention the other reason: that her offer of a place to study architecture had been withdrawn.

She looked down at her hands and observed that, while she'd been talking, she'd shredded her paper napkin. It lay in ribbons on her lap. With nothing more to shred, her right hand automatically adjusted her watchband. Although it was wide, it barely covered the scar on the underside of her wrist. She continued, 'I've got to be careful what I put in letters and what I say on the phone. Anyway, I don't care about my painting's history. I just want it back.'

'Of course you do.'

'It's all I have of home. Have you got any idea of how it feels to be so far away from your family? That picture's a connection to my parents.'

'Leaving family behind is the fate of most immigrants,' he said slowly. 'At least your parents are alive. A lot of my parents' generation lost their entire families.'

It hurt that he was accusing her of something: self-pity; a deficit of courage; a shortage of empathy. 'I'm really sorry that happened, Daniel.' Her cool voice was in stark contrast to the anguish that began to swell up like a geyser inside her. Though she might have deserved his comment, she knew she had to get away before exploding. 'I can't listen to this right now, I'm going home.'

Standing up, she knocked the metal milk jug on to the ground. For the barest instant she watched as the milk trickled across the concrete and began to form a rivulet. It was all too much to bear. She ran across the grass under the darkening sky. Weaving around groups of picnickers packing their things, she soon found the path she and Daniel had followed earlier.

In the bush there were no people about. The gulls were now silent. All she could hear, as anger and suspicion propelled her along the track, were sticks crackling, leaves rustling underfoot, and the pounding of her heart. With the sun screened by ever-thickening black clouds, the trees began to seem threatening. Suddenly she felt that someone was watching her. Halting a second, she glanced around. No one in sight, yet the bush was expectant. Dark and brooding, it might have been waiting to pass judgement.

Again she broke into a run. A sudden loud crack of thunder made her jump. Increasing her pace, she started to feel more frightened. The bush was too quiet, too dark. She might almost be back in the forest near the Danube Bend. Another clap of thunder but she'd seen no lightning. The pounding of her sneakers on the path became a syncopated rhythm. Thud thud thud went her feet, and there was a separate rhythm in between. She ran faster, her heart pumping harder and air rasping into her lungs.

'Anika,' Daniel called. 'It's only me!' She slowed, sweat

dribbling down her forehead and beading on her upper lip. When Daniel caught up with her, panting with the effort, he said, 'Don't shoot the messenger.'

'Why not?' Anika said, breathlessly. 'What was good enough for the Greeks is good enough for me.'

He thought she'd made a joke and started to laugh, but stopped when he saw her expression.

'I'm taking the ferry home.'

'Don't do that, Anika. It's cutting off your nose to spite your face. You'll have to wait ages for a ferry and then for the bus at the quay. It'll be hours before you get home.'

'That's what I want. I'm sorry, Daniel, but I need time on my own to think.'

'I know you're upset. I've made things worse. I'm sorry too.'

She glanced at him. Again, his black eyes were drilling into her face. She averted her gaze. Her body had become numb and her brain was blocking messages, all except for the one that was urging her to get away. The silence between them was broken by another rumble of thunder, louder this time. Without a word they hurried along the path. When they reached the road, he leaned towards her as if to kiss her cheek. She backed away and, with a quick nod, headed down the hill. A ferry was steaming slowly across the choppy water of the harbour towards the Taronga Park jetty. A sheet of lightning slid down the purple sky and twelve seconds later came another clap of thunder.

When the ferry pulled into the wharf, Anika was among the first on board. Sitting on a slatted wooden bench at one side of the boat, she stared unseeing over the shifting green water. Her body felt anaesthetised. Only when she was on the blessedly empty bus from Circular Quay and the rain began did the numbness start to wear off. There was now a dull sort of pain in her chest, as if someone or something was pressing down on her ribcage. Like a tongue seeking out a mouth ulcer, her mind kept returning to the conversation with Daniel, running through every sentence they'd spoken. Sentences that were as clearly written on the surface of her brain as a script of a play. *Raising Doubts*, it would be called, the play that Daniel had written for her. Raising doubts about her family and her past.

Chapter 17

That evening Anika made a start on the Butler's Stairs design project. Work provided an escape, she told the framed photograph of her family that sat on one of the bookshelves next to her drawing board. Work was a glorious retreat from the trauma of engaging with people, she told them. *Carpe diem*, that was how she should be living. Seize the moment when it was good, and bury it under mounds of work when it was bad.

After spreading out the sketches and photos of the arches at Butler's Stairs, Anika put the cassette *Tender Prey* by Nick Cave and the Bad Seeds into her Walkman and began to rough out a design. She'd already decided that the purity of that colonnade with its high arches had to be retained. The way to do this was to set a wall of glazing back a metre or so and make the glazing uninterrupted, or as much as possible, given that there would have to be joints in the sheets of plate glass and somehow air allowed into the building. There had to be some way of getting an updraught into the space through openings that could be concealed at the very top and bottom of the glazing so they wouldn't be visible from outside. Joining the glass panels would be relatively straightforward. One advantage of working part-time at Barry Oreopoulous and Associates was that she'd seen how it was done in Barry's buildings.

She roughed out a floor plan on a piece of butter paper and then scrunched it up in irritation and chucked it across the room. Nick Cave and his Bad Seeds were starting to grate;

out with the cassette, off with the headphones. It was past midnight when she had a sketch plan that she was happy with. For a few minutes she was on a high. It was while she was collecting the rejected plans from the floor that her conversation with Daniel bubbled up once more in her mind.

She looked at the space where the portrait had hung and saw only Daniel's face and those beautiful dark eyes. For Daniel, life was a series of exchanges, that's what he'd said. Sometimes of gifts; sometimes of punishments. He took her out not because he wanted to spend time with her but because he wanted to pump her about her painting. Maybe he had something to gain from this. Last week he could have taken her out to dinner as a ruse, a means of getting her out of the house in order to allow someone Julius employed to steal the picture.

Or someone Daniel hired himself – that was possible too. He'd kept her out all evening, given her a few glasses of wine at the pub – she must have drunk at least two-thirds of that bottle of Riesling – and injected a hint of romance into the air. That interlude would have given the thief plenty of time to nip into the house when Tabilla was distracted, and creep up to Anika's room and remove the painting. Yet why would Daniel have contacted her again afterwards if he'd organised the theft of the Rocheteau? Again she dismissed this possibility. She was going around in circles and getting nowhere.

She squashed the scrunched-up pieces of butter paper into her wastepaper basket. Daniel was also an art expert, she reminded herself as she changed into pyjamas, and perhaps he was right about the painting's provenance. If it really was looted all those years ago – and she was beginning to think this was likely – what should she do about it? Give it back, of course, but it was too late to do anything now it had gone. Unless Julius Singer had arranged to have it stolen but she couldn't really believe he'd do that. If only she could discuss what to do with someone. Tabilla maybe. Yet Anika didn't want to worry her aunt or worse, upset her by raising suspicions about her beloved Tomas. Besides, Tabilla was a friend of Julius's; not a close friend, admittedly, but a friend nonetheless.

Suddenly she remembered Jonno's offer that now seemed almost tempting. It was not that she wanted him to write a human-interest piece about her but he was someone to talk to – and someone who knew about her painting. Yet a moment later Daniel's words bobbed up in her head like a red warning balloon: there was something odd about the way Jonno had latched on to her at the art gallery that day.

And she began to feel more confused than ever.

* * *

People who hadn't studied history of architecture mightn't realise how judgemental it could make you, and sometimes Anika wished she could stifle that inner critic. At its worst, it slotted every building into an historical timeframe and when, several days later, she went to the Mitchell Library she immediately noticed how derivative its façade was. Neoclassical architecture in the early twentieth century. Ionic columns that might have graced an ancient Greek temple grafted on to the front of a sandstone building. Just like the Art Gallery of New South Wales, only the library had windows in its façade. She didn't need Professor Smythe, the history of architecture lecturer, to tell her that both buildings were designed by the same architect. But at least they brought some consistency to the hodgepodge of downtown Sydney, she thought, where developers were keen to knock down the past and construct their own interpretations of the present.

Once she was through the library portals, it took a while to calm her inner critic and settle down. This wasn't because the place was noisy; the only sounds were the background thrumming of the air-conditioning and the occasional rustle of papers and clunk of a spool rolling forwards. Not hers though. She spent half an hour in the reading room tracking down newspaper records and now, perched on an uncomfortable chair in front of one of the microfilm readers in the library's basement, she struggled to come to terms with the instructions on the laminated sheet in front of her. Her English was failing her, and once more she began to read the instructions. When she felt a gentle tap on her shoulder, she looked up to see an angel in the form of a middle-aged librarian with a kind face and a halo of curly fair hair.

'Let me help you.' Effortlessly the librarian slotted in the spool of film and spun the dial. White text appeared on the backlit screen and the instructions Anika had been labouring through suddenly made sense. The librarian's expression was benevolent, as if nothing gave her more pleasure than helping novices like Anika. 'What are you looking for?'

'Articles by Jonno Jamison.' Anika showed her Jonno's business card.

'I'll teach you how to search.' Within seconds the librarian had brought into focus an article from a few months back. 'There may well be earlier ones,' she said. 'But this is the latest. Let me know if you need any more help.'

Anika read carefully. The article was prompted by a politician's outburst against migration. There were too many migrants, the politician claimed, they were changing the character of Australia. In response, Jonno had written that Australia as we knew it was a country of migrants. Even the Indigenous Australians were migrants, out of Africa. Much later the migrants had been European. And in 1947, two per cent of the Australian population comprised displaced persons.

Two per cent. That was quite a few. Jonno's article then mentioned the displaced person camps scattered across Europe post-war and the enormous task of repatriating people where possible and of finding them new countries where impossible. Anika imagined the refugee ships collecting migrants from stopping points along the route. She imagined them arriving at the major ports in Australia. She imagined the shock of arrival: the incomprehensible accents, the blinding sun, the prejudice. And perhaps the friendliness too and the plentiful food. Her mind flickered to her own arrival. Her nervousness, her apprehension. It had been a major step to come to a new country, where no one knew of her apart from her Aunt Tabilla.

Next, Anika retrieved one of Jonno's earlier articles. It contained a number of interviews with people who'd fled immediately post-war from Europe to Australia. An issue, Jonno wrote, was that when an old order vanished – together with most of its records – new opportunities arrived for the perpetrators of crimes: they could change their identity as well as their destiny, and escape justice. Of the refugees, deeply traumatised by their experiences, some had made good in their new home, while others had not. They told him how they felt if they saw their guards and captors walking free in Australia, somehow evading war crime charges, somehow gaining visas. They told him about their different coping strategies when they saw a former guard. Averting their eyes, taking revenge – a brick through a window, a tip-off to the police – and sometimes people they had known committing suicide.

This pulled Anika up and she wondered what might happen in Hungary now it was liberalising. Would the secret police somehow evade being punished, would they become part of the new establishment? Might she come across the man who'd interrogated her, walking the streets? That was possible.

And at this point she decided that she couldn't be interviewed by Jonno. He was a fine journalist, and after reading his work she felt a growing respect for him, but the situation was still too fluid in Hungary. She didn't want to draw attention to herself. You couldn't trust a journalist, even in a country with a free press. Even a journalist who wrote as well as Jonno. She'd been wrong in thinking he'd be a good friend to talk to about her anxieties. You couldn't believe in someone you'd only recently met. And you certainly couldn't call them a good friend.

* * *

Barely two minutes' walk from the library, the large man stepping in front of Anika made her jump. 'Hello, Anika,' Jonno said. 'It's good to see you.'

She stepped back a pace and Jonno grinned in a knowing way. This startled her – it was as if he knew she'd been investigating him, or maybe he thought she was bowled over by his good looks.

Jonno said, 'What are you doing in this part of the world?'

'Working in the library. What are you doing in Macquarie Street?' Only now did it occur to her that it was strange the way he'd started turning up everywhere. It could have been coincidence but it could also be that he was stalking her.

'I had a meeting.' He gestured vaguely in the direction of the city. 'You didn't phone me. About that interview, remember?'

From the Moreton Bay fig tree next to the pavement a small fig dropped. Jonno gave it a gentle kick and it rolled into the gutter. The air smelled of fermenting fruit overlaid with a hint of car exhaust.

'I haven't forgotten. It's serendipity that our paths just happened to cross.' She scrutinised his face but his expression remained unaltered, until he began to sing the last few lines of 'Simple Twist of Fate', which was her favourite Bob Dylan song, and how could he have known that?

'Everyone's favourite Dylan song,' he said, as if reading her mind.

'Maybe,' she said, smiling. 'Anyway, I was going to ring you tonight. I'm sorry, Jonno. I don't want to be a human-interest story. But thanks for offering.'

'There's another way I can help you.'

'How?'

'I'm thinking of doing a piece about artworks that go missing. Like yours.'

'How will that help me?'

'Your painting might turn up somewhere attributed to a different artist.'

'That's unlikely. Rocheteau's signature shows quite clearly in the bottom right hand corner of the canvas.'

In fact, the name was virtually illegible. Anika would have been none the wiser about the identity of the artist without the assistance of the silver-haired curator from the art gallery.

Jonno narrowed his eyes. 'I've already interviewed Olivia Cousins.'

'Who's Olivia Cousins?'

'She's one of the curators. The one Daniel got to identify your painting. She had some interesting things to say.' His antipathy to Daniel manifested itself in the note of contempt that had crept into his voice. 'Maybe you've forgotten I was there that day. Daniel didn't have a clue.'

This irritated Anika slightly, in spite of her own annoyance with Daniel for what happened on their Clifton Gardens walk. 'Of course he had a clue. He was just being careful.'

'He had to get the real expert. I was there, remember? Anyway, Olivia was more than happy to be interviewed. We had lunch yesterday. What about you and me having lunch on Friday?'

'What did Olivia Cousins have to say?'

'If you have lunch with me I'll tell you.'

Anika hesitated. She'd already decided that she didn't want to tell him anything. But on the other hand, maybe she could get information out of him. Like what he was planning and why he was pursuing her and what Olivia Cousins had told him.

When Anika agreed to lunch, he asked where her office was. 'That's not all that far from where I live,' he said after she gave him the address. 'There are some nice little restaurants near there.'

They arranged to meet outside the building where she worked. As Jonno strode down the street, she observed the spring in his step, as if he were about to break into a run.

Only when he was out of sight did it occur to her that he could have lied about interviewing Olivia Cousins. He might have fashioned that as a hook to draw her in and she'd swallowed it in a matter of seconds.

Chapter 18

On Friday morning Anika dressed carefully for lunch with Jonno, in the shift dress Tabilla had made for her the previous year out of some black-and-white Marimekko fabric that Anika had been unable to resist purchasing. As Anika came out of the office building, Jonno bobbed up in front of her, an engaging smile on his face and hair striped with comb marks. He was wearing beige chinos and a blue Oxford shirt with a button-down collar and carrying a brown leather attaché case that she wouldn't have minded purloining as a handbag. There was something spicy about his aftershave, with an overtone of peppermint.

Jonno had booked a table at the Mezzaluna restaurant; it was by the window, with a view of a quiet lane bordered by palm trees and recycling bins. The restaurateur, a small man with an Italian accent, greeted Jonno like a long-lost friend. He referred to Anika as Jonno's beautiful companion and winked at her. Although she didn't like winkers she smiled back, a social smile that she couldn't make reach her eyes, though no one would notice in this restaurant, not when they were discussing the intricacies of the menu. She ordered a pasta dish and tried not to worry about the cost. Jonno chose a bottle of wine that was far beyond her budget and when she told him she didn't drink at lunchtime he changed his order to a glass.

'I used to practise as a lawyer,' he said. 'My boss brought me here when I started, and I fell in love with the food. So when I gave up the law I kept on coming.'

'You don't look old enough.'

'To have given up the law?'

'Yes. I hope that didn't sound rude.'

'I assure you I'm easily old enough. I'll be thirty-three next birthday.'

The two middle-aged women sitting at the table nearby halted their conversation and swivelled their heads to inspect Jonno. Anika took the opportunity to register what they were eating: grilled barramundi on one plate and what could be veal on the other. The women grinned at each other before resuming their conversation. Did they recognise Jonno from his journalism or was it his childish emphasis of his age that amused them? Or maybe it was just that she and Jonno seemed like an unlikely couple to be on a lunch date. But of course they were not, this was a working lunch and Anika was here only to obtain information. 'Who did you work for?' she asked him.

'When?'

'When you were a lawyer.'

'Oh, back then. That was a while ago. It seems almost like a different lifetime.' He mentioned the name of a firm that she'd never heard of. But why should she have? So far in Australia she'd had nothing to do with the law and she wanted to keep it that way.

'I like to take the legal angle,' he continued. 'Property rights, human rights, that sort of thing. They underlie everything, don't they? Or at least everything I'm interested in. In fact, that's what intrigues me about you and your stolen painting.'

'You mean who the legal owner is? That's me.' She picked up a breadstick from the basket on the table and crunched into it. Crumbs flew everywhere.

'But you don't have the provenance, do you?'

'No.' The word *provenance* sprung out of everyone's mouth and yet she'd never heard of it a month ago. She brushed the crumbs off the tablecloth and took a sip of water.

'That's not a huge problem in the art world. It can be faked.'

'Is that what you're offering me, Jonno?'

He laughed; his head flung back so far she could see the arch of his top row of teeth with not a filling to be seen. 'Well, you don't have the painting any more, so having a provenance now isn't going to be much help.'

'But whoever took the painting could forge the provenance. Do you know people who do that? It might be one way of tracking down where the painting is.'

'That's a clever idea, Anika, but it's not only your painting I'm interested in. I'd like to investigate a few thefts. I want to find out who they belonged to originally. Whether there's a story that can be told if I can examine enough cases.'

Their conversation was interrupted by the waiter bringing their food. Jonno had ordered osso bucco and Anika was having spaghetti carbonara. After the waiter figured out who was having what, he waved a very tall pepper grinder in front of her and it took her a few seconds to understand that he was offering to grind it for her. Shaking her head, she waited until he'd gone before asking Jonno, 'Isn't that the job of the police?'

'Yes, and they might be doing it for all I know. But they're unlikely to be following up the story I'm after.'

'I read your articles in the Sunday supplement from a few months back.' She wiped the spaghetti sauce off her chin – it left a greasy mark on the napkin – before continuing, 'That's what I was doing in the Mitchell Library when you saw me the other day. Checking up on you.' Ever since then, she'd wondered why he was so interested in her. It might have been a journalist's natural curiosity or maybe was there something else going on.

'I'm flattered.'

'You said when we bumped into one another near the library that day that Olivia Cousins had some interesting things to say.'

'She did.'

'What were they?'

'She said it was surprising the Rocheteau had turned up in Australia.'

'Was that all she had to say?'

'Yes.' He grinned in a way that might have been disarming if Anika hadn't felt flooded with irritation at how he'd duped her into lunch.

He continued, 'What I'm now fascinated by is the global market for stolen paintings.'

'Like, my painting could be sold outside Australia, is that what you mean?'

'Sort of.' He finished his glass of wine and looked at it in some surprise, as if he'd expected it to hold more and was now regretting not ordering a bottle.

'I haven't told my parents it's been stolen yet.'

'Is that where you got it from, your parents?'

'Yes, just before I left Budapest.'

'Are they likely to give you another one?' Jonno raised his empty glass to the waiter.

'I very much doubt it.'

'Do they have any more paintings?'

'No.' Her heart began to thump so hard it must surely have been audible. Uneasily she thought of Nyenye's flat, with its shabby large rooms with lofty ceilings, and her living room walls filled with pictures. Pictures that no one was supposed to know about. She wondered if Jonno knew more than he was saying, or at any rate suspected more than he was letting on.

Jonno finished his meal and nodded at the waiter as he put a glass of wine in front of him. 'Do you have any idea of where your oldies got the Rocheteau from, Anika?'

'I don't know.' Avoiding his eyes, she picked up her waterglass and took a few sips.

'They're introducing reforms in Hungary.'

'Yes, it's been on the news.' Only now did she make the connection, that if the Iron Curtain were lifted, her family might easily be able to sell some of the collection.

'Look at this.' He pulled a newspaper out of his attaché case. It was yesterday's edition that had been folded so that the article about Hungary was immediately visible.

'I've read it,' she told him. 'They reckon the borders will come down in a year or two, and there'll be free mobility of people.'

'There'll be free mobility of paintings too.'

'I wouldn't know about that,' she said carefully, and wondered why Jonno was talking of free mobility of paintings. A coldness gripped her, as it her body had been suddenly packed in ice, and it was only with the greatest effort that she prevented herself from shivering. There was no way Jonno could know about Nyenye's collection. Anika had never mentioned it to him or to anyone else. Perhaps his words were another hook that he'd baited and tossed into the waters, in the hope that it might provoke some reaction. The iciness abruptly left her body and she began to feel unnaturally hot, her cheeks tight as if with sunburn. Her appetite gone, she put down her spoon and fork.

Her family were honourable people, she told herself, and she was proud of them. Her grandparents had resisted the Nazi occupation and the Russian occupation, that's what she'd always thought, and her parents had struggled against the communist regime in their own quiet way. But could she be wrong about them? After all, Nyenye's flat was crammed with paintings. How did her grandparents get hold of them?

Jonno was looking at her closely. He'd be marking her reaction, you could bet on that. She moved her chair to escape a spear of sunlight that was slicing through the palm trees outside the window and threatening to blind her. There was no way she could talk to Jonno about Daniel, let alone Daniel's idea that her painting was stolen by the Nazis. Clearly that was Jonno's view too. This was why he wanted to get friendly with her. He would buy her lunch and see what more information he could extract. Well, she would let him pay for her pasta but he was not going to get any more information out of her. Not today or any day.

Chapter 19

It was the third week of the semester and Professor Smythe was about to give a history of architecture lecture. He was a remarkably tall man, and stooped with it, as if for too many years he'd been ducking his head to get through doors. Soon after he dimmed the auditorium lights and the slideshow began, Sally – who was sitting next to Anika – whispered, 'Wait for the soundtrack.' A few seconds later they heard gentle snoring from the rows at the back of the hall.

Professor Smythe didn't notice, so caught up was he in Gothic architecture and those glorious stone cathedrals with the flying buttresses and huge windows, a miracle of construction out of heavy stone. This was history of architecture on the comparative method, he reminded them. This was how cathedrals were built in Northern Europe, and he flashed up a few pictures. This was how they were done in the south, and a few more images appeared on the screen. Climate and available materials, that was what guided builders and architects over the millennia.

Usually Anika loved Professor Smythe's lectures but tonight she was so distracted she could barely take in his story. A worm of anxiety had for days been burrowing through her brain. If only she could have talked to Nyenye about where the painting had come from and a hundred and one other matters but that was impossible. Not by phone, not by letter. Anika was stranded here, with Tabilla her only connection to home, and a tenuous connection that was too. The loneliness she suddenly felt was more than the familiar little ripple of isolation that sometimes washed around her. Rather, it was like a large wave that could crash down on her in the shallows. Her family was too far away. She'd give anything to go home for a visit. Anything to find out if they knew about provenances. Anything to know where all those paintings came from.

After the lecture ended, Anika and Sally were descending the staircase when Anika saw, in the side corridor, their design tutor Howard Meyer talking to a striking woman. Her grey hair was cut very short and gelled up into little peaks on the top of her head, and she was wearing an elegant black shift with a deliberately irregular hemline that would give Aunt Tabilla the horrors.

'That's Judith Armstrong,' Sally said. 'I saw her picture in *Architecture Australia*.'

Armstrong was an architect with a one-woman practice and a penchant for sun-control and designing imaginative houses made out of corrugated iron. She was talking animatedly to Meyer, who nodded from time to time, his head a metronome to mark her progress. Though Armstrong's voice was low, Anika distinctly heard her mention the name of Barry Oreopoulous.

In response, Howard said, 'I don't get on with him.'

'Why ever not? He's a lovely man.'

'Maybe to you but not to me. Now, Judith, when are you going to give me your answer? You said it would only take a day or two to come to a decision and that was over a week ago.'

They moved away and Anika heard no more. Sally said, 'Do you think it was a proposal of marriage?'

'Howard's already married and anyway she's at least ten years older.'

'Age is just a number, that's what my mum always says.

About her own age and her own birthdays, I should say, not about mine.'

* * *

When Anika got home just before ten o'clock, the house was in darkness apart from a light in the kitchen. On the kitchen bench there was a note in Tabilla's large looping hand and weighted down by a bunch of nasturtiums packed into a jam jar. *Daniel rang and wants you to call back.*

For an instant Anika felt such a longing to hear his voice, such a regret that she'd missed his call, but that was before her head stepped in and decided that enough was enough. She was beginning to feel shallow-rooted, as if she might be blown away in any breeze that might spring up. The trouble was that Daniel was undermining her origins, she decided. He was undermining who she was.

She put the kettle on and rummaged in the pantry cupboard for the can of Milo. The shrill ringing of the phone made her jump. It would be Daniel again. Quickly she picked up a cushion and pressed it down hard over the handset. She could feel it vibrating through the feathers. After eight rings it stopped. There was the sound of footsteps down the stairs and Tabilla appeared, her hair dishevelled.

'Don't look so concerned, the phone didn't wake me,' she said, doing up the buttons of the old green cardigan she was wearing over her nightie. 'Was it a wrong number?' When Anika nodded, she continued, 'I can't get to sleep. Besides, I heard you come in and wanted to make sure you saw Daniel's message.'

'I did.' Anika washed her hands in the sink and wiped them over her eyes and face. 'I'm too tired to call anyone now.'

'You look dreadful,' Tabilla said. 'Dark rings around your eyes. You're not crying, are you?'

'No. That's just water and mascara.' Slowly Anika patted her face dry with a paper towel and inspected the black marks. 'Tabilla, can you do me a favour?'

'Ask away.'

'You'll think me ridiculous.'

'Don't I already?' She smiled and ruffled Anika's hair.

'Can you ring your friend Julius Singer and ask him if he knows Daniel's uncle?'

Anika watched Tabilla's expression closely. It remained unchanged, although she didn't reply immediately. Then she said, 'What's his uncle's name?'

'Rubinstein. Jake Rubinstein.'

'Why do you want to find that out?'

'It's just something Daniel said about his Uncle Jake knowing Julius Singer. It was when we went to Clifton Gardens last Sunday. He said Julius and his Uncle Jake were old friends and I wondered if that was true.'

'You don't trust Daniel?'

'I don't trust anyone at the moment.'

'You need to have faith in people, Anika. You should open up a little, like Hungary is beginning to. You don't need to be so suspicious any more.'

'I trust some people.'

'But not Daniel. I suppose that's fair enough, you hardly know him. Yet he was good enough to offer to introduce you to a valuer and he's obviously keen on you if he's asking you out. He sounded really nice on the phone. We had a very pleasant chat.'

'What about?'

'Just small talk, you know the way it is. He has lovely manners.'

'You can't judge a man on the basis of one phone call.'

'I know that, Anika. It was quite a long phone call though. He sounded a bit reticent at first but I drew him out and we talked about the heat and Bob Hawke and the advantages of having a fan in a heatwave. And we bonded about Fred Williams – Daniel loves Fred Williams's paintings too.'

'Would you like some Milo, Tabilla?'

Tabilla shook her head and continued talking. 'I never liked that boyfriend of yours, that Frank. I disliked him right from the beginning but I knew you'd hate me to tell you that. What turned me off was that comment he made the afternoon you introduced us. His father worked in construction, he told me, and he hated architects poncing around on building sites, poofters the lot of them.'

Anika remembered that comment well. It had hurt at the time and had resonated for days afterwards, and at first she'd blamed Frank's father not Frank. It had taken longer than it should have for her to realise that Frank had chosen to report his father's words that he could have kept to himself. Months later, she'd understood that he was belittling her because she'd got accepted into architecture.

Tabilla said, 'So what's wrong with Daniel?'

'I'm not sure.'

'And you're not going to tell me why?'

'No.'

'Well, I trust you, my darling. I'll phone Julius tomorrow morning.'

'Before I go to work?'

'If you wish. I suppose that's so you can listen to the conversation.'

'Please don't tell him that I asked you to call.' Anika's mouth was dust-dry and she knew her words sounded strangled. She prayed that Tabilla wasn't going to ask why she wanted this information concealed.

Tabilla sighed. 'I expect that one day you're going to let me know what this is all about.'

'I will, I promise.'

Anika hoped that this was a promise she could keep.

* * *

That night Anika dreamed of Daniel, as a boy of no more than nine or ten. She would have known him anywhere. It was in the shape of his head and his profile and the set of his shoulders. In the dream she was sitting on a sofa next to him; her adult self whom he was trying to shock. He was slowly turning the pages of a book about Hieronymus Bosch, the mediaeval painter, looking at the grotesque images that Bosch specialised in.

She turned away for the barest instant and, when she looked back, Daniel had metamorphosed into an elderly man whom she recognised right away, Julius Singer. Julius remained sitting on the sofa while Anika began to drift around the room like a phantom listening to what he was saying. His voice was raised as he told her that her past was not hers, it belonged to someone else, a woman with half her ambition but twice her talent. His words became louder and louder and more accusatory. Details about how she was about to be sacked and that by rights her position at Barry Oreopoulous and Associates belonged to him. She had stolen it from him and left him with only an aching emptiness. But one day soon the tables would be turned and justice would be meted out and her life would become his life. The words came faster and faster, louder and louder. She put her fingers in her ears but still the noise escalated. So frightened did she feel that she wrenched herself awake, breaking through the fragile dome of sleep into the reality of her bedroom. She realised then that it was her voice and her screaming that had woken her.

When she stood up too quickly, the room began to spin.

She knew what the dream meant. That she was going to lose her job. She would lose her job as well as her painting. Catching hold of the wall, she navigated her way to the drawing board but misjudged where the stool was and banged her shin hard on one of the metal legs. Her annoyance found an outlet in Hungarian expletives as her fingers fumbled to switch on the planet lamp. After throwing open the window, she listened to the distant swish of traffic. Though the sky was whitening, a lopsided moon still shone faintly. Her watch showed six o'clock. There was no point in trying to sleep again. Not when she had a bad case of the jitters.

Chapter 20

After showering and dressing for work, Anika took Tabilla
a mug of tea in bed. Her bedroom door was wide open and
she was sitting propped up on pillows, reading the Hungarian
novel that Magda had lent her. In a barely focused way she
peered at Anika over the top of her reading glasses and smiled
when she saw the Clarice Cliff mug. After putting it on the
bedside table, Anika perched on the end of the bed. Through
the double doors leading on to the glassed-in back verandah,
she could see the brilliant sapphire blue of another lovely day.
It didn't do much to cheer her though. She said, 'You said
you'd phone Julius Singer this morning.'

'So I did and I haven't forgotten. I'll be down shortly. Just
let me finish my tea.'

Finish my tea in peace was what she really meant, so Anika
returned to the kitchen to eat a slice of toast and honey. Not
long after the clock in the lounge room chimed seven-thirty,
Tabilla came downstairs wearing her royal blue kimono with
the golden dragons embroidered on the front and back. She
looked at Anika quizzically before punching into the phone
the digits of a number that she had written on a scrap of paper
in her hand. When Anika headed towards the lounge room,
Tabilla beckoned her back so she was close enough to hear the
conversation.

After speaking a few nothing words to Julius, Tabilla said,
'I was wondering if you know someone called Rubinstein.
He's probably about your age. Do you know anyone by that
name?'

'The only person I know of with the name of Rubinstein is Daniel Rubinstein. He's a curator at the Art Gallery of New South Wales but he's much younger than me.' Julius's voice was so loud that Anika could hear every word.

'And does he have an uncle by the name of Jake Rubinstein?'

'Not that I know of. Daniel's a good man though, one of the best.'

Abruptly Anika sat down. It was as she'd suspected. Daniel had lied to her when he'd said on that Clifton Gardens walk that Julius and his uncle were old friends. Anika could see his expression as clearly as if he were right in front of her still, fixing her with his lovely black eyes as if willing her to believe him.

'And you definitely don't know any Jake Rubinstein?' Tabilla said.

'No,' Julius replied. 'Why do you want to know?'

For one horrible second, Anika thought Tabilla was about to tell Julius about her request. But she simply said, 'A friend was asking, that's all. She couldn't find his number in the directory.'

'Sorry I can't help. We must go to another concert, Tabilla, maybe when my wife is well again. We had so little time at the concert to talk.'

The jab of pain in the palm of Anika's hand made her realise she'd been pressing her fingernails into the soft skin there. She felt sure now that she was right to be suspicious of Daniel. On that walk to Clifton Gardens, his words about his mythical Uncle Jake had led her to blurt out the whole story of what had happened when she took her painting to Julius's gallery. Her forehead started to hurt as adjustments were made in her brain. It was as if she could sense the neurons making connections, sending new messages, reorganising her consciousness. Although she recognised that Daniel was untrustworthy, she felt a deep sense of regret.

Yet how could she regret something she'd never had? Maybe that was what regret was all about, thinking about someone as a possibility when really it was only a chimera in her head, nothing more than that. Daniel meant nothing to her, she decided, and she wouldn't see him again. He was too unsettling; he was someone to be avoided.

* * *

That morning Barry didn't come into the office. This didn't help with Anika's apprehension, for none of them knew where he was. To stay awake she had too many cups of coffee, which kept her alert but didn't help with the jitters. When she got back after lunch, Barry was lounging in one of the Mies van der Rohe chairs in the waiting area. Sitting opposite him was the woman Anika had seen talking to Howard Meyer after Professor Smythe's lecture. As soon as Barry saw her hovering by the door, he waved her in and introduced her to Judith Armstrong. Anika shook hands with her and asked if they would like tea or coffee.

'No thanks,' Barry said, beaming. 'We've just eaten. Judith is going to join the practice. From tomorrow.'

'As the missing Associate?' The words were out before Anika had time to consider what she was saying.

Barry looked surprised and Judith amused. 'No,' he said. 'She'll be a partner. The practice will be Armstrong and Oreopoulous once she joins. There'll be no more Barry Oreopoulous and Associates.'

No more associates. That meant they were all going to be sacked. Anika's throat constricted and an icy coldness gripped her stomach.

'Can you pull out the McConnachies' site plans and bring them into my office?' Barry said, as casually as if he hadn't just hurled a grenade into the works. 'Judith is going to take over that job.'

After Anika handed over the drawings, she backed unacknowledged out of Barry's office. A moment later she saw, through the glass partition, Barry's and Judith's heads bent cosily over the drawings, grey spiky hair and black curls almost touching, like they'd been working together for years. Quickly she told the others what she'd learned.

'We're not going to be sacked,' Tim said confidently. He meant he wasn't going to get sacked. 'I'd heard that Barry was competing with Howard Meyer to hire her.'

'Why didn't you tell us?' Anika said.

'You know me, I never gossip.'

'There'll be more work for us all,' Greg said.

Anika saw that Greg was trying not to show his unease, though the jiggling that had started up in his left leg gave him away. It made his shoe scrape against the metal footrest of his draughting stool in an irritating squeak. She wasn't so sure there'd be enough work for them all. With another partner on board there'd be less need for one of them, and that one would be her. She went into the ladies' room by the lifts and locked the cubicle door behind her. There was a new poster on the back of the door about genital herpes that further depressed her. Sitting on the closed lid of the WC pan, she considered her options.

She hadn't seen any advertisements for draughting jobs though she'd been keeping an eye out. If something came up, Barry would probably give her a good reference although she'd been getting mixed signals from him lately. According to him the other day, when he was so grumpy, she was a poor draughtsman. Yet the rational part of her pointed out that there could have been another reason for his bad mood last week. If Tim was right, he and her tutor Howard Meyer had been competing to induce Judith Armstrong to join their practices.

And Howard Meyer would have to be Anika's second referee. He'd definitely give her a glowing reference; she was convinced of that from his enthusiastic reaction to her sketch plans for the Butler's Stairs apartment project. *A sensitive design*, he'd said, *that takes away none of the integrity of the nineteenth-century arches.*

Of course, if her painting hadn't been stolen she could have put it up for auction. That might have solved all her job insecurity problems. She unbolted the cubicle door and dashed back into the office. Picking up the phone extension near her drawing board, she dialled the number for Balmain Police Station. Eventually, after endless minutes on hold, she was connected to Tom Warburton, the taller of the two rugby forward lookalikes who'd come around after the robbery. Sounding harried, Warburton told her they'd found nothing.

Sadly, Anika put down the receiver. She would give up on the Rocheteau now. There was no point in brooding over its loss, no point in drawing up her own list of suspects. The painting could have been taken by anyone. Anyone who knew her, knew her friends and their friends, knew the gallery curators, knew the curators' contacts. Someone who'd seen her coming and going with a package that was obviously a painting. It could have been stolen by any one of a lot of people.

When it was time for her to leave the office, Judith and Barry were still deep in conversation. No chance for Anika to ask if she still had a job until after the weekend, and the prospect of that delay filled her with gloom.

Waiting for Anika when she got home was a heavy cream envelope. Her name and address were inscribed on it in a spidery hand that she didn't recognise. On the back was the sender's address: 137 Gallery, Queen Street, Woollahra. She ripped open the envelope, panic clutching at her throat. Inside was a postcard. A picture of a painting, Impressionist in style, of a man standing in an overgrown garden and reading a newspaper. On the other side of the card, tiny printed letters indicated that the artist was Antoine Rocheteau. The message on the card was written in the same handwriting as that on the front of the envelope.

Dear Miss Molnar,
   I was sorry to read of your loss. Your loss is not my gain. Let me assure you that I had nothing to do with this and I hope that the whereabouts of the painting will soon be known so it can be restored to its rightful owner.
      Yours sincerely,
      Julius Singer

Anika was startled by these words. Contrition was not something she expected from Julius and he could hardly have been sorry. Not when on her visit to his gallery he'd said the painting wasn't hers. With a trembling hand she shoved the card back into the envelope.

Yet perhaps the message was genuine. She pulled the card out and read it once more. Julius didn't need to deflect attention from himself; after all, he had an alibi for the night of the robbery. Maybe he really was hoping the painting could be restored to her. Puzzled, she put the card and envelope in her bottom drawer. This was where she kept the things she never looked at, never thought of. Things like her passport and hairdressing qualifications. Maybe by osmosis this card might absorb their irrelevance to her everyday life.

But she felt unnerved anyway. Sitting on the edge of the bed, she rested her head in her hands and stared at the carpet. Breathe, breathe, get that air deep into your lungs, think of something else, something calming. All at once she felt inundated by an overriding desire to go home. For a visit, that was all. For a chance to throw her arms around her mother, for a chance to feel her mother's arms around her. To feel Nyenye's arms around her too, and to see her father and Miklos. And most of all to pose those questions that she so desperately wanted answered but at the same time didn't want to have to ask. For she had to discover the truth about how that painting came into her family and the only person who would know for sure was her beloved Nyenye.

Chapter 21

Saturday morning and Anika was at the corner shop far too early. The mesh security screens were bolted in place across the shop front, and on the pavement outside there were piles of packaged newspapers waiting to be lifted inside. There was a chill in the air and she was in such a hurry when she rushed out of the house that she hadn't thought to put on a jacket. Hopping about to keep warm, she resisted the temptation to untie the string around one of the bundles of the *Sydney Morning Herald* and yank out the classifieds section.

The Cataldos were surprised to see her loitering outside when they opened up not long after six. 'We could deliver, you know,' Mrs Cataldo said.

Anika muttered some excuse. Tabilla used to get the morning paper delivered but it came erratically. She suspected it was being picked up from the front path by passers-by, and anyway she wanted to be able to pick and choose daily which paper to buy. To *behave promiscuously with broadsheets* was how she described it.

'You look tired,' Mrs Cataldo said after Anika had paid for the paper. 'Burning the candle everywhere, are you?'

Once Anika understood what Mrs Cataldo meant, she laughed, and the lovely thing about laughter was that it drew some of the tension out of you, and before she knew it Mrs Cataldo had drawn her close in a warm embrace. 'Don't work too hard,' the newsagent said. 'You must remember to have fun too.'

'That's a bit rich coming from you,' Anika mumbled into

Mrs Cataldo's springy grey hair. 'I bet you've worked hard every day of your life.'

When Anika got the newspaper home, she found that Tabilla was already up, and sitting, fully-dressed, at the kitchen table in front of the cafetière. 'I heard you go out,' she said. 'I couldn't sleep either.'

Anika unfolded the *Sydney Morning Herald* and gave her aunt the front section. Then she spread out the classified sections at the other end of the table.

'Anika, why are you looking through the jobs classifieds with that felt-tip pen? I thought you were happy where you are.'

'I am. But I'm not sure Barry is all that happy with me.'

Anika told Tabilla about developments at work and the transition from Oreopoulous and Associates to Armstrong and Oreopoulous.

'You can't possibly let things run on like this,' Tabilla said. 'Why don't you just call Barry? The phone is not an instrument of torture. It is something to be used for your own benefit.'

'Maybe I will. But I'd like to have a fallback position first.'

'That seems illogical to me. Why not call him this morning?'

'It's the weekend, that's why.'

'Well, for heaven's sake, ring now. Or give him till eight-thirty if you must. You want to get him before he goes out shopping or sailing or running or whatever he does on a Saturday morning. I don't see why you should have to wait until you go in to work again.'

Anika decided to take her advice. At eight-thirty, after a furtive tot of Tabilla's medicinal brandy that was kept at the back of the pantry cupboard, she dialled Barry's home number. The phone rang on and on. Eventually there was a pickup. She was ready to launch into her prepared speech but

152

it turned out it was only Barry's recorded voice suggesting that she leave a short message after the beep. She wittered on, her message so lengthy that she'd only just got around to leaving her phone number and name before the machine cut out.

* * *

The next morning Barry called back. 'I'm so sorry, Anika, I should have explained things to you last Friday. It was really too bad of me.' His tone was apologetic. Like a criminal on trial waiting for the verdict, Anika braced herself for what he was going to say next.

As he carried on in this contrite vein for a time, her anxiety increased. While he was berating himself, she thought of the advertisements for part-time work that she'd found in the classifieds. One was at St Leonards and much too far to travel each day from Rozelle, and it would be difficult to get from there to uni for lectures. The other one was over at Bondi Junction; this would be a bit easier but it would still involve a lot of travelling. And neither job was with a good firm of architects. Sitting on the floor with her back against the wall, she waited nervously for Barry to get to the point.

'We certainly don't want to get rid of you,' he said at last. 'I'm really impressed with your design skills and your drawing has improved. In fact, I'd like it if you could work some more hours but I understand that you can't because of your studies. Anyway, don't worry, your job is secure.'

Your job is secure. She felt like a prisoner who'd just been acquitted. Before the conversation was even finished, she began to dance around the kitchen as far as the phone cord would allow her, hip hop, she was a teenager again, and in the money, and a little bit in love with Barry who was impressed with her design skills, and how wonderful that was! After she'd hung up, she heard the front gate open and was out the front door in a flash, thinking it might be Tabilla back early from her jaunt. But it turned out to be Mrs Thornton's gate not theirs, and Anika was left standing like a statue of an athlete in mid-action while Mrs Thornton beamed at her across the low fence dividing their yards.

'You look happy, love,' Mrs Thornton said. 'Happier than I've seen you for a while.'

Anika told her about her job and the firm's name change. Mrs Thornton listened all the while so sympathetically, nodding her head and tut-tutting from time to time, that Anika started to wonder if she'd misjudged her, for she could receive news as well as give it. Perhaps Anika had never given her a chance before. She'd certainly never told her anything much. It struck her that it was an act of generosity to talk to other people about what had been happening to you, and an act of trust too. Trust that they wouldn't exploit you, trust that they wouldn't use to their own advantage the information that you'd given away.

Their chat was terminated by the sound of Tabilla's phone ringing. 'Have a good day,' Anika said and dashed inside again to pick it up.

Jonno's voice was mellow rather than sharp, and yet she felt his call as an intrusion into her life, a piercing of her bubble of happiness.

'Can I come around this afternoon?' he said. 'There's something I need to tell you.'

'Is it about the painting, by any chance?'

'No. It's something else.'

'Can't you say it on the phone?'

'I'd prefer not to. Will it be OK if I drop around at about three? We can go somewhere for a drink if that's not too early for you.'

Jonno seemed tense when he collected her and she wondered if his news was bad. They managed to find a table in the small and crowded beer garden of a pub not far from Balmain Wharf. 'What's been happening with you?' he asked, ripping the top off a packet of dry-roasted peanuts and pushing it her way.

'I haven't lost my job.'

Although he congratulated her on her job stability, he took the news with equanimity. Anika supposed this was because he hadn't known that only this morning she'd thought she was going to lose it, so to all intents and purposes what she'd told him was an item of non-news, a bit like saying, 'I didn't get run over by a bus this morning', or 'the earth didn't stop spinning today'.

'What's your news?' she said, thinking he could have tried harder to rustle up some enthusiasm. She sipped her beer and waited.

'I'm going away.'

This gave her a jolt. If he was going away he wouldn't be inviting her for interviews or turning up unexpectedly or making her uncomfortable in the variety of other ways at which he was expert, and that was all to the good. But why then was his news making her feel a little unsettled? It was another option closing, that must be it. She avoided his eyes by grabbing hold of her glass and swilling down a few mouthfuls of beer, looking nonchalant all the while, as if she didn't care whether he went or stayed.

'Did you hear me, Anika?'

'Yes, I'm just rather thirsty. Where are you going?'

'I've been posted overseas.'

'Congratulations, Jonno, that's wonderful. But I thought you were freelance. Are you posting yourself? Or are you giving up being freelance?'

'Well, in a sense I'll continue being freelance but I've also been commissioned to write a series of articles on what's happening in the Soviet Bloc countries.'

The Soviet Bloc countries. That made her nervous. Hungary was one of those. She said with an assumed calmness, 'Any particular country?'

'Poland and East Germany,' he said. 'Roving between the two.'

'When are you going?'

'Next week. I won't be able to do that article, Anika. I'm so sorry.' He leaned forward and did the staring into her eyes thing that he'd done when they'd first met. The eyes are a portal to the soul, that's what he'd said when they sat together in the café opposite the Art Gallery of New South Wales. As she looked at those beautiful blue eyes flecked with topaz and fringed with sandy eyelashes that glinted in the light, she felt as if he were willing her to fall for him. It must be an automatic thing with him. Since he was leaving next week there was no point in him sweeping her off her feet. He said, his voice as intent as if making a declaration, 'You will let me know if anything happens, won't you?'

'Like what?' She made her voice flat.

'Like getting your painting back.'

That wretched painting that Jonno was much too interested in. 'I've given up all hope of getting it back,' she told him.

'I'll send you my address when I get there.'

She smiled to herself, doubting she'd ever hear from him again.

When he dropped her back at the house he came into the front yard with her. She was astonished when he bent down and kissed her on the lips. But it felt good, very good, and it was not long before she was kissing him back. When they came up for breath, she pushed him gently away.

After he'd gone, she congratulated herself on her gift for choosing men to pash on with. A dishy man who was just about to go overseas looking for stories was an excellent pick. She was pretty safe here.

He was a top-notch kisser though, she'd say that for him.

* * *

On the bench in the kitchen was another note from Tabilla saying that Daniel had called. Of course, Anika wouldn't phone back. But the message was disquieting. Any interaction with Daniel, any mention of his name, resurrected all those anxieties that she tried to keep suppressed, for she could see no way of resolving them without going back to Budapest. Tabilla's note was letting the genie out of the bottle and her first thought now was to wonder if Daniel was right when he'd hinted the Rocheteau was looted art. And if he was, it might well be the case that some of the other artworks in Nyenye's flat had been looted too, and this was an even more disturbing thought. They could have been bought unwittingly by her grandparents thinking there were no issues of ownership.

Or worse, maybe her family had been involved with the SS or the Arrow Cross. Her grandfather, for instance, who'd died ten years ago leaving Nyenye alone and her parents in charge of the butcher's shop. Yet her grandparents would have hated the Arrow Cross, Anika felt sure of that. She knew who they were: industrious and astute people who'd managed to survive under a tough regime. But was it possible that they were too astute? Perhaps Nyenye wasn't the naïve collector of art as Anika had assumed before the Rocheteau was stolen. This thought filled her with alarm. Nyenye had been a bulwark all Anika's life and it would rock her to her foundations if her grandmother was not who she seemed. Anika had to come up with some strategy to find out what her family was.

But perhaps the only strategy was to wait. Hungary was liberalising. If she were patient she might be able to talk to Nyenye. You never could tell what the future might bring.

PART III

Sydney, November to December, 1989

Chapter 22

When the Berlin Wall came down in November, Anika and Tabilla were as good as there, leaning forward in their chairs with the television on loud. Anika's heart was dancing the polka, Tabilla's face was so jubilant she looked ten years younger, the journalist's voice was as animated as a commentator for the footy grand final. People jammed the Berlin streets, the gates were open, crowds were surging through from the East. The green-uniformed guards, who a week before would have shot anyone trying to cross to the West, were standing idly by, watching it all.

Anika's eyes misted over as the television camera closed in on the hugs, the reunions, the faces wet with tears, tears of joy as families reunited after all those years they had been apart. People were scrambling up the wall and dancing on its top. Others were bashing at it with sledgehammers, intent on breaking down this division between East and West, while some began to knock off bits of concrete to take away, souvenirs of this miracle that countless numbers of them would never forget.

'We'll celebrate too,' Tabilla said once the news item had ended. She got the wine box out of the fridge and poured them each a large glass. 'To reunification.'

'To the end of a regime,' Anika said, and after half a glass added, 'I'd love to go home for a visit.'

'I never want to go back,' Tabilla said. 'But I'm over the moon this has happened.'

Anika found herself telling Tabilla that she'd been saving

for months. She had begun to save after the Hungarian share of the Iron Curtain was rolled up in early May. That was when the electrified fence between Austria and Hungary was removed; that was when the authorities hacked through the barbed wire that was too expensive to maintain. But in May she had nowhere near enough to pay for a ticket. By late September, she had more savings but still not enough. That was when the Hungarian Communist Party voted itself out of existence and announced that there would be free elections the following March.

'How much more do you need?' Tabilla asked.

When Anika told her, she said, 'I can lend you some money. Add it to what you already have and it should be enough to get you a return ticket.'

'Are you sure you can spare it? It will be months before I can pay you back.'

'I wouldn't offer if I wasn't sure. You've seemed withdrawn for ages. I guessed you were homesick. You need to go back to recharge your cultural batteries.'

The next day in Anika's lunch break she visited the travel agency on William Street. All three of the booking clerks, clad in navy and red uniforms like flight attendants, were engaged in advising customers. Anika hovered around the waiting area, trying to curb her excitement, ready to leap forward when a position became available.

'I'd like to book a return ticket to Budapest,' she told the woman behind the counter when it was her turn and the clock on the wall said 1.45pm. The woman wore her dark hair cut in a bob, and a smile that might be glued-on it looked so fixed.

'Give me some dates.' Even when she spoke, the booking clerk's smile remained unperturbed.

'I'm pretty flexible. I can leave any time from two days before Christmas right up to Australia Day. But I can only be away for three weeks in total.'

'You've left it very late to book.'

'It's not even mid-November,' Anika said.

'But it's Christmas, you see. People plan months ahead for that. But I'll see what I can do.' The clerk's voice was soothing.

'I'll fly any route,' Anika told her. 'Any route as long as it's not via Moscow.'

'There aren't any direct flights from Sydney to Budapest. You'll need to go to London or Paris or Rome or somewhere and then get another flight onwards. London, probably, that might be the cheapest. I'll have to get back to you.' The woman made a note of Anika's office and home telephone numbers.

A few hours later she called Anika at the office. 'If you're willing to travel on Christmas Day, I've got a really good deal for you: Budapest via London and Bahrain and Singapore.' She told Anika to drop in to the agency in a few days' time.

Afterwards, Anika danced around the office and Barry, bless the sweet man, burrowed in the tearoom refrigerator and came up with a bottle of champagne that had been sitting there for months waiting for something to celebrate. They all had a glass or two and everyone shared Anika's euphoria.

In the late afternoon, she rang the police station. They were tired of her, even that taller policeman Tom Warburton, and made it clear that she shouldn't call them again. If there was any change in the situation they would contact her.

That evening she phoned her parents to let them know she was coming. There was no click on the line after her mother picked up, there hadn't been for months, although this hadn't made their conversations any less guarded. Anika's mother was overjoyed but anxious about how she was paying for the flights. Three weeks in Hungary, that was not long, her mother said, already counting down the days until she must leave again. She's got a job, Anika's father said. She has commitments. Then Anika told them the office shut for just over three weeks from Christmas Eve. We are lucky then, said her mother. It's all a miracle. She was right about that, it was.

* * *

It was early afternoon, two days before Anika was to fly to Budapest, when she popped into David Jones in her lunch hour to buy a present for her mother. Afterwards, as she was waiting at the stop for an Oxford Street bus – while the breeze agitated the reindeer antlers on a teenager's head and fingered women's skirts and flapped men's jacket fronts – she heard her name being called.

'Anika,' Daniel said. 'I'm so pleased to see you.' In the bright sunlight his skin glowed golden and his dark eyes were unfathomable. Anika thought of the name she'd given him when they first met all those months ago: Mr Black Eyes.

'One pronounces my name *Uh-nee-ka*. I told you that before.' Anika's heart was thumping too hard but her voice was calm.

Daniel smiled. He looked as if he hadn't visited a barber for weeks. His hair was smooth and shiny, and he was wearing a rumpled cream linen suit and a black T-shirt.

At this moment she caught sight of the Oxford Street bus pulling up at the stop further down the street. 'My bus will be here in a moment.'

'Why don't you miss it? We could have a coffee.'

'I can't.'

'I was lucky to see you,' he said. 'I don't know why you won't return my phone calls.'

'You only called three times and that was months ago.'

'*Uh-nee-ka*. I know when I'm not wanted.' He said this so comically that she couldn't help but laugh. He added, 'I don't normally come this way, I just popped into Angus and Robertson for a couple of books.'

'I don't usually come this way either.'

'Let's meet another time.'

'I don't think so.' There was no point telling him that she was going to Hungary the next day.

'What's the matter, Anika? I didn't mean to upset you that day at Clifton Gardens. I just wanted you to be aware of the possibilities.'

'That wasn't what upset me, though it did make me rethink a few things.' The bus was still stationary at the stop up the road, allowing what seemed like scores of passengers to alight, while there was a score more waiting to get on.

'Why won't you at least do me the courtesy of telling me honestly what's upsetting you?'

'Me tell you honestly? I've always been honest with you. The trouble is that you haven't been with me.'

'What did I do wrong?'

'It was about your Uncle Jake.'

'What about him?'

'You tricked me into telling you what happened when I took the Rocheteau to Julius Singer's gallery.'

'How did I do that?'

'You said your uncle knows Julius.'

'And he does.'

'Julius told my aunt that he doesn't know any Jake Rubinstein.'

Daniel laughed for rather too long. 'But that's not his last name. And he's my *great*-uncle actually, though he's the same age as my other uncles. And what's more, he's called Jacob Lacey. He's my grandmother's youngest brother.'

'Julius would surely have known that.'

'Why would he? As far as I know, Uncle Jake's only called Jake within the family. To everyone else he's Jacob. And there's no reason why Julius would know how we're connected. Uncle Jake is hardly likely to go around saying to every acquaintance of his, "Oh, do you know my great-nephew?" If you'd ever met Jake you'd know that.'

The surprise of this took her breath away. When she'd recovered, she said, 'I remember very clearly what you said that day. I wouldn't have told you what Julius told me if you hadn't mentioned that your uncle knows Julius.' Her palms suddenly felt sticky and she wiped them on her skirt.

'But I just told you, he *does* know Julius. You're acting like an ostrich burying your head in the sand. I would have thought someone like you would want to know the truth.'

'But the trouble was, Daniel, that I wasn't sure that you were the right person to tell me.'

'I was only trying to help, Anika.'

There was something about the way he said this that moved her, but at this point her bus pulled up. After taking a seat, she twisted around to look for him. In his rumpled linen suit, he was still standing on the pavement, his too-long black hair flopping forward on to his forehead. Although she could have leapt out of her seat, jumped off the bus and run back to him, she stayed immobile. There was an errand that she had to run and there wasn't much time left.

As the bus lurched off, she began to feel overwhelmed with sadness. A sadness that, she told herself, probably had more to do with nostalgia than regret. Nostalgia for that glorious day at the beach when Daniel took her into the surf and hauled her up from where she'd been dumped on the sand. Nostalgia for that evening at the pub at Watson's Bay when he'd drawn her out of her usual reticence about her past.

She let the bus carry her beyond the turnoff for Armstrong and Oreopoulous and on towards the 137 Gallery in Paddington. Thoughts swirled around her brain, churned up by what Daniel had told her, as she formulated questions that she planned to ask Julius. She hoped he was there. There were some things she had to find out before flying home. She wanted to have as much information as possible from Julius before confronting her family. All those things she'd avoided thinking about after her first visit to his gallery. All those things she'd wanted to forget. Now she wanted to remember them.

Chapter 23

Inside Singer's gallery, the assistant – the burly man with a face like a full moon – was engrossed with a sale and barely noticed Anika. She weaved her way around intricate wire sculptures and past an exhibition of abstract expressionist paintings by Indigenous artists from the Kimberley that lit up the white walls. Mr Singer's office was at the back of the gallery. The door was open. He was sitting behind a desk with a pile of papers in front of him, his face half turned away from her. Strands of his comb-over were displaced, as if he'd been running his hands through what was left of his hair.

When she coughed, he looked up, startled. He'd aged since she last saw him, his face appeared lined and his mouth sinking at the corners. How could a man age that much in only half a year? She must have caught him at a bad moment. Surprised, she let go of her bag and it crashed on to the floor. By the time she'd picked it up, he had collected himself. Those strands of hair were now neatly spread across his scalp. Only his eyebrows remained unruly. Thick and bushy, it was as if they were trying to compensate for the balding pate.

His expression was still unwelcoming though. Standing, he said, 'Miss Molnar,' the old-fashioned way, no Ms here. His face was thinner than when they'd last met, and the eye sockets deeper than she'd remembered. He cleared his throat before saying, 'I was sorry to hear of your loss.'

'Thank you. I got your card.' She watched him closely for any signs of guilt.

His face was now expressionless and his light brown eyes

gave nothing away. Quietly he said, 'As I wrote on that card, your loss is not my gain.'

'I'm glad to hear it.' Anika's voice came out too high and the words too fast. 'I've come because I've been thinking about what you said to me the day I brought in the Rocheteau.'

Gesturing to the chair in front of his desk, he said, 'You'd better sit down.'

'When I was here last you told me the painting wasn't mine. I've thought a lot about that.'

Julius said, 'So have I.'

'I wonder if you might tell me why you thought it wasn't mine.' She stumbled on her words, though this was one of the questions she'd prepared on the way and rehearsed again and again.

His face contorted as if he had a toothache. She looked away. Behind him, outside the picture window, there was a courtyard. It looked as if a piece of rainforest had been transplanted to Paddington and at any moment she might see a monkey swinging from an umbrella tree.

Turning away from the rainforest so she could watch Julius's expression, she continued. 'Perhaps you don't know that the painting belonged to my uncle, Tabilla's husband. It belonged to him.'

Julius looked alarmed. Anika's words hung in the air like a fence dividing them. Tabilla had told him all those months ago, when Anika was listening to their phone conversation, only that a *distant* relative had given it to her. It was the news that this *distant relative* had been Tabilla's husband that shocked him so much. Anika persevered. 'Did you know, Mr Singer, that it was her husband's?'

'No,' he said slowly. 'I thought you said you got it from your father.'

'All I told you was what my father thought. That the

painting must have come from the consignment store or a state auction, I can't remember which. But it belonged to my Uncle Tomas and I haven't got a clue where he got it from. When I left Budapest, I brought it with me for Tabilla. But she didn't want it. She insisted that I have it. She gave it to me.'

There was a pause during which Julius began lightly tapping his fingers on the desk. He seemed to be struggling to marshal his thoughts, and when he began to speak again, his words emerged slowly. 'The painting was once ours, Anika. Ours, not yours or your uncle's.'

Anika felt the room start to swim and her mouth suddenly dry. She wondered if she might be going to vomit. There was a wastepaper basket by Julius's desk. Maybe she could reach that in time, if she didn't keel over first. She breathed deeply and the nausea faded. All the while Julius's fingers continued to drum on the desk and he appeared lost in thought. Above her head a ceiling fan slowly circulated. The air-conditioning unit made an irregular rattle as it blasted cold air across the room.

'Mr Singer, all you said last time was that the painting couldn't be mine. You didn't say it was once yours.'

When he spoke again his voice was gravelly. 'I'm going to tell you how it came into our family, Anika. And then I'll tell you how it left again.' His left eyelid began to twitch and he paused for a second to rub at it. 'I was very young when my mother turned thirty-five, I was only seven. *I want a quiet birthday in the bosom of my family,* she said. Those were the same words she used every year. The bosom of the family was just the four of us, Mama and Papa and my younger brother Emil.'

Julius's eyes shifted to a point somewhere behind Anika's left shoulder. When she turned to follow the direction of his gaze, she saw only the blank white wall. Then she realised it was the past that he was peering into. Although his voice was faint when he continued speaking, the words came fast. 'My father came home the day before my mother's birthday with a parcel. Emil and I watched when he hid it in his study behind the drawn curtains. It was large and flat. "It's a secret," my father whispered, one finger raised to his lips. "Between you and me. You mustn't tell Mama."'

At this point Julius began to cough and Anika feared he might be choking. But when she stood, he waved her back to her seat. The gallery assistant stuck his head around the door. Taking no notice of the coughing, he said, 'There's a man here to see you, Julius. Your afternoon appointment.'

Julius croaked, 'Tell him to come back in half an hour, James. And bring some water, there's a good chap.'

The assistant returned with a bottle of sparkling mineral water and two glasses that he placed on the desk. Julius gestured him out of the room. Still coughing a little, he fiddled with the screw cap until Anika took the bottle from him and poured two glasses.

After half-emptying his glass, Julius started talking again, his eyes once more trained on that patch of wall behind Anika's head. She braced herself in her chair, feet planted firmly on the floor. 'The morning of my mother's birthday I watched her open the package,' he said.

It was clearly a struggle for him to speak. He swallowed noisily before continuing. 'And that's when I first saw the painting of the auburn-haired woman. I'll never forget that day. When Mama looked at the canvas her face lit up. She seemed to glow like the woman in the painting. That's when I realised that they looked a bit alike. Not in feature, you understand. The woman in the portrait was more classically beautiful than my mother. But their hair was similar. Mama wore her dark red hair piled on top of her head. It was thick and wavy and was always slipping out of its pins and threatening to tumble on to her shoulders.'

What he said moved Anika deeply. Only when Julius wiped the back of his hand across his eyes did she realise that his cheeks were wet, and she found that her own eyes were filling with tears.

'But it wasn't just that,' he said. 'Appearances are only ever part of a story. Do you remember that question mark on the face of the woman in the portrait? She had that same defiant look that was often on my mother's. I've sometimes thought since then that my mother knew what was to come and was challenging the future.' He paused and after a few seconds he looked directly at her.

At this point the assistant, James, reappeared at the door. 'Your visitor's back again,' he said, his face severe. 'He's only got a few minutes and I promised you'd see him now.'

'He'll have to wait,' Julius said.

'I'm so sorry,' Anika said when the assistant had gone. 'There's one more thing I wanted to ask, I hope you don't mind. You said you'd tell me how the painting left your family. When was that?'

'Didn't you guess that, Anika? We had to leave the painting behind when we fled Vienna. And my mother died in Auschwitz, together with the rest of my family.'

His words were a minefield between them and she longed to leap over it, to hug him, to tell him that she'd had no idea that this was how they'd lost the painting. How obtuse she'd been, for it was obvious that he was Jewish and she should have guessed that this was what had happened to his family. For a moment she didn't know what to say, English words seemed to have suddenly deserted her. All she could manage was to spit out a phrase that was like an awkward lump of gristle in her mouth. 'I am so s-s-sorry. I didn't know that.'

Julius continued, his voice low, 'We left Vienna in 1938 and got as far as Prague. Of course, we'd left everything behind but at least we still had each other. Then in 1940 the situation got much worse for people like us. My parents managed to get me on to a Kindertransport to London. Emil was too young though. I was the only one of our family to get out.'

Anika became aware of James standing outside the door again, glaring at her as if he wanted to bundle her out of the office, and she didn't know how long he'd been standing there.

Julius stood up and nodded at her, before taking her right hand. She felt that this sealed a pact between them. She put her left hand over his and might have hugged him if James hadn't been standing so close. Julius said, his voice low, 'Thank you for visiting me, Anika.'

'Thank you for telling me about your mother, Mr Singer.'

'Call me Julius. You and I are linked by the picture. I hope it can be traced.'

* * *

That night Anika had trouble sleeping. She turned on the radio and listened to the World Service. They were talking about Eastern Europe again. Economists were queuing up to offer advice to the former Soviet Bloc countries about how to clean up the shambles left by communist mismanagement. *These countries need to take a swift and dramatic leap to private ownership and a market system*, recommended a Harvard professor, *so that financial instability can be avoided*.

The news item finished. Turning over in bed, Anika rolled into darkness, into an embracing sleep. Abruptly she was in the back of a police wagon with three or four faceless protesters. Her breathing was uneven and her legs trembling. Miklos was no longer with her. He must have got away.

The bruise on her shoulder began to throb as the wagon bounced along an unpaved road in the dense forest. A thick mist swirled about the trees and formed tendrils that curled into the wagon through cracks around the door, around the windows. Tendrils that began to wrap themselves around her throat, around her chest, stifling her breath.

An instant later, she was in a cold and windowless cell that stank of cigarette smoke and stale sweat. Unforgiving lighting illuminated the room. There was that grey man, sitting opposite her, the same one as before. Grey-faced, grey-haired, grey-uniformed, this man peppered her with questions. He smirked as she stumbled through replies that were always the wrong ones. Smirked as she struggled against the straps that were holding her down.

After a while, he grew fed up with her. He lit another cigarette. While he sucked hard at it, she stared at the cement floor with its gutter and drainage outlet. There would be worse to come; she knew there would be. She had to be strong. Too soon, she felt a movement in the air as he leaned towards her and seized her left hand. Turning it over, he exposed the underside of her wrist. She pressed her lips tightly together. She would not shout as he stubbed out the burning cigarette on her white skin, she would not. But, oh, that smell! Never ever would she forget that smell.

Fighting against the constraints and slippery with sweat, she forced herself awake and out of the tangle of bedclothes. It was that old dream, that recurring nightmare that she might never be rid of. Panting as hard as if she'd been running a race, it took her a few moments to realise where she was.

Slowly her breathing became less ragged. Shivering, she crept on to the landing. The sound of gentle snoring came from Tabilla's bedroom. She crept down the staircase, clutching at the bannister and avoiding the treads that squeaked. When she turned on the kitchen light a cockroach scuttled across the floor; a shiny repulsive thing that she couldn't cope with, not in the middle of the night, though the spray was in the broom cupboard and there was a shoe by the back door that she could have thwacked it with. Instead she let it run under the kitchen sink.

The can of Milo in the pantry was nearly empty and she made a hot drink with what was left. The back garden was bathed in shades of bluish-grey, the shrubs faintly illuminated by a crescent moon that looked sharp and dangerous. In the few moments that she stood by the back door, draining her mug, the moon was stationary. But as soon as she went upstairs it would resume its progress. It would continue cutting through the dark velvet of the sky.

The wailing of a fire engine from Victoria Road made her jump. In just a few hours she'd be leaving Sydney. Her thoughts were all muddled, longing and apprehension warring against each other. She yearned to see her family, to put her arms around them, to feel the security and warmth of their love, to see her home. Yet at the same time she didn't want to think about what she might discover there.

Ever since hearing Julius's story she'd felt confused and unsettled. Julius's revelation had been a shock to her, but once he'd told her what had happened to his family, events started to slot into place. The Singers had escaped from Vienna at the time of the Anschluss. They'd left the Rocheteau behind. It would have been looted by the Nazis and somehow made its way to Budapest. What had happened to the painting after that, before Tomas had acquired it, was a mystery, but one that she hoped to solve.

It was strange how quickly the mind adjusted without you really noticing. After the Rocheteau was stolen last March, she'd desperately wanted it back but as the months passed by she'd resigned herself to never seeing it again. And once she'd learned this afternoon that it had belonged to Julius's family, she'd known that the painting was rightly his. This thought had become not a sad thing but a relief. A washing of the hands.

But though her hands felt clean, she wasn't too sure about Nyenye's and Tomas's. She felt sick at heart about what she might discover in Budapest. It could blow her family apart. She would have to take things slowly, very slowly. One question at a time.

PART IV

Budapest, December 1989

Chapter 24

At the top of the Budapest funicular, Anika and her mother alighted into a biting wind. Above them, the sky, whipped clear of clouds, was a cold harsh blue. Walking on Castle Hill, on the Buda side of the Danube River, was Anika's mother's idea: a good brisk walk would prepare Anika for sleep tonight. This had made Anika smile: walking was her mother's solution for everything. It was as if the interminable plane ride and transitions through too many time zones hadn't already been preparation enough.

The winter sunlight slanted off the glazed walls of the funicular station. Below them, the Széchenyi Chain Bridge led from Buda across to Pest, the flat land on the other side of the river. Pest was where Anika's parents lived, a thirty-minute walk away, in an apartment on the third floor of a late-nineteenth century building that had seen better days. Paint fading, stucco crumbling off the walls, gutters leaking; it was one of the many shabby neo-Baroque apartment blocks constructed around central courtyards.

The wind, channelled through the narrow streets of Castle Hill, found freedom in the cobbled area around the funicular station. It fretted at the coats of the few hardy people alighting there, tourists mostly, and filled the air with dust.

'It's lovely having you here,' Anika's mother said. She was wearing her favourite brown overcoat that she'd had for at least a decade and around her neck the blue and red silk scarf that Anika had bought for her before she left Sydney. That silk scarf would be inadequate for these temperatures, Anika realised; it would have been more practical to have bought her a woollen scarf instead.

Anika took her mother's arm as they turned into a side street that was slightly more sheltered. Mama had put on too much make-up for her homecoming and, though Anika found this touching, the colours were garish: the eye shadow too green, the lips too orange. She was lovelier without it, Anika thought, with her high cheekbones and intense green eyes, her turned-up nose and long upper lip. Suddenly guilty at these disparaging thoughts, her heart filled with love and other emotions that she couldn't immediately put her finger on. Perhaps it was a touch of regret mixed with trepidation. Regret that she'd missed chunks of her mother's life. Trepidation about what the future would bring.

A football tapped its way along the pavement towards them, controlled by a towheaded boy of eleven or twelve. He didn't notice them, so intent was he on bouncing the ball in front of him. He would be dreaming of being selected on the team, dreaming of playing for his school, dreaming of playing for Hungary. This boy might have been Miklos some years ago, Anika thought: that mindless rhythmic bouncing, that ferocious concentration. Miklos, completing a PhD at the University of Szeged, was very busy, he'd told her on the phone that morning when he'd rung to welcome her not long after she reached her parents' apartment, but he would be home soon.

While they were battling the breeze, Anika's mother wanted to know all about her job and the course; she asked rapid-fire questions that Anika tried to answer clearly. 'And the climate too, Anika, it is surely too hot for you? Maybe you'll come home now we're no longer a Soviet satellite.'

'I'll see, Mama.' Her voice was non-committal. 'I love it in Australia and I have to finish my degree.'

At this moment the wistful notes of a cello began to filter through the morning air. Her mother tightened her grip on Anika's arm but she didn't need prompting to stop in front of a large bay window. Inside was a spacious living room filled with empty armchairs. On an upright chair in the middle of the room a young woman sat, her dark hair falling across her face, sunlight slanting on to the mellow wood of the cello that she supported between her legs. She was wearing an orange dress and an expression of fierce concentration. At once an image flashed into Anika's mind of one of the paintings in Nyenye's flat – the picture of a woman in a cobalt blue dress playing the cello. The woman in the room finished her piece and flexed her wrist.

'Beautiful,' Mama breathed, squeezing Anika's arm as they moved on. As her hair whipped across her face, Anika saw the few white hairs that were mingled with the dark brown.

Although autumn was long gone there were still a few scraps of leaves blowing about, rustled up as if from nowhere. The cellist began to play again, a melancholy refrain that faded as they descended the hill, down cobbled streets of the old town. Perhaps it was the sadness of the music or maybe it was the memory of Nyenye's painting of the cellist in the cobalt blue dress that made Anika think of the stolen Rocheteau. She still hadn't told her parents of its loss and she wasn't looking forward to doing so. To crowd out this prospect, she deliberately conjured up the walls of Nyenye's flat. All those glowing paintings began spinning in her head like in a kaleidoscope, until suddenly she felt dizzy. Where did they come from? What was going to happen to them and what were they hanging there for? No one ever looked at them, no one knew about them except for the family. Abruptly she asked her mother, 'What are you going to do about those paintings?'

Mama gave a start. 'What paintings?'

'The ones hanging in Nyenye's flat. If Nyenye sold a painting or two you could all afford to visit me in Australia.'

'We don't talk about those paintings.'

'But things have changed. I thought they were only there because they were by Hungarian artists and their paintings couldn't be taken out of the country. If you need the money, surely they can now be sold on the international market?'

'You'll have to ask your grandmother about the paintings.' Mama's voice was taut.

'Ask Nyenye?'

'Yes, Nyenye. Those pictures are nothing to do with me.'

'But they're by Hungarian artists, aren't they?'

'I don't know. Your Nyenye and Nagyapa bought those.'

'But you do know about Hungarian artists.' Mama had always seemed well informed about the history of Hungarian art, especially of the late eighteenth and the nineteenth century. Not erudite like Daniel and his ilk but knowing enough to recognise a painter's style and era without reading the small print.

'I can like something without being an expert on it.' She turned away from Anika, who was unsure if she really did want to lean her elbows on the balustrade that looked over the Danube River, or if this was an excuse to drop her arm.

Below them, the yellowy green waters of the river surged between the substantial stone pillars of the suspension bridge. The wind, whistling through tree branches, formed an accompaniment to the metallic buzz of the Trabants puttering along the road by the water. Always Anika found this river sobering. It connected people and regions that history had shown might well be irreconcilable. It had been life-taker and life-giver. A theatre of war. A graveyard. A demarcation between East and West.

Towards the north, on the Pest side of the river, she noticed that the Parliament buildings were under renovation, scaffolding climbing up the side of the dome. Beyond this was Kossuth Square, and nearby were the copper-green cupola and twin spires of St Stephen's Basilica. To the right of this and a few blocks further away from the river, her father would be busying himself in the butcher's shop, not all that far from her parents' apartment in Erzsébetváros. Though he and Mama had met Anika at the airport that morning, he'd decided to go back to work for a few hours. He could not imagine that his assistants would do the job as well as he could. They could not tell you about every animal that he bought: where it came from, what it ate and what age it lived to. And they were not always mindful of his edict – that every cut of meat was the best cut, and that what really mattered was the purpose of the cut.

After a few minutes Mama started to shiver again, and they carried on walking down the hill, Mama with her hands sunk deep into her pockets, her handbag banging against her hip with each stride. The streets were dirtier than Anika remembered. There were scraps of rubbish blowing about – paper and bits of plastic – and they had to watch where to put their feet to avoid the dog turds. Underpinning Anika's exhaustion was a vague sense of disappointment. She'd been looking forward to this homecoming for so long, with yearning as well as with apprehension. For too long; perhaps nothing would live up to her expectations. Everything was changing, including her, and for a moment she longed for Boggabri Street.

'Let's have a hot drink. I'm freezing,' Mama said when they reached a coffee shop. The interior was warm and lined with dark panelling to shoulder height. Above that, a row of mirrors reflected light in a thousand images from a handful of art deco wall fittings. There was only one vacant table, towards the back of the café. Mama sat on the worn leather banquette and Anika sat opposite her, on an awkwardly curved wooden chair.

'Did you ever know Uncle Tomas?' Anika asked after the hot chocolate, and the strudel they were to share, had arrived.

'No, I was only ten when he died.' After a couple of sips of her drink, Mama look revived, and spots of colour returned to her cheeks. She said, 'My mother and I were living in the countryside then. Ask your father about your Uncle Tomas. It's natural that you want to find out more about him. I expect Tabilla has spoken of him a lot.'

'She hardly ever mentions him. And when she does, she gets very sad.'

'Your Nyenye will also appreciate it if you ask her about him,' Mama said, shrugging off her overcoat. 'There are so few people left who knew him. Most of her friends and Tomas's escaped Budapest at the time of the Revolution. Your father adored his big brother. I wish I'd met him. I've never met Tabilla either. Apart from on the phone, if you can call that a meeting.'

'Of course it's a meeting. Everyone's voice is unique. Think if you were blind, that's all you'd ever know someone by.'

'There's touch too,' Mama said.

'Well, I doubt if you'd be touching up Tabilla.'

Mama chose to ignore Anika's little joke. 'If I were to meet Tabilla, I would hug her.' Her voice was dreamy. 'She is a generous woman who has taken in my daughter and she's my sister-in-law too. Even if I were blind, if I hugged her I would feel her warmth and get an idea of her height and whether or not she has square shoulders and learn what soap and face cream she uses. And that would be far better than viewing a photograph.'

She cut the strudel in half and pushed it towards Anika. They ate in silence until there were only a few crumbs scattered across the plate.

'When you left,' Mama said, 'I thought I would never see you again. You see, I hadn't imagined that Hungary would ever be free. All that was left to us was letter-writing and endless days of waiting for your replies. That wasn't because you wrote infrequently, it was because they checked our mail.'

For the first time in a long while Anika looked at her mother, really looked at her. The frumpy clothes meant nothing and neither did the ill-applied make-up. Immutable as a statue, she radiated kindness and love. Anika's heart went out to her, the fulcrum of their family's life. Leaning across the table, she squeezed her hand and told her how wonderful it was to see her again.

* * *

Anika's parents' apartment seemed shabbier than she'd remembered. Her bedroom was crowded with furniture that she kept tripping over when unpacking. She couldn't unpack her anxiety though, it was wedged too tightly in her head. They were a family of worriers. Anxiety was like a trait picked up on leaving the family home, along with a passport and a suitcase. Anika had hoped she'd abandoned it when she'd first left Budapest, but this useless piece of baggage was with her still – a family failing or the burden of history, she had never worked out which.

While Mama was in the kitchen preparing dinner, Anika sat with her father in the living room. She felt dissociated, as if she'd been flung back into another era. Some things remained the same – the predictability of her parents and their unconditional love – but others had changed. The apartment no longer felt like home and her father looked older and seemed somehow more fretful, or perhaps it was simply that she was observing everything now with greater detachment. There were streaks of white in her father's hair. His face was lined and his forehead permanently creased from a lifetime of raising his eyebrows. It was as if he were permanently surprised by all the changes he'd witnessed to this country of theirs, that had lurched – in less than one century – from being part of an empire to communism to fascism and back to communism, though to a more relaxed sort – that *gulyás* communism that everyone talked about.

'I've got something to tell you.' Anika spoke quickly, wanting to get it out into the open.

An apprehensive expression appeared fleetingly on her father's face, like a cloud blown by a strong wind, soon to be replaced by a bright blankness. He said nothing but his face had already told it all, his concern about her, his concern about everything.

'It's about that painting you gave me to return to Tabilla.'

'Tomas's painting.'

'I tried to give it to her but she insisted I keep it. I didn't want to tell you before, not when I was away, because of the phone-tapping and that other business.' Anika's trouble with the police over the Danube Bend project – her arrest and interrogation – was always referred to in her family as 'that other business'. Their shorthand in case anyone was listening.

He looked surprised. 'That was good of her.'

'Yes, she's very generous. But unfortunately it's gone now.'

'Gone?'

'Yes, it was stolen from my bedroom wall where it was hanging. Don't look so concerned, we weren't home when it was taken.'

She censored her account so she didn't worry him further.

186

It was not necessary for him to learn that the theft took place with Tabilla in the house watching the television.

'Was anything else taken?'

'No, nothing. I kept hoping the picture would turn up again but it hasn't.'

'Never mind. It wasn't worth much. We just wanted Tabilla to have something that was Tomas's.'

'But it *was* worth something, you see. It turns out it was by a famous artist.' Anika explained what had happened, that whole chain of events from when she first took the picture to the Art Gallery of New South Wales. She didn't mention that it was looted art though. She wanted to talk to Nyenye about that first.

He was silent for a while, his face pensive. After some moments he stood and began to pace around the room, as if marshalling his thoughts.

'Your grandmother will give you another,' he said at last. 'Though not yet. No one is to know about her collection yet.'

'Why not?'

'She'll tell you some day.'

'I don't want another painting.' And she certainly didn't want one from that collection. *You've got to keep distinct Tomas's painting and the collection,* she reminded herself. All she wanted at this stage was to discover how Tomas came by the picture. Whether she liked it or not, she was caught up in its provenance – or lack of provenance. She fixed her father with a stern eye and said, 'Where did Tomas get his painting from?'

'I don't really know.' Her father shrugged and his tone was vague. 'He had it for as long as I knew him. Someone gave it to him, that's what your grandmother always said.'

'It doesn't bother you that it's gone?'

'To be honest, I didn't like it all that much. And after

Tomas died I didn't really think of it as his painting, I thought of it as Tabilla's. Anyway, it might turn up again.'

'Unlikely,' Anika said. 'Not if it's worth that much.'

His face became grim. 'Your grandparents had no idea that the painting was valuable either. It's because they hadn't bought it, I suppose. Not like the other ones in Nyenye's flat. They had to pay for those.'

Anika filed this comment away to think about later. Right now she wanted to check on something that had been niggling away at her ever since Tabilla mentioned it all those months ago. 'Have you heard of someone called Sebestyén Tinódi?'

'The name sounds familiar. Didn't Nyenye mention him the day you left? I think he was one of Nyenye's friends. And your grandfather's too.'

'How old would he be?'

'Nyenye's age, I imagine, although I never actually met him.'

There was a pause while Anika thought about the implications of her father's words. He and Tabilla had different stories and she didn't know who to believe. The only way to settle this was to check with Nyenye. But after all that had happened over the past months – the rearrangement of her loyalties, the worries about looted artwork – she didn't know if she would be able to believe her grandmother. Perhaps the best approach was to tell her that Sebestyén Tinódi was dead and see how she reacted. Anika said to her father, 'How could my grandparents have afforded to buy all those paintings?'

Her father shrugged. 'They worked hard. They were always in the shop. Savings weren't allowed and I think you know how to put two and two together.' He took a sip of his beer and stared at the heater.

Anika knew then that, if the paintings were legitimate purchases, they must have been bought outside the system.

Under communism, only the consignment store and the state auction house could buy and sell paintings, but there was sure to have been a black market for pictures, there were black markets for just about everything. Of course, Nyenye's paintings might not have been purchased at all – they could have been looted, looted by the Nazis when they took over Budapest in the Second World War. Or looted by Hungarians when the Jews were sent off to concentration camps. Yet if that was the case, why had her father said that her grandparents had to pay for them?

She was back to the same old questions that had been plaguing her for months. Were her grandparents hard-working people who might have taken a few risks operating outside the system when their business became more successful than they'd anticipated? That's what she'd once believed. But ever since that afternoon with Daniel when they'd walked to Clifton Gardens her thoughts had been shifting. Perhaps her grandparents were calculating entrepreneurs providing a safe depository for looted art. And patiently waiting for the collapse of the communist regime before slowly releasing artworks on to the international art market. Maybe they were not as smart as she'd thought. Maybe they were criminals.

Her father said, 'The pictures Nyenye has in her collection now are certainly much loved.'

There was something in the way he said this, the emphasis he put on the word now, that unsettled her. She said, 'Did Nyenye not like the Rocheteau?'

'She was glad to see you take it away.'

'Why?'

'She never liked it much.'

This puzzled Anika, for she knew Nyenye had a good eye for artworks and that – unlike Tabilla – she didn't care for more modern paintings. Maybe she had thought of Tabilla as having ownership rights to the Rocheteau, just as Anika's father had. Anika decided to change her approach. 'What was Tomas like?' she asked.

'He was funny and kind and handsome. Everyone liked him.' Her father stared into the distance, as if that would help him conjure up the past, and she waited for him to go on. Eventually he said, 'Don't mention anything about Tomas's painting to Nyenye just yet. It might upset her that it's been stolen. She's been looking forward so much to seeing you and it would be a shame to spoil her happiness.'

'I can't wait to see her.'

Anika didn't want to spoil her happiness either but she did want to learn the truth and she'd choose her own time to talk to her grandmother about the painting.

Chapter 25

Anika still found it hard to believe that the old regime had gone and here she was waking at noon in her parents' apartment. Opening one eye, she saw her mother silhouetted against the light from the hallway; she reached up for a hug like she used to when she was a child.

'It's lucky that Nyenye's coming for dinner not lunch,' Mama said, smiling. 'She'll be here at five. Your father's at work and I'd hoped to spend some time with my daughter but it looks as if she just wants to sleep all day.'

Anika was in the entrance hall later that afternoon when Nyenye arrived.

'Dearest girl, how well you look!' Nyenye said, laughing. 'And I would swear you've grown but I know that can't be the case, it's more likely I've shrunk. Such a pretty young woman! Mind my strudel, don't hug me too hard. It's poppy seed, I hope that's still your favourite, do let me put it down. Oh, your mother's taking it, now I can give you a proper hug.'

Anika held her grandmother tight; how thin she seemed, had she always been this slight? Over her shoulder, Anika saw, through eyes blurred with tears, Mama's expression. She too had made a poppy seed strudel and Anika could guess what she was thinking; if Nyenye would just get the phone installed she could have called to let them know she was planning to bring a dessert.

Kissing Nyenye's cheeks now, Anika noticed how much more wrinkled she had become. Gravity and age had done their work and her throat and chin had lost their definition but when she smiled Anika forgot all about appearances.

'This is like a miracle,' Nyenye said. 'Do you know, I'd thought I might never see you again?'

'But here I am. And I'm so happy to be back.'

Soon after, Miklos arrived. He seemed taller than Anika remembered, and stronger. Broad-shouldered and a head taller than her, he was rather handsome too, with that broken nose from football several years ago giving his otherwise symmetrical face some interest. But he was also instantly recognisable as her occasionally irritating big brother who used to tease her about anything and everything. Pulling her hair. Hiding her toys. And, when she was older, ribbing her about boyfriends. They hugged and he lifted her up and twirled her around a few times until, breathless, he had to stop.

'You are so heavy, Anika,' he said. 'Too many *fasírozott*. Those meatball patties always were your weakness.'

'You are so feeble, Miklos,' she replied. 'You need to eat more *pörkölt* to build up those puny muscles of yours. Pork stew with dumplings is just what you need.' They collapsed laughing at this point. Meat was not something they took seriously enough, being the progeny of butchers.

Anika's mother lit candles and her father opened a bottle of wine, and Miklos pulled out a chair for Nyenye like a waiter in a restaurant. The candlelight flickering over their faces made them look like a painting from a previous century, Anika thought, and she felt grounded for the first time since leaving Budapest years before. But she watched Nyenye closely. Although she appeared the same – a sweet old lady who loved her family – after what Anika had learned in Australia, she was no longer sure of who her grandmother was.

Just one glass of wine went to Nyenye's head. No sooner had she swigged it down than she embarked on scurrilous anecdotes about her neighbours in the apartment block, many of them her friends for decades, but there were also some informers living there, she reckoned, for everyone knew that the secret police could never have learned about what was going on in people's lives without a network of spies everywhere. You never knew who might be one, and no one ever talked about what the AVO did to its prisoners. People who'd been released after a spell with the AVO were as silent as if they'd had their tongues cut out.

Suddenly uncomfortable, Anika shifted in her seat. It was just as well those days were in the past, for why would the secret police need informers when a bottle of wine would release such a torrent of information from her grandmother? She glanced at Mama and knew right away what she was thinking, that Nyenye was going on too much.

Yet Anika was maligning Nyenye; the old regime had gone, she was with her family and letting her hair down with the five of them sharing a meal. It was significant that Nyenye spoke about those days in the past tense: could her old suspicion perhaps have gone away? And if she was willing to be so unusually open over dinner, maybe tonight was a good time for Anika to find out more about Tomas and the painting. When Nyenye got up to leave, Anika offered to walk her home.

'No need,' Nyenye said. 'It's only three blocks.'

'I feel like a breath of fresh air, Nyenye. It will help me sleep better.'

Her father nodded his approval. When Nyenye turned away to find her bag, he winked at Anika. It was clear that he thought his mother was too tipsy to go home alone.

'I could go,' Miklos said, 'but I have to phone Irma first to let her know I've arrived.' Irma was his new girlfriend, the latest in a series, Mama had told Anika earlier. Miklos was pursued by women for reasons that Anika didn't quite understand, for though funny and kind he could also be obnoxious and too keen to get his own way. Irma was different, Mama had said. This time it was serious. So serious that he would go back to Szeged a couple of days after New Year's Eve to be with her.

'I want the walk,' Anika told Miklos. 'You go and phone your girlfriend.'

When he had untangled the phone cord enough to get the receiver into his bedroom with the door shut, Nyenye whispered to her, 'Miklos has to do the running with this one. Irma knows how to pull his strings and push his buttons and generally keep him to heel.'

Nyenye and Anika walked down the wide spiral staircase that led from the apartment into the old carriageway with its cobbled surface, and out into the street. The evening was icy cold, it was like they'd just stepped into the cool room of the Molnars' shop. When Anika tripped over the kerb, Nyenye seized hold of her arm. The street was dark, though the sky was light enough to suggest the moon must be visible somewhere, but not from the floor of this canyon with its array of five storey buildings looming up on each side. There were a few people about, couples mostly, arm in arm, hurrying against the cold.

They turned right at the first corner. Diagonally opposite was a bar full of elderly men; inside, the light was poor so you couldn't make out their faces clearly. They could be in an old black-and-white film from the 1930s, Anika thought, and at any moment a spy would materialise and hand over secret documents.

Rounding the next corner, she could see the gibbous moon, its aureole making it seem larger than it was. Her grandmother might look frail but she was a fast walker and Anika had to hurry to keep up with her. They strode past shabby once-grand apartment blocks, with broken neoclassical features and chipped stucco and pockmarked stonework, and turned into Nyenye's building. She shut the heavy door behind them and leaned against it for a moment to catch her breath. Ahead was the central courtyard and to the right rose the dimly lit but rather grand staircase with its wrought iron balusters and elegant stone treads. The staircase wound up around a space that might have been big enough to put a lift into, if only someone could find the will and the money.

A middle-aged man with a figure like Humpty Dumpty's was coming down; he nodded and stopped on the first-floor landing to talk to Anika's grandmother. She introduced him to Anika as Tibor, who had recently moved into her apartment building. She described Anika not as her granddaughter but as a visitor. Perhaps it was because of this that Anika got the impression that she didn't trust him, but her reserve might also have been because she didn't trust many people. Anika shook his hand and mumbled a few words. When he asked where she was from, Nyenye didn't let her reply, as if she wanted to protect her or to save herself embarrassment. 'Australia,' she said firmly. 'Her Hungarian is excellent, no? But we must get on.'

She gently pushed Anika in front of her and they continued up the staircase. Her response was automatic and Anika realised with startling clarity that Nyenye was an expert at concealment, even when there was no apparent need. She had never understood that about her before.

On reaching the second floor, Anika looked down on the man who was now standing on the carriageway below. He was going through his pockets as if he had forgotten something important, but it was only a handkerchief that he needed. Pulling it out, he blew his nose energetically, a loud trumpeting that echoed around the hard walls.

It took Nyenye a while to find the door key, though she had it in her hand only seconds before. 'Come in.' She was smiling now. 'I'm guessing there's a reason you wanted to walk me home, no? We'll have a cup of tea while we talk.'

She double-locked the front door behind them and hooked the door chain into its slot before heading into the kitchen. While she was filling the kettle, Anika opened the door that led from the hallway into the living room.

'Don't turn on the light,' Nyenye said quickly. 'I can't remember if I drew the curtains.'

By the borrowed light from the hall, Anika could see that the curtains were pulled across all the windows. The walls were crowded with paintings, as they had always been. Nyenye returned to the kitchen while Anika groped her way around the furniture to the fireplace. She looked to the right of the chimney breast, where Tomas's painting used to hang, and ran her hand over the wallpaper. The Rocheteau had left a gap here, just as it had in her bedroom in Rozelle.

Anika blundered back to the hallway and followed Nyenye into the kitchen. Her heart filled with an emotion that she couldn't immediately put her finger on. Shivering, she realised it was foreboding. If only she'd never seen that advertisement in the *Sydney Morning Herald* all those months ago. If she'd tossed it into the wastepaper basket and given it no more thought, she wouldn't need to ask Nyenye any questions.

'It's really lovely having you here.' Nyenye gave her a quick hug.

Anika hoped she'd still be saying that at the end of her visit.

'Something's bothering you, no?'

Anika's mouth opened as if it had a mind of its own, and she found herself saying, 'Do you remember a man called Sebestyén Tinódi?'

'Of course.' Nyenye began to take cups and saucers out of one of the cupboards and had her back to Anika. 'He was one of Tomas's friends. A couple of years younger, I think.' The cups clattered on to the table. 'He worked in the Rákosi Metalworks at Csepel. We heard he escaped after the 1956 uprising.'

'He died in the marshes near Andau.'

'Did he? So many did. Poor Sebestyén. Why are you asking?'

'The day I left, you said he gave the painting to Tomas.'

'Did I? Maybe I got confused. There was so much happening at that time I must have misremembered.'

A cobweb of lies and concealments, that's what a police state was. That's what families became. Anika felt the air around her thickening, slowing down her reactions. It was the jetlag, she told herself, nothing more. Longing to throw open the kitchen window and let in a draught of cold air, she wondered who Nyenye had been hoping to protect by mentioning Sebestyén the day Anika left Hungary. Was it her granddaughter or herself? It was probably both of them. If she'd been stopped while leaving Hungary with the painting, she would have relayed Nyenye's story.

She said, 'I'd like to talk to you about Tomas.'

Nyenye plugged in the kettle and right away it began to vibrate. Nyenye had heard her words though, Anika could tell by the way she squared her shoulders.

I'd like to talk to you about Tomas, though? That's not what she should have said, it was much too general. Quickly she added, 'It's Tomas's *painting* I want to talk about.' But Nyenye didn't hear these words with that antiquated kettle of hers juddering away on the bench in front of her.

'Ah, Tomas, my first born,' she said sadly, once the kettle had switched itself off and she'd poured water into the teapot.

'You never expect your child to die before you do, never.' She turned to face Anika, a questioning look on her face. 'Even though it happened all around us during the war years. In those days, people were dying everywhere: children, adults, soldiers, civilians. We grew to expect that there'd be no natural order to death. It could happen anywhere to anyone at any time. But a decade later the Revolution took us by surprise. I wasn't prepared for it.'

'How did it happen?' Anika made her voice gentle. She was relieved that Nyenye hadn't heard her say that it was Tomas's painting that she wanted to talk about. His death had been like a taboo topic until now. Anika had only ever heard a brief account from her parents about how Tomas died. Shot in the massacre at Kossuth Square was all they'd told her.

'It began with a demonstration,' Nyenye said. 'Tomas and Tabilla were so excited before the march. I told them not to go but Tabilla was insistent.'

Her voice when she mentioned Tabilla's name was harsh and she took a deep breath before continuing. 'Everything would change, people thought. Everyone was shouting *Russians go home*. And on that first day people even managed to pull down the huge bronze statue of Stalin. That was quite something. It was a massive bronze thing. They left only his boots in place, and someone stuck into one of those boots the Hungarian flag. It had a hole in the middle where the Soviet hammer and sickle emblem had been cut out.'

Nyenye distractedly reached for the teapot but she seemed to have forgotten why, and her hand dropped to her side again. She said, 'Then the Soviet tanks arrived and there was a curfew.'

'You sit down. I'll pour the tea.' Anika put a cup of tea on the table in front of Nyenye but she ignored it.

'Nobody understood what the Soviet strategy was,

especially when the curfew was lifted on the third day. That was when thousands of people gathered in front of Parliament, Tomas and Tabilla among them.' She stared at the cupboards but Anika knew it was not them that she was seeing. 'Then suddenly, with no warning, the shooting started. And that was the day Tomas died.'

'I'm so sorry, Nyenye.'

'What I have trouble understanding,' Nyenye continued, her voice hoarse, 'is why Tomas died before me. And why him rather than somebody else. There were thousands of demonstrators in Kossuth Square. But a random shot got him, before he'd had a chance at life, before he and Tabilla had a chance to start a family. It seemed so unjust. We never got over it, your grandfather and I. One day we had two sons and the next day we had one. Afterwards, all those memories kept flooding back, of when Tomas was a young boy and a teenager and marrying Tabilla, and the realisation that there was to be no future.'

'Was Tabilla wounded?' There had been something in Nyenye's voice when she mentioned Tabilla's name that Anika didn't understand.

'No, she wasn't. We heard about the shelling on the news and from the shop we could hear all the firing going on. Not long after it stopped, Tabilla came running to us. She was wet with rain and there was blood on her clothes. She said that Tomas's body had been taken away with the others on the back of a truck. She'd tried to get on to it so she could see where they were taking Tomas but they dragged her off.' There were tears pouring down Nyenye's face but she seemed oblivious to them as they plopped on to her blouse, darkening the fabric.

'I'll never forget that moment when Tabilla told us. "Tomas died in the arcade of the Agricultural Ministry," she said. Then a minute after, she said, her voice as strident as could be, "I'm leaving Hungary. There's nothing left for me now and already they're hunting down people who were fighting yesterday. They took photos, you see." In a way I hated Tabilla at that moment. Hated her for telling us the news and then going away again, looking after her own skin. She managed to get over the border into Austria, and there was a refugee camp on the other side. We heard from her once she got there and later when she arrived in Sydney.'

'And you found Tomas's body in the end?' After handing Nyenye the worn tea towel to dry her eyes with, Anika put an arm around her shoulders and thought of Tabilla's decision to get out. It had been the right thing to do. If she'd been picked up by the AVO her life would have been over. But Anika could see how her flight might have looked like abandonment to Nyenye. Her kind-hearted and loving grandmother had a tough streak and probably resented that Tabilla had survived but not Tomas. Anika wondered if this was one reason why Tabilla hadn't wanted the painting when she'd tried to give it to her. It was too tied up with unresolved issues with her mother-in-law.

'Your grandfather and I found where they'd laid the coffins on the ground at the cemetery,' Nyenye continued. 'They weren't labelled. No one had a clue who was in which box. I lost count of the number I opened before I found my son. The gravedigger dug a hole that wasn't long enough. Your grandfather got really angry then and he grabbed a spade to make it longer. We buried Tomas that evening.'

She dabbed at her face with the tea towel and blew her nose on it before continuing. 'Later, much later, I decided that Tabilla was absolutely right to get away before the AVO could come for her. Do you know that for months after she'd gone, I kept hoping we might get a letter from her saying she was pregnant with Tomas's child? But that never happened.' She sighed deeply. 'And you know we didn't dare take his personal papers to the authorities for a long, long time. We were afraid of what they'd do to us.'

'I'm so sorry, Nyenye.'

Nyenye batted away Anika's words as if they irritated her, and continued speaking, her voice a monotone. 'Your father was too young to remember much about that time, although sometimes I think he might have blocked it all out. For months afterwards, he would wake up at night screaming but he never could remember what he was dreaming about. I could guess though. Who wasn't scarred by all that?'

Absent-mindedly, Nyenye began to pleat the edge of the tea towel, as if that were what she needed to focus on. After a minute or so she looked intently at Anika. 'You've got a lot of Tomas about you,' she said. 'Not in appearance so much as the occasional expression and the way you sometimes hold your head.'

Anika liked that: it made her feel more connected to the uncle she'd never met. She said, 'In the photos of the two of them, I think my father looks a bit like Tomas.'

'He does, though he doesn't have the same facial expressions.'

Nyenye appeared drained. Now was not the time to raise any more questions, Anika judged, but she didn't want to leave her grandmother yet. She made some fresh tea and after a while Nyenye asked Anika about her job and her course. She seemed to listen attentively to the answers, though Anika knew they were becoming less and less coherent, for her diurnal clock was protesting and the temptation to lay her head on the table was almost too strong to resist.

'I'm exhausted, my darling, and you look tired too,' Nyenye said at last. 'You've got dark smudges under your eyes and you're starting to repeat things. The thing is, jet travel is unnatural, no? It doesn't give you time to adjust. You get into an aluminium canister and twenty-four hours later you're dumped on the other side of the world. No wonder your body complains. It must be like being in one of those metal capsules the drapery shop used to have, that whisked your money through a tube to the cashier and then back again with the correct change. If only flying were as easy as that! But it's brought you back to us for a visit and I'm certainly not objecting.'

At the front door they embraced warmly. 'Walk fast, my love,' Nyenye said. 'I've kept you out too late with my talking.'

After Anika took her leave, she heard the rattle of the chain as Nyenye secured the door and the click of the barrel bolts at the top and the bottom. There'd better not be a fire, she thought: Nyenye had pulled up the drawbridge for the night and only a battering ram could break down her defences.

On the way home, Anika began to feel uncomfortable. Maybe her grandmother's nervousness was affecting her. The streets were empty, silent. There weren't enough streetlights and the moon had vanished behind a thin layer of cloud. In the bar on the corner the old men were still sitting, now avidly watching a televised football game. The light from the television flickered across their faces and they didn't seem to notice that the volume was turned up too loud.

In her parents' street, Anika suddenly heard footsteps behind her, making her jump; hard shoe leather clicking down on the pavement like some tap-dancing routine. She quickened her pace and the tapping sped up too. Pulses pounding, she turned to see a tall figure coming fast her way on the other side of the street. The collar of his bulky overcoat was turned up and a woollen hat was pulled down low over his ears. She walked faster and turned again when the tapping changed tone. The man had rounded a corner into a side street and, by the time she reached the double doors into her parents' block, she could no longer hear him.

PART V

Budapest, January 1990

Chapter 26

Anika's time in Budapest was flashing by; it was like flicking over the pages of a calendar that had already been lived through and looking for the entry that said *talk in private to Nyenye*. She spent a riotous New Year's Eve with Miklos and their old friends, when they saw out the old year – an amazing one for Hungarians everywhere and they drank to that again and again – and welcomed in the new.

After Anika and Miklos got home, she made her New Year's resolutions. In private, of course; she thought there was something lovely about finding a sheet of blank paper and thinking you could start afresh just because the clocks had rung midnight. *Discover the truth*, she wrote down carefully on her little list: *try to see the good in people; try to forgive; try to pay Tabilla back quickly the money borrowed for the air ticket.*

When she had finished, Miklos burst into her room with two glasses of brandy and she hid the list in a book on the bedside table. They sat on her bed like they used to when they were young and sneaking an illicit drink, while he told her about the wonderful Irma and the thesis he'd nearly completed.

'I'd love to meet her,' Anika said.

'Next time you visit. Irma's so busy.'

While he carried on enumerating Irma's many virtues, Anika remembered Nyenye's tone of voice when she spoke of Irma the other night. It had been the same as when she'd mentioned Tabilla. Both women were outsiders, both were apparently viewed with some suspicion. Anika wondered if Nyenye might have felt burned by her boy falling too passionately for Tabilla, and now here was Miklos falling for Irma in a similar way. Yet Nyenye wasn't suspicious of Mama, or if she had been, that had vanished long before Anika began forming memories.

'And what about you, Anika?' Miklos said, once he'd finished cataloguing the wonders of Irma. 'What's preoccupying you?'

'Am I preoccupied?'

'You've seemed distracted ever since you got here. Is it that damned painting of Tomas's? It wasn't your fault it got stolen. Our parents should never have given you such a valuable painting to take out.'

'No one knew it was valuable. Papa said he'd never liked it much.'

Taking a swig of brandy, she started to tell him that the Rocheteau was almost certainly looted art and that she was scared Tomas and their grandparents were somehow implicated in it.

'How could they have been?'

'By receiving stolen goods that they knew were taken by the Nazis.'

'They wouldn't have known if the painting was looted, Anika. How could they have?'

'But shouldn't we try to find out? I can't bear living with this uncertainty. I'm going to ask Nyenye. In a way that's why I'm here. As soon as I heard that it might be looted I felt I had to come and find out.'

'Well, don't let anyone know that's why you're here.' Miklos's tone was rather tetchy. 'They all think you came because you missed us. You've no idea how much they've been looking forward to seeing you.'

'I've been looking forward to seeing you too, of course I have. Don't deliberately misinterpret me.'

Anika wondered if he was trying to deflect her. He'd never been one to take things seriously enough. This made him charming most of the time but now she decided it also made him exasperating. She put the brandy glass on her bedside table. The last thing she wanted was to become even more befuddled than she'd been when they got home from their celebrations. Miklos was silent. When she glanced at him, he was frowning at the carpet, as if those worn threads were annoying him.

'That painting of Tomas's isn't the only thing that's worrying me, Miklos. There's Nyenye's paintings. Everyone's always so secretive about them.'

'Everyone's secretive about all that stuff from the past. You are too. You're as paranoid as the rest of them. I wouldn't worry about it. Asking Nyenye about the provenance of Tomas's painting is hardly going to help.'

'I haven't even told her that it's been stolen.'

'Didn't Papa tell her?'

'No. He said I should wait a while. She doesn't know yet.'

'I wouldn't bother her about it. Just get on with your life, Anika.'

She glared at him but he didn't notice. He was probably thinking about Irma again. *The trouble with you, my darling brother, is that you always want to take the easy way out. You should get a coat of arms with a couple of ostriches on it, with their heads buried deep in the sand.*

'Don't you want that brandy, Anika?'

When she shook her head, he picked up the glass from the bedside table and raised it to her. 'Here's to a quiet life, Anika,' he said, laughing.

He downed the lot in a gulp and kissed the top of her head.

And then he was gone and she was left feeling alone. She'd hoped that he would support her but he wasn't interested. It saddened her that she no longer knew who he was. In part this was because she'd changed, probably beyond all recognition. But so too had he: she'd thought of him as always staying the same but of course that couldn't have been true. What she did recognise, though, was that he was so busy looking forward that he couldn't afford the time to take a glance at what lay behind.

Chapter 27

New Year's Day was a sober affair. Anika spent it in the company of a hangover that went only with a ten-hour sleep that night. Miklos returned to Szeged the day after. She was sorry to see him go. Before he left, he repeated those words she hadn't been able to get out of her head: *just get on with your life, Anika*. She didn't argue with him, though she wanted to say that if they applied that mantra to everything, they would wipe out every injustice, and by doing so they'd let bad deeds go unpunished. And that would make it more likely they would happen again.

Still she delayed asking Nyenye about how Tomas got hold of the painting. It was partly getting on with her life. It was partly cowardice on her part, but it was also that she didn't want to put Nyenye through that grief again. And overlaying it all was that sense of foreboding, for she dreaded having to ask Nyenye difficult questions, knowing that her grandmother's answers might change everything that she'd ever thought about her family. She'd been working herself towards this for months and, now the time was near, she couldn't bear the thought of what she had to do. Of what she might discover. Of course, she didn't need to do it right away. She could wait a few more days before doing anything to upset Nyenye.

It was easy to compartmentalise her life. After Miklos's reaction and his advice, she steered away from suspicions as if they were poison. She lived each day in the present. Like a horse without blinkers, she was distracted by the pleasures of seeing family and friends, the delight of being on holiday.

But sometimes she woke at night in a hot sweat, tangled in sheets so taut they might have been a straitjacket, and full of fear that the construct of her family that she'd held in her head all her life was an artifice. Simple honourable people, that's how she'd thought of her family while she was growing up and through the years she'd been away. That thought had sustained her. It had defined her identity. But what if they were instead opportunists, profiteers from war? Unless she asked more questions, she'd never know the truth. Yet she didn't want to hurt anyone: she didn't want to hurt her family. And also, she told herself on those long nights when she awoke sweating and full of dark fears, her inner critic at its harshest and accusing her of weakness, that she didn't want to hurt herself.

*　*　*

Early one morning Anika went to the market, her first visit for years. She'd always loved its vast lofty space and today the sky blazed cobalt blue through the glazing, and the oblique light illuminated stalls laden with produce, all so well-ordered and beautifully arranged that it almost seemed a shame to buy anything that destroyed this symmetry. She filled her carry bag with the vegetables Mama wanted. For a while she lingered before the stall displaying strings of garlic bulbs and dried paprika. She'd thought of these sometimes when she was away; they seemed to symbolise home, for there was always a string of each hanging in the kitchen and she'd never seen garlic and paprika arranged like this in Sydney. The sunlight sluiced over the display, the brilliant white of the garlic bulbs contrasting with the peppers that glowed in shades of red and ruby and maroon. Today Anika found them impossible to resist, although they were not on Mama's list, and she bought five bulbs of garlic on a raffia plait and two dozen or more Kalocsa paprika threaded together. She knew that Nyenye would love them.

When she rang the bell to Nyenye's flat, her grandmother took a while to answer, though Anika could hear her footsteps in the entrance hall. She called out her name and, soon after, bolts clunked open and there she was, peering around the edge of the door, the chain allowing it to open no more than a few centimetres. Grumpy was the best way to describe her expression but annoyance and anxiety vied for second place. Her face didn't alter when she saw Anika but without a word she unhooked the chain and the door swung wide open.

'There was a man here first thing this morning looking for you,' she said at once, her body barring the way. 'He was really pushy. He went on and on and on about how he knows you and was really hoping to see you while he's in Budapest.'

'Who was he? Did you ask?' Right away Anika thought of Jonno. She knew he was in Eastern Europe somewhere and he was given to stalking her when he wanted something. Journalists had big strides and after the Berlin Wall had come down a few borders were unlikely to block him.

Nyenye ignored Anika's questions, so tangled up was she in the skeins of her irritation. 'You know he actually put his foot in the door when I tried to shut it. What a cheek, I couldn't believe it. You'd better come right in, Anika, instead of hanging about on the landing so the whole world can hear our conversation.'

She ushered Anika into the flat and shut the door behind her. 'Fortunately, Dori Nagy came by just when that man was becoming really annoying. So I called out to her and told her he was being a nuisance. "I'll phone the police if you don't go," she told him. I would have had to ask her not to though.

213

I don't want the police coming here either. He's not your boyfriend, is he, Anika?'

'I don't have one. Did you ask for his name?'

'I clean forgot, I was so upset.'

'If he comes again, don't let him in.'

'You bet I won't. I'm keeping the chain on all the time now. I don't like being pushed around.'

'Did he actually push you, Nyenye?'

'No. He just put his foot in the door. He said you'd mentioned that I have some pictures. I really wish you hadn't done that, Anika. No one is supposed to know about these paintings.'

'I didn't tell anyone about your paintings, honestly. What did this man look like?'

'Hard to say. I only caught a glimpse of him over the chain and the light was behind him. He was all rugged up in winter gear and quite big. Anyway, I was more focused on getting him to go away. Oh, and one more thing: he had a funny accent.'

'He spoke Hungarian?'

'No. German.'

'Nyenye, I promise that I didn't mention your paintings to anyone.' Anika put the strings of garlic bulbs and paprika on the kitchen table. 'These are for you. I went to the market.'

Nyenye gave her a hug. 'You're a darling,' she said. 'Was it crowded?'

'I went early.'

'Let's have some coffee, no?'

Once Nyenye had made it, she picked up the tray and Anika followed her into the living room and avoided looking at the walls where the paintings hung. After putting the tray on an occasional table near the door, Nyenye flicked the light switch. Only one of the bulbs in the chandelier lit up and Anika thought it couldn't have been any more than sixty watts. No artificial lighting would be necessary if only Nyenye would open the curtains; the morning light would stream through the three tall windows along one side of this room. Two of them had ancient velvet curtains drawn across, but not much daylight came in the window with the curtains open, for behind the velvet there was a layer of net curtains so thick and bunched up that, even standing by the window as Anika was doing now, she could see little of what was outside. If she spread the netting smooth and taut, she could just make out the shadowy outline of a building on the other side of the road and the shape of a tree, its branches bare. She lifted the material slightly to see better.

'Don't open the curtains.' Nyenye's voice was suddenly harsh.

'No one can see in.'

'You never know,' she said. 'They might have binoculars.'

'Those days are over,' Anika said firmly. But suddenly she felt an acute sense of foreboding that made her shiver. There must be more to Nyenye's paranoia than fear carrying over from the old regime, for who would pursue her now if the paintings were bona fide purchases? But if they weren't, she could well be in trouble.

'I'm not so sure those days are over,' Nyenye said. 'Some of the secret police will be hanging on to the files of certain people. They'll use the information for blackmail if they need to. You can never be sure that the new regime won't change into the old. When you've lived as long as I have you'll realise that.'

After they were settled in their chairs, with the tray between them, Nyenye said, 'Is something bothering you, *szeretet*? You look like you have another question for me.'

'I'd like to know more about Tomas.'

'You have only to ask,' she said slowly. 'But of course memory is a funny thing. No two people remember something in the same way. My brothers and I had wildly different recollections about our childhood. They were much older than me so that might be part of it, and they were boys too with more freedom.' She hesitated. Neither of her brothers survived the wars; one had died in the First World War and the other in the second. 'But everyone sees the world in their own way and they process what they've seen in their own peculiar brain. And it's not just that people notice different things. Some of them are in their own world half the time and a lot of things pass them by completely.'

'And they block out things too, Nyenye. Even if they've observed them.'

'People do that to survive. Some are better at it than others. Such terrible things we've lived through, some of us. The only way we can cope is to bury them deep inside us and carry on.'

Is that you, Nyenye? That's another question Anika would have liked to ask but it seemed too bald, especially as she could hear the sadness in Nyenye's voice. Anyway, there were more pressing questions that required answers and she needed to be more direct. 'Did you know that Tabilla didn't want Tomas's painting? She said it brought back bad memories, so she gave it to me.'

'It brought back bad memories to me too, darling. But not of Tomas. And I'm very glad you have it.'

Anika took a deep breath before she told her. 'I don't have it any more, Nyenye.' She explained about the robbery.

Afterwards, Nyenye bombarded Anika with questions. Were any other things taken. Were the police called in? What did they do? Was there any likelihood she'd get the picture back? At the end of her interrogation, she said, 'The most important thing is that you and Tabilla were unharmed.'

'All that was taken was the painting.'

'So someone knew about it. That's another reason not to tell anyone about my collection. Once people know you have something of value they start to envy you or want if for themselves or start thinking you got it illicitly.'

Anika didn't want to tell Nyenye about Julius Singer, not yet. Nyenye was glancing around the room, and Anika hoped she was not going to offer her a replacement picture. If she did, she'd have to decline. Provenance was all, and Nyenye almost certainly didn't have any. The sad thing was that Anika used to love this room and all the paintings on the walls but at this point she felt she simply couldn't bear to look at them. All she wanted to discover today was how Tomas got hold of the Rocheteau. Thinking about this gave her the heebie-jeebies. Her hand started to shake and the cup rattled in the saucer. Carefully she put it down before beginning to speak.

'Do you know where Tomas got that painting from, Nyenye? Papa told me he thought you'd said it might have come from the consignment store.'

'It didn't.' There was not a trace of doubt in Nyenye's voice.

'But you and Nagypapa got some of your pictures from there, didn't you?'

'Yes, and from collectors who needed the money. Your grandfather and I worked really hard and we did well with the butcher's shop. People have to eat, you see. And later we expanded into pickles. That was my idea, and I made them right here in this kitchen using my grandmother's recipes. They were a great success; people came from all over Budapest to buy them. But in those days, before the regime loosened up, you wouldn't want to have a savings account that might alert the state to your profits. And neither of us thought it would be a good idea to put our hard-earned cash under the mattress, so we bought paintings instead.'

'And was that where all these came from?'

She looked away. 'We took advice on what we should buy.'

'Who from?'

'Collectors, mostly. Richer people who'd fallen on hard times.'

'But you told no one?'

'That's right, Anika. We didn't want to get anyone into trouble. Private art sales were illegal.'

'That's what Papa said.'

'These are all by Hungarian artists.'

'All of them?'

'All of them. I insisted on that. And Hungarian artists' paintings couldn't be taken out of the country so we got them cheap.'

For a few seconds Anika felt a sense of great relief that the paintings were purchased not stolen by her grandparents. That was before she remembered they could have got the paintings cheap because they'd been looted by someone else and offloaded on to her grandparents. She pushed that thought to the back of her mind. Right now, she needed to concentrate on the Rocheteau. She said, 'What about Tomas's picture?'

'I never knew who painted that. It was Tomas's, you see. But I was pretty sure it wasn't Hungarian. There was something about it that didn't look Hungarian. And anyway, it came from a different source.'

'Well, we know it wasn't from Sebestyén Tinódi. So where did Tomas get it from?' There was a fluttering sensation in Anika's chest. *Please God, don't lie to me, Nyenye.*

Nyenye looked at her in surprise, as if she'd never heard

of Sebestyén Tinódi, and Anika wondered if her grandmother had already forgotten that lie or the conversation they'd had only a few days ago. Nyenye said, 'It was after the siege of Budapest.'

'When the Russians came?'

'Yes. After the Germans had been driven out. The city was in a terrible mess because of all the bombing. There was rubble everywhere, shelled buildings, dead bodies lying in the streets, homes in ruins. We were living in the cellar that was all that was left of our apartment block, we lived closer to the river then. And we shared that cellar with a lot of other people. When we went out sometimes there was so much debris lying around you couldn't even tell where the streets were, and the place stank. Everywhere the Russian soldiers were drunk and out of control and there was looting. And worse.'

She paused and Anika watched her face and the twitch that had started up below her left eye. Anika's own stomach began to churn and she felt conflicted about what she was doing. This need of hers to know the truth was costly for Nyenye, putting her through a painful revisiting of the past.

'They were not all barbarians,' Nyenye continued. 'Just most of them. There was a Russian man who befriended Tomas. He had children of his own and he said that Tomas reminded him of his son. He was an officer, very kind, and he visited us a few times. The last time he came he gave Tomas the painting. I don't know where he got it from, stolen probably.'

'Stolen?'

'Oh yes, it must have been stolen. The Germans left things behind. Things they'd taken, for who goes into battle with paintings or antiques? Or things they'd looted from Hungarians. And then the Russians looted them back again. The Russians were like that, Anika. Their commander had granted them three days of looting and more to celebrate their victory. But Tomas loved that painting. Not because we thought it was valuable but because it was something beautiful after all those months of shelling and violence and hunger. He hid it as soon as the Russian officer, Sergei was his name, had gone. In case there were more visits from other soldiers who might take his painting away again.'

A veil had come down over Nyenye's eyes. Although they were still open, the light had gone out of them. The skin under her eye continued to twitch as she began to speak again, so softly that Anika had to lean forward to distinguish the words. 'And we did have more visits, Anika, but they were not from Sergei. It was me and the other young women the soldiers were after.'

Anika's throat suddenly became so constricted that she could scarcely breathe.

Of course, she had known of the rapes by the Russian soldiers but she hadn't thought that Nyenye might have been one of the victims. Yet she knew it was a failure of her own imagination not to even contemplate that her grandmother might have been affected. 'We won't talk about this, Nyenye,' she said gently. 'There's no need.'

'But I want to tell you about it,' Nyenye said. She picked up her coffee cup with a trembling hand and took a sip. 'It was hard to start telling you but now I've begun it would be harder still to stop. When the fighting and looting and raping were all over, and we were struggling to rebuild our lives, Tomas retrieved the painting. It meant a lot to him. He was an artistic boy.'

'Like you.'

'Your grandfather and I both loved paintings.'

Anika could understand why. Beautiful objects after a violent history, after all those months of shelling and violence and hunger and ugliness, and after the police regime that followed. Barely registering what she was looking at – the fusty curtains over the window, the feeble light – Anika felt her suspicions slowly trickle away, to be replaced by admiration for this strong woman, her grandmother.

They sat on in silence apart from the ticking of the grandfather clock. The tight band of anxiety around Anika's throat began to relax as the seconds passed by, and then a minute and another. She started to feel her identity slipping slowly back into place, enveloping her like a reassuring pashmina. Knowing who Nyenye was meant that Anika better understood who she was, and this lightened the burden of suspicion she'd been carrying around ever since the Rocheteau had been stolen.

But there were more questions that she needed to ask, and when the clock finished chiming the hour, she said to Nyenye, 'Do you know why Tabilla didn't want Tomas's painting?'

'Maybe it's not so much that she didn't want it,' Nyenye said carefully, 'but that she wanted to pass on something to you. Something from the past. Something from home.'

Nyenye's tone as she mentioned Tabilla's name was warmer than it had been when she'd told her about the Revolution and Tabilla's escape, and Anika was pleased at this.

'I'll make some more coffee,' Nyenye said, struggling stiffly to her feet.

'I'll do it.'

'I make it better than you.'

While Nyenye was clattering about in the kitchen, Anika wandered around the room peering at the paintings in the gloom. She felt a bit better about the collection after what Nyenye had told her but without having the provenances Nyenye would have no way of proving they weren't looted and she guessed that her grandmother could be in trouble.

Distractedly she inspected a little watercolour of the Danube Bend. The hills were blue smudges and there was a grey lilac mist along the river banks. Although the sky was not in the painting it was still a presence, reflected in the water. The scene looked peaceful, a far remove from the time she'd been arrested in the nearby forest.

Turning away, she noticed that her grandparents' collection had a remarkable number of blue paintings. Or perhaps it was just that the predominantly blue ones appeared at eye level all the way around the three sides of the room. Many shades of blue. Darkness and light. There was the cellist in the cobalt blue dress, her face pale, the cello glowing. There was the procession of women in brightly coloured hoop dresses – red and orange and yellow – winding their way through a blue landscape. Above this picture was the gap where the Rocheteau used to hang – that painting that was never theirs – and Anika averted her eyes from that blank space. Instead she stopped in front of the picture that Nyenye had once told her was of the Italian Riviera, though it didn't look in the least bit Italian but more like some northern landscape, with an extraordinary sense of depth and enclosure. It was beautiful but bleak, with the merest touch of warmth in the ladder of reflections from the sun on the water's surface.

How many of these paintings were stolen, she asked herself. Not by Nyenye and Nagypapa, but by the people who were selling them. Perhaps you never owned anything but were just the custodian of it for a generation or so. No one was able to see all these beautiful pictures, it seemed such a shame. They were just stored here in this fusty room worrying Nyenye. They were supposed to be an investment from which she could reap returns, and Anika wondered when she would realise them. She was still healthy enough to enjoy travel and she could certainly do with some nice clothes.

'You've got so many pictures,' Anika told Nyenye when she returned with the coffee. 'You could sell some and travel a bit. Or give them to the National Gallery where everyone could see them.'

Nyenye looked shocked at this. 'Never ever mention anything about these paintings, Anika. Not to anyone, do you hear? You don't know what sort of trouble you might get me into.' Her voice cracked and that twitch appeared under her eye again.

There was something not quite right here. Nyenye had told Anika so much about Tomas and the Rocheteau but Anika now thought she was concealing something about her collection. She wondered if it was the provenance of the collection, or perhaps the lack of it. Or it could be her fear that the communist state – they were still in power and the free elections wouldn't be held until March – might prosecute her for accumulating wealth over those years when savings were not allowed.

Nyenye was too upset for Anika to push her for answers, and looked so drained that Anika left soon after, knowing they would have to revisit these issues before she flew back to Sydney.

That night she fell into a deep sleep from which she woke with a start, fear striking her like a hard slap to her face. In her nightmare the woman in the Rocheteau painting was no longer beautiful. She had become an ogre, her hair a writhing mass of red-bellied snakes, her eyes glittering, and her face a ghastly painted mask that belonged in some grotesque expressionist painting. This cursed thing was Julius Singer's history, her uncle's history, Nyenye's history. And although Anika didn't want it to be her history, there was no escaping it. Once you knew about something it became stuck in your head and there was no way of avoiding it.

Chapter 28

A reunion of Anika's old friends from years back, a dozen of them squeezing around a long table in the café on the Buda side of the river that was once a favourite meeting place. Their voices were loud, the volume escalating, they were laughing at nothing and everything. Candles stuck into old wine bottles illuminated their faces. This friend was doing this, that one was doing something altogether different; some of them were married or partnered, some were single, and one of them had come out as gay and turned up with a boyfriend Anika had never met before. Funny how you couldn't always tell whether or not a man was gay. Somehow she found it easier with women to know right away which way they were inclined. This random thought made her think of Daniel. He could well be gay. The kiss she might have given him the night the Rocheteau got stolen would have been unwelcome. She had another swig of wine.

At around eleven o'clock, after her fourth or fifth glass of wine – she'd somehow lost count – fatigue hit her and she got up to go. Three of the group joined her while the others stayed put. Together they went out into the cold crisp night and one by one her friends peeled off, going their different directions, a metaphor for their lives, she thought, and perhaps this was the last time they would meet like this. Already they were different to the way they'd been at their last meeting.

Soon she was walking home on her own through lonely streets by the river. The too-many glasses of wine she'd consumed, coupled with fatigue, made her feel slightly out of control, as if her legs were being operated by someone else, a tipsy puppeteer pulling the strings. Lurching to a stop, she clutched on to a tree for support. Suddenly her stomach felt too full and for an instant she wondered if she was going to throw up. She inhaled deeply and after a while the nausea passed. For a moment longer, she held on to the tree. Her loyal supporter. No criticism from you, my friend, you would have seen a few drunks in your day.

She looked up at the bright moon: if she were a wolf she might bay at it. Almost full, it loomed large and low, casting bars of light on the smooth-flowing river. A cloud blew across the moon and blocked out some of the light. It was then that she saw a solitary figure standing on the quay. A few hundred metres away, he was staring out over the water. He hadn't been there when she passed by that spot a few minutes ago. She wished there were people around. Perhaps he hadn't noticed her. He was tall with broad shoulders and what she assumed was a head of thick dark hair until realising it was a dark woolly hat pulled down over his ears.

She shifted behind the tree so the man moved out of view. This lonely stretch of river was not the place to loiter when you were drunk. It wasn't safe any more for a young woman to be wandering through the streets on her own. Only yesterday Mama had told her that she'd seen a bunch of skinheads throwing their weight around in the old Jewish quarter. And muggings had become more common. Under communism, people had been too afraid to commit crimes. Not so any longer.

After a few seconds, Anika squared her shoulders and stepped out from behind the tree. The man had gone. Perhaps he was a trick of her imagination, a fantasy brought about by too much alcohol. More likely he was a man on his way home from an evening out and struck by the beauty of the Danube.

Suddenly sober, she hurried on through the streets of inner Pest, heading away from the river. She knew this route well, all the back alleys and shortcuts, the dark bits and the less dark bits. This evening was so cold you could almost feel frost forming in the air. She ducked into the shelter of a long colonnade with ponderous pillars and heavy Romanesque revival arches. Trapeziums of moonlight fell across the stone flags, interspersed with strong diagonals of shadow. There was no one else around, and little sound apart from her footsteps and the distant clattering of two-stroke engines from the main road. Racing along the colonnade, she breathed through her mouth to avoid the stench of urine. She was nearly at the end when a figure popped up a dozen or so paces away. Tall, with a dark coat and a dark scarf wound around the lower part of his face, and a dark woolly hat pulled down low on his forehead.

Fear grabbed hold of her heart and squeezed it. Pulses pumping too hard, she stepped through an archway and into the square. Automatically she arranged the fingers of her gloved hand into a vee. What a fool she'd been to come this way, anything could happen and no one would know. She thought of the self-defence classes she'd done when starting university. If he attacks you, drive the forefinger into one of his eyes and the middle finger into the other. Crouch low if he puts his arms around you. Jump up so that the top of your head crashes into the underside of his chin and raise your arms to wriggle down and out of his clasp.

'Hello Anika,' the man said.

She stared at Jonno Jamison, relief and anger fighting it out in her breast. 'What are you doing here?'

'I'm sorry if I frightened you,' he said, grinning. 'I thought you might be pleased to see me after that fond farewell in Sydney.'

'That was months ago.' Her cheeks grew hot at the memory.

'Only half a year.'

'You're following me.'

He didn't deny it and this inflamed her fury even more. 'How long have you been doing that for?'

'I wanted to know where in Budapest you're staying so I could drop by.'

'What for?'

The moonlight illuminated half of his face, casting the rest into deep shadow. 'To ask you out for dinner,' he said. The one eye she could see was staring fixedly at her, as if willing her to swallow his story, but she didn't believe a word of it. He continued, 'When I saw you last time you did say that if ever I was in Budapest I should drop by to meet your parents. It's a shame you forgot to give me their address.'

'I can't remember saying that. I think you're making it up. As I recall, you said you'd send me your address.'

He carried on as if she hadn't spoken, a ruthless bulldozer ignoring obstacles in his way. 'I met some of your friends who told me where your grandmother lives but not your parents. Your grandmother wouldn't give anything away when I dropped around there. She's a bit protective, isn't she?'

The smallest criticism levelled at family by an outsider was guaranteed to raise the passions of anyone, let alone someone who'd just seen a large man bob up in front of her in a lonely part of the city. But Anika's voice was calm when she said, 'If you'd been through what I have, you'd be defensive too.'

'I'm sorry I offended you. Can I walk you home?'

She would have liked to refuse but there was no point in that. Since he would follow her anyway, he might as well be useful and she could possibly charm him into telling her what he was up to in Budapest. Smiling, she said, 'If you're going my way, we can walk together. What are you doing in Hungary?'

He didn't answer. It was not like him to be without words, so she prompted him. 'I saw a couple of your pieces in the colour supplement just before I left Sydney, one on East Germany and the other on Poland. They were good. A different slant. Interviews with lots of different people. I particularly liked that article about the children. The ones in the East German village, I've forgotten its name.' After the Berlin Wall came down, people from Western Germany were driving over the border and throwing the kids sweets – that the children had never had much of before – and this was one of the things that Jonno had written about. 'The photographs were very touching.'

'Thank you.'

'Did you take the pictures as well as write the text?'

'Yes.'

'Clever you. What are you doing in Hungary?'

'More human-interest stories.'

'What are they?'

'I'm not really sure yet. I'm just nosing around to get a feel.' His eyes flickered, before their focal point wandered off into the distance.

'Do you speak Polish as well as German?'

'I had a translator with me for the Polish story but I do speak a bit of German.'

'So my grandmother told me. You didn't win hearts and minds there.'

'I only asked her about you and the paintings.'

'I didn't realise you were an art collector. I thought it was just your relatives who collected. You know, the ones whose artworks you took into the Art Gallery of New South Wales to get identified every month or so.'

228

'How did you know about that? Let me guess, it was Daniel.'

'Well actually, Jonno, it was just a wild stab in the dark on my part,' she said. 'And so my hunch was right.'

The lie came out easily. For reasons that she didn't fully understand, she wanted to protect Daniel. It was as if learning from Nyenye how the Rocheteau came to be in her family's hands had somehow knocked a few more holes in the barricade she'd constructed between herself and Daniel.

'Do you know why I turned up at your aunt's Rozelle place that time? I'd just read in the newspaper about your stolen painting. I knew from my research that quite a few Impressionist paintings found their way into German hands, confiscated from Jews after the Anschluss. And only a handful were recovered after the war ended.'

'But you've always said you're not an art expert.'

'I'm not, but I'd read something about SS men who got into Australia masquerading as refugees from displaced persons' camps, and I thought that there are probably more Nazis in Australia who haven't been detected yet. I reckoned that I might be able to track one or two of them down through works of art that come up for auction. I even thought there might be a supply of paintings trickling into Australia from stashes hidden in Central and Eastern Europe.'

'So you thought that by turning up each month at the art gallery with another painting for identification you might get some information.' Anika made her tone incredulous and for some reason he found that funny. He laughed so much he started to choke and she banged him on the back harder than warranted.

When he'd recovered he said, 'You're a bright woman, Anika. My trick was to hang around near the art gallery cloakroom on the first Tuesday of every month. I'd wait until someone turned up with a European accent and a picture in their arms. Then I'd follow them downstairs and listen to what the curators had to say. I'm lucky to have plenty of aunts and uncles who've accumulated a tidy collection between them, most of the pictures not worth anything much apart from my aunt's Lister Lister. After I made that discovery, all the other relatives started queueing up, wanting to get their paintings identified. Of course, I had to string them out and only take in one at a time.'

'So that's why you invited me for coffee that day. You thought I was likely prey.'

'That was one reason. The other was that I thought you were gorgeous.'

'But you wouldn't have had to buy me coffee if it hadn't been for that chatty old dear.'

'I would have asked you anyway. But you're right, she did bend my ear just as I was trying to learn the name of the artist who'd done your painting. All I heard was that it was by an Impressionist in the French School. And that was all you told me too. No wonder I was intrigued.'

She remembered that morning when Jonno had tried to get her to talk about the painting over coffee. While she'd resisted his overtures, apart from telling him the suburb where she lived, she'd given him a perfect excuse to drop by on his way to his old mate's house. He could have taken the painting and this story he was now spinning could be an elaborate concoction to find out how to steal more. But she decided this was all much too complicated. There'd be other easier ways to track down what to steal and his journalism was clearly not faked. On the other hand, while his strategy might have been complicated, it was also rather clever. She had to concede that, however reluctantly.

When they reached her parents' place, he bent his head

to kiss her. Surprised, she pushed him away. For some reason he found this funny and that riled her. With fumbling hands, she unlocked the door to the apartment block. Murmuring goodnight, she glanced back through the door opening. That glimpse of his face unsettled her even more. He looked satisfied, as if he'd got out of the conversation everything that he'd wanted.

'I'll drop by again in a couple of days' time,' he called. 'Let's have that dinner.'

Confused, she slammed the door and leaned against it. The entrance way was shrinking around her, the walls drawing in. Her breath came unevenly and she felt her face flushing with annoyance. Jonno was using her to further his career. He was handsome and talented but she had no intention of dining with him. She listened to his footsteps as he strode away, back in the direction they'd walked from.

All men were hopeless, it wasn't worth bothering with them. That spark of feeling she'd felt for Daniel only a few minutes back, that sudden surge of protectiveness, was completely misplaced. Daniel could look after himself. He'd been right about the Rocheteau and Jonno seemed to have guessed too. That was the reason each man was interested in her. That was the only reason each was interested in her.

Chapter 29

The next morning Anika woke up hungover. Not again, she told herself. Really, she had to take more care of her liver. A quick inspection of her reflection was enough to show that her ghostly-white face looked ghastly from every angle. Never again would she touch alcohol, never. And she felt so grouchy; it was only with the greatest effort that she stopped herself from snapping at her blameless mother.

Not long after breakfast and some paracetamol, she received in the post an airmail envelope from Tabilla. Inside was a brief note from her aunt and an envelope with her name on it and the Rozelle address, handwritten in an elegant script that Anika recognised instantly. This at once resuscitated her thought from last night. All men were hopeless, it was simply not worth bothering with them. Crossly she tore the envelope in half and put it in the garbage bin.

An hour later, after another cup of coffee, she had second thoughts and retrieved the ripped envelope and its contents. Once she'd brushed off the bacon rind and bits of eggshell, she managed to join up the damp pages along the tear. Some of the ink had smudged but she could just about make out what Daniel had to say.

Dear Anika,

I cannot get our last conversation out of my head, and I'm writing to say how sorry I am that we had that misunderstanding about my great-uncle. It never occurred to me that my comments about Jake when we walked near Clifton Gardens might be misinterpreted, and I very much regret that this caused you distress, as it so obviously did.

An apology from Daniel, she never expected to have this. But here it was, and it was such a sweet thing. The armour she'd constructed around herself shifted a bit.

But also I can't help but wonder if, when you get upset about one thing, you immediately start looking for something else you can vent your anger on. You were upset at what I said about looted art that day when we were walking, so you started searching for other things about me that you don't like, or that you might be able to work yourself up into not liking.

Probably I shouldn't be writing this to you tonight, just after our Christmas party when I've had too much to drink. But at least now I'll write what I think and not censor my letter. Perhaps I'll regret it either way.

I have become very fond of you, and I think that you might have been growing fond of me in spite of yourself and this is why are you are always on the lookout for things about me that are unsatisfactory. You're looking for reasons to dislike me.

I know you are going through a difficult time and I would like to help you in any way I can. Do please give me a chance. We could be friends. I would hate for this not to happen.

With much love,
Daniel

Irritation mounting, Anika read the letter again. OK, it contained an apology but it also contained an accusation. If he really wanted them to be friends, he wasn't going about it the right way. She ran her finger over his signature and the line above it. *With much love.* What did that mean?

She'd felt so close to him that evening they'd spent at the pub at Watson's Bay, the night the painting had been stolen. The night of that almost-kiss. He'd probably been relieved once Mrs Thornton appeared; he'd moved away quickly. *With much love* meant nothing special; it must be how he always signed off. She put the letter away, this time in the top drawer of her bedside table rather than in the garbage bin.

Just before going to sleep, she got it out once more. It stank of bacon fat. She looked at those words 'With much love.' Then she reread the whole letter.

He'd mentioned looted art once more. That was what upset her. OK, that and the insinuation that she didn't think things through. How could she be a friend to someone so in-your-face? Impossible. And he thought she was fond of him. Such arrogance.

After this she got into a state: thoughts all over the place, black thoughts mainly that she couldn't control even by deep breathing. Daniel's letter on top of Jonno's words last night had reawakened all her anxieties. 'I'm just nosing around to get a feel,' that's what Jonno had said, and this made her deeply apprehensive. She picked up a book to read but couldn't get into it. Her anxieties wormed their way on to the page and lined themselves up in neat rows waiting to be confronted.

The bed covers pulled up to her chin, she began to shiver, not so much with the cold but with her anxiety about Nyenye. The Rocheteau was picked up by a Russian after the siege of Budapest. Somehow Sergei, the officer Nyenye mentioned, had got hold of it; maybe it had simply been abandoned by the retreating Nazis and Sergei had discovered it. Missing his own children and liking the young Tomas, he had given

234

Anika's uncle a beautiful object whose origins he didn't know, because he felt sorry for him. And her uncle had kept it for years, perhaps because of the memory of the kindness he'd seen in the officer's face as well as his love for the picture. Then eventually it ended up in her hands, only to slip away.

And if the Rocheteau was looted, what about the others that Nyenye had on her walls? OK, they weren't stolen by Nyenye, but they might have been looted beforehand. And why was Jonno hanging around? Clearly he had a story in mind about stolen artwork turning up in the Eastern and Central European countries now that the Iron Curtain had been lifted. If Nyenye had no documentation for how she and Nagypapa came by the paintings, Anika guessed that Jonno could write any damn thing he liked about them. His story didn't need to be based on fact; you could get a long way with generalities and a little innuendo.

* * *

The next day Anika's head seemed stuffed with cotton wool and she knew the only way to clear it was to go for a walk. Her parents' apartment had become too small, its walls were pressing in on her, almost like a prison. She needed to see things in perspective.

It wasn't until late afternoon that she got home. Before she'd even had a chance to shut the front door behind her, Mama said, 'Where have you been?' She was standing in the hallway, hands on her hips, her face a question mark like it used to be when Anika was years younger and had gone out without telling her mother what she was doing.

'I went for a walk up Gellért Hill and then I met up with my friend Lena. You'd already gone to the shop when I got up this morning, otherwise I would have told you.'

'I was only gone a couple of hours. Nyenye's been around

looking for you. She stayed for ages and I was hoping you'd turn up. I gave her lunch and afternoon tea and I thought she'd never go home. She was just sitting at the kitchen table looking sad and worried and she wouldn't tell me what the matter was. Do you know anything about it, Anika? In the end she left but she wants you to go and see her. Please do it today. She looked so – oh, I don't know – so vulnerable and tired and old.'

It was dark when Anika reached her grandmother's apartment block. She rang the bell and called out Nyenye's name so she'd know who it was. Nyenye opened the door slightly and peered through the crack with suspicious beady brown eyes, like she was checking that it wasn't someone else masquerading as her granddaughter. When she'd made sure, she unfastened the bolts and the chain, and pushed open the door barely wide enough to let Anika through. 'Quick, help me with the bolts, Anika, we've got to get this secure. I don't want him coming back again.'

'Who?' Anika slid the top bolt up while Nyenye struggled with the bottom one.

'Your boyfriend.'

'He's not my boyfriend. So he's been around again? Is this what you wanted to talk to me about?'

'Yes to both questions.'

Nyenye was wearing a chunky red cardigan over a black dress and the labels were sticking out of both. When Anika tucked them in, Nyenye swatted her hand away irritably.

'I stupidly opened the door without checking first. But I did have the chain on and managed to get the door shut again before he had a chance to put a foot through the gap. He wanted to talk to me, he said through the door, and there was no harm in that, was there? He knocked again several more times and I could hear him striding up and down the landing. After half an hour he went away, clattering down the stairs. I thought that noise might be a ruse, that probably he was biding his time one floor below. So I peered out one of the front windows overlooking the street and there he was, sloping off towards the river.'

Nyenye hurried into the kitchen and Anika followed more slowly. 'I wouldn't believe much of what he tells you. You're right to be suspicious of him. I do know that he's a bona fide journalist though. I've seen stuff he's written.'

Nyenye looked horrified, the blood draining from her face as quickly as water down the plughole. 'Why would a journalist want to talk to me?'

'It could be your paintings.'

'You shouldn't have told him about my collection.'

'I've told you, I didn't.'

'Well, how did he find out then?'

'He's probably been pumping your neighbours, sussing out what they know. A bit of flattery and a few dollars can get people to blurt out all sorts of stuff they might regret later. You know how it goes. Journalists are really skilled at that.'

'Like the secret police.'

'I know you keep the curtains to that room drawn all the time but there are bound to be rumours. And some of your neighbours might even remember you acquiring the paintings. They might have seen them being carried into your apartment.'

'I doubt it. None of the paintings are big. And if they had been seen, an informer would surely have snitched on us years ago.' Nyenye's face was pale, the age spots more noticeable than ever against that blanched skin.

'But you never invite anyone in.'

'No one invites anyone in. You've got to stop that man bothering me, Anika.'

'I'm not sure that I can do that.'

In an apartment block like Nyénye's, and like Anika's parents' too, where the flats were distributed over five floors and arranged around a central courtyard, it was easy for neighbour to keep an eye on neighbour. Anika could imagine the whispers. *Why does Mrs Molnar keep the front curtains drawn? Why does Mrs Molnar still never allow visitors beyond the entrance hall?* It would have been straightforward for a charming man like Jonno to gossip in German with a resident or two; easy as well for him to drop a few hints to provoke some reaction, and a handful of dollars to get more detailed information.

'Maybe I'll have a glass of water now, Anika.' A pulse was beating too fast at the base of Nyenye's throat. Anika got ready to catch her; she looked as if she were about to keel over.

'Water and a touch of palinka,' Nyenye said. 'There is some in the cupboard next to the sink.'

'You sit down first.' Anika guided her into a chair before filling two glasses with water.

She found the palinka at the very back of the cupboard, behind some containers of cleaning products that were so neatly arranged they might have been up for sale in a grocery shop. Resting upside down on the top of the palinka bottle was a small shot glass. When Nyenye had taken a sip of water and a swig or two of brandy, a little colour returned to her cheeks. Anika stood opposite, watching carefully, and wondering if it would be too much to ask what she needed to know. Only another two days in Budapest and who knew what other opportunities there'd be for a tête-à-tête like this. Probably none, she thought. Once you were close to something like a departure, time passed at an accelerating rate, confounding the laws of physics. People would be dropping by, old friends inviting her for drinks, her parents' friends turning up for a chat. Even Miklos was tearing himself away from his beloved at the University of Szeged and catching the train up for a farewell dinner tomorrow evening.

The palinka in Nyenye's glass had almost gone when Anika blurted out, 'There's something else I need to find out, Nyenye.'

Her grandmother's cheeks were rosy pink as she drained the last of her drink. 'You're a great one for questions. You'd better get it off your chest.'

Anika had a couple of sips of water before asking, her words as hesitant as a trickle of water from a leaky tap, 'Do you have any documentation for your paintings?'

There was a pause that she couldn't decipher. Nyenye was now studying the label on the palinka bottle as if she would find inspiration there. The pulse at the base of her throat was no longer visible and her voice was steady when at last she spoke. 'Of course I have, *szeretet*. Your grandfather and I were always very careful about that.'

'That's wonderful, Nyenye. Just wonderful.' If Anika hadn't had the back of a chair to grab hold of, she might have keeled over with the shock. 'Can I see them?'

'Not at the moment. Later maybe, but not when I've drunk too much palinka.'

'Every man and his dog wanted to know where the provenance for Tomas's painting was,' Anika told her, 'once they thought it was by Antoine Rocheteau.'

'Tomas wouldn't have known the provenance. It was a gift in wartime when the city was in ruins and people had lost everything, or nearly everything. But your grandfather and I made sure we had documentation for all the artworks we bought.'

Nyenye's face grew dreamy as she continued. 'We came to learn quite a bit about art, your grandfather and

I. To begin with we knew nothing, or next to nothing. Our education started the day we got chatting to one of the regular customers, Mrs Szabo was her name, about a picture. It was just a reproduction of a Dutch still life of pheasants that we had hanging near the cash register. Customers often made comments about it. Everyone was hungry, you see, and it was hard to get good quality meat then. Just the sight of those pheasants was enough to make your mouth water. It turned out that this customer was an art historian, and that's how our collecting began. She gave us some good tips. Who was selling what, which paintings were good, which were pastiches, that was a word she often used.'

Anika imagined Nyenye and Nagypapa in their shop, both in the white coats that Anika had seen them wearing in a photo in one of their albums. She could see Nyenye with a scarf over her head, the walls of the shop covered in white tiles as they still were, and the art historian attired in a rather shabby fur coat and well-worn shoes, advising her grandparents about art.

Nyenye continued, 'When we took her advice and made a purchase, we always gave her a commission. In kind, that's what she wanted. We usually gave her prime cuts of beef rather than pork – she was very happy with that – and sometimes a jar of my pickles. And she was a real expert, she could tell a forgery right away. There were quite a few of those about.'

She reached for the palinka bottle and tipped a little more into her glass before continuing. 'It wasn't just collectors we bought from; we had another source at BAV, the state auction house. We got to know a lovely man there, Sigmond Andor was his name. Poor thing, he was always so thin and hungry looking. He'd been in Mauthausen concentration camp and lost all his family. He and your grandfather became really close friends and we had him over for dinner sometimes.

They'd talk for hours about art and everything else. He was a real carnivore, loved his beef and talked up my pickles too.'

'Nagypapa was a great talker. I remember how he was interested in so many things.' Anika swallowed too large a sip of brandy and gasped as the fiery liquid hit her throat. Once the coughing was over, she asked, 'Do you have the provenance for *all* your paintings, Nyenye?'

'Of course. Weren't you listening properly, Anika?'

'I just wanted to make sure. Where do you keep the documents?'

'Well hidden.' Nyenye's voice had suddenly become sharp. 'And I'm not going to tell you where, not with that friend of yours hanging about all the time. Who knows if he really is a journalist. He could just be after my art collection.'

'I think he simply wants to know how you came by them. I checked him up before I left Australia. He really is a journalist, and he's published some good articles.'

Nyenye looked at her intently, as if wondering what to believe. Anika held her gaze for what seemed a minute before her grandmother visibly relaxed.

'Do you keep your documents in a safe?' Anika asked.

'As good as.'

'Does anyone else know?'

'I'm planning to tell your father.'

'You mean he doesn't know yet?'

'No.'

'But if anything happened to you...?'

'Don't think I haven't thought of that, Anika.'

'Papa's a bit of a worrier, is that why you haven't told him?'

'It's more that I've learned over the years that the fewer people know something, the safer things are. I keep only essential things and I keep them very well hidden.'

Again Nyenye reached for the palinka bottle but hesitated, hand held mid-air for an instant. Sighing, she returned her hand to her lap and laced her fingers together, while her thumbs began to worry at each other as she stared vacantly at the kitchen sink. Anika kept very still. As she observed her grandmother, she began to feel an immense sadness. Something had changed between them tonight and she wasn't sure quite what that was. For a long moment they sat on in silence, until Nyenye said, her voice hoarse, 'I think you'd better come with me now, *szeretet*. Maybe I should show you something.'

Chapter 30

Nyenye flicked on the light switch to her bedroom. Three bracket lights feebly illuminated what was the ugliest room in Nyenye's apartment and Anika couldn't understand how her grandmother could live with it. She loved beautiful things and this room certainly couldn't be described as pleasing let alone beautiful, although the faded crimson velvet curtains would once have been splendid. They covered the large window in one wall, and the rest of the space was crowded with enormous pieces of furniture.

'Look under the bed, Anika,' Nyenye said. 'You'll have to do a bit of crawling about for me.' She settled herself on the chair with its ugly turned legs and gestured towards the bed. 'I don't relish the thought of getting down on my hands and knees. But there's something I want to show you.'

The provenances, Anika thought. If Nyenye really had them, rather than documents that she thought were provenances. But surely she wouldn't have put them under the mattress. Anika knelt on the rug next to the bed and slipped her hands under the mattress.

'No, not there, *szeretet*. That's way too obvious, no?'

On hands and knees, Anika peered under the bed. As a child she used to hide from Miklos in this space between the wire mattress-base and the floor. There was a china chamber pot here, decorated with roses. There had for ever been a chamber pot here, blessedly always empty. Next to it was a rust-freckled tin trunk some seventy centimetres square, and

243

nearly reaching the sagging wire base on which the mattress rested. 'Not in the trunk, I hope,' she said.

'Nowhere so obvious,' Nyenye said. 'But pull it out anyway.'

Anika slid it out, slowly, ducking her head below the bed-beam, but not enough to prevent her head knocking against it painfully.

Nyenye said, her tone impatient now, 'Get right under, Anika, so you don't damage yourself again.'

'It's all dusty, Nyenye. You haven't mopped under here for a while.'

'No matter. You've got your old clothes on; I've already noticed that your jumper has a hole on your right elbow and another one on your right cuff.'

It was dark under the bed and hard to distinguish the floorboards clearly. Anika ran her hands over them; each was about fifteen centimetres wide. Beneath the film of dust, she could feel how smooth they were. Then she encountered two rough-sawn raggedy-edged boards. Fingering her way along them, she discovered they were each cross-cut in the same place, and that forty-five centimetres along they were sawn again. When she exerted pressure on them, they jiggled. They were loose. Not nailed in place, not screwed down. A real giveaway, this. After she managed to manoeuvre up one of the boards, lifting out the other was easy.

Nyenye, kneeling on the floor next to Anika's feet, directed a wavering beam of torchlight in her direction. 'Stick your hand into the hole.'

Anika had enough experience with Australian spiders to think it was folly to be shoving her hands into small dark places. But she pulled down the sleeve of her jumper so that it covered her hand to below the knuckles and slipped her thumb through the hole on the right cuff, before feeling her way into the opening. In the gap between the floor joists there was a large plastic-covered box-file. After pulling it up, she backed out from under the bed using her foot to guide the box ahead of her.

'This is my documentation,' Nyenye said, beaming.

'You need a better hiding place than this.'

'Yes, yes. But let's open the box, Anika, after we have gone to all this trouble.'

'Can I look?'

'Of course, that is why you have been crawling under the bed, no? It is not for your amusement. But hand-on-heart you must tell no one. No one.'

Inside the box-file there were a number of manilla folders tied with black tape. Anika sat cross-legged on the bed and Nyenye perched beside her. 'Your grandfather organised these documents. So meticulous, always. That's one reason we did well.'

Inside the top folder were some papers and two black-and-white photographs. Anika picked up the first photo; it was of a young woman standing next to an easel on which a painting rested. This was one of the paintings hanging in Nyenye's living room: the watercolour with its strong diagonal movement of girls in pale dresses on a green-gold hillside, against a background of dark red-brown mountains and sky.

'This lady is the artist,' Nyenye said, pointing to the woman next to the easel. 'See her name? It's Kodály.'

Anika thought the photo looked convincing, though she was no expert. In the second photograph, an elderly woman wearing a cloche hat and a fur coat was holding up the same painting.

'That's our art historian friend, Mrs Szabo,' Nyenye said. 'She passed away in the 1970s. We had to take that photo secretly, for no one was to know what we were doing. It was the black market, you see. Mrs Szabo was such a lovely woman. She taught us of the importance of the provenance. We didn't buy anything where there was no proof of ownership.'

Under the photos were some stamped receipts, a page torn from an auction catalogue dating back to the 1920s, and a few sheets of foolscap paper describing the work and its passage from owner to owner and tracking its appearance in several exhibitions. This was more like it, Anika thought. This was what she had imagined a provenance would be like.

'This is a full history,' Nyenye said. 'Some of our paintings only had one or two owners. Those are the ones that are easy to follow. But others were more difficult. So much was destroyed in the war.'

It took more than an hour to go through the documents in the box-file. Nyenye looked happy, Anika thought. She might have been stimulated by this exploration of the past or perhaps she was pleased to share it with Anika, though she did regularly punctuate her comments with exhortations about secrecy. 'Nothing is safe, Anika. Nothing. You can trust only close family, no one else.'

'I know that, Nyenye. I know that. But for some things it's possible to open up a bit.'

'As I have done this evening,' Nyenye said. 'With you. And I trust that what you've seen and what I've told you will go no further.'

'Of course.'

At the bottom of the box-file was a small black-and-white photograph.

'*Ó, Istenem,* I'd forgotten about this,' Nyenye said, her words ragged and torn. 'Your grandfather must have put it there.' She handed Anika the picture.

It was of a boy aged eleven or twelve standing in front of a ruined building, a boy with an open smiling face and thick brown hair.

'Tomas!' Anika felt her heart start to hammer too hard as she stared at Tomas. He was holding the portrait of the auburn-haired lady skew-whiff in front of him. Though it was only a black-and-white photo, you could see the sun was catching her hair and glowing from her shoulders. It was unmistakably the Rocheteau.

'Maybe you'd like to have this photo,' Nyenye said. 'I've got plenty more of Tomas. Take it with you.'

Anika turned the photo over. On the other side was written, in her grandfather's hand, the words *Tomas Molnar, 1946*. Her eyes filled with tears. Tomas looked so young and he was only to live another ten years. 'Thank you, Nyenye. I'll show it to Tabilla.'

'And now, my darling Anika, we are going to pack everything away again and get the box back between the floor joists.' Nyenye's voice cracked, and when she continued it was almost falsetto. 'And after that we shall have another little tot of brandy and then you will go home to your parents who will be wondering what is keeping you here. And you will tell them nothing.'

Anika put an arm around Nyenye's shoulders. 'OK,' she said. 'But you really do need to speak to my father.'

'I shall indeed speak to György. Although isn't there a saying in English, *don't teach your grandmother how to suck eggs?*'

'There is, Nyenye. But that saying is about *how* to suck eggs. It says nothing about *when* to suck eggs.'

She could tell from the way Nyenye was pursing her lips that she was trying not to smile.

'You have become so wise, Anika. Let me tell you again

that I shall indeed speak to your father. But that will be in my own good time, *szeretet*.'

Anika hugged her, feeling the smallness of her, that tiny frame housing her indomitable spirit. Her darling grandmother was safe. No investigative journalists were going to be able to come up with a story of her being a conduit for looted art. And at that moment Anika suddenly realised that Nyenye almost certainly wouldn't have been quite so willing to reveal the truth about her documentation if Jonno's visit hadn't given her such a fright.

Nyenye said, her voice slightly muffled, 'Surely you didn't think your grandfather and I would be so naïve as to buy things without proof of purchase. We were traders, Anika. That's who we were. A family of traders. Meat and pickles and paintings.'

'A diversified portfolio.' Anika's words were rendered indistinct by laughter that might at any moment turn to hysteria.

'But in fact it's only the meat and pickles that we trade nowadays,' her grandmother said firmly. 'The paintings are not for sale.'

'Of course they're not. They belong to you.' Anika's voice was shaking. Abruptly, face averted, she collapsed on to the floor next to Nyenye and rested her head against her knee.

'You're a good girl, Anika,' Nyenye said, smoothing her hair. These were the words she used when Anika was very young and used to trail around after her. 'You're a good girl.'

At first, Nyenye said nothing about Anika's sniffles that morphed into tears of relief. Tears that were spiced with a dash of remorse that she'd ever thought that Nyenye might be the receiver of stolen goods.

'There is no need to cry, Anika. We're not thieves in our

family, we never have been. Though you were not to know that.'

'The trouble is, we don't talk about those things.'

'We don't talk about them because it's too painful. And also because it's too dangerous. You know that, darling. Even your generation can remember the knock on the door at night, the people vanishing. We've avoided thinking about those things by withdrawing into ourselves, by trying to appear invisible.'

Anika blew her nose and dried her eyes.

'That's partly why your grandfather and I loved our paintings so much,' Nyenye continued. 'And I still do. We could escape into the worlds the artists created. We didn't need to run away when we had those other places accessible on our walls. Art became an escape from the regime. And after a while the secretiveness becomes ingrained. It becomes a part of who we are.'

She carried on stroking Anika's hair, her touch infinitely comforting. 'I'm sorry you've suffered, Anika,' she said at last. 'You thought my paintings might have been looted, no? Not by us, perhaps, but by those who sold them to us. I hadn't realised that you were so worried.'

'I didn't know, that's the thing. I didn't know anything until ten months ago when I took Tomas's painting to be identified. After that, it was like everything was unravelling.' Anika didn't tell her that she'd wondered if her family was a mob of crooks as well as traders.

But she felt as if a weight had been taken off her shoulders, that burden of worry she'd been carrying ever since the afternoon Daniel took her on the walk from Taronga Park to Clifton Gardens.

In the kitchen, Nyenye poured two glasses of palinka. Anika raised her glass in a toast to her grandparents. Hardworking people with an eye for beauty. Hardworking people who took a few risks operating outside the system when their business became more successful. That's what she'd once thought. That's what, for months, she'd hoped for.

And that's who they were.

Chapter 31

The phone started ringing when Anika was in the bath. She heard her mother's lively voice but not her words. When ten minutes later Anika came out of the bathroom, hair wrapped in a towel, her mother called out, 'Tabilla's on the phone. We've had such a lovely conversation.' Mama was looking very pleased with herself as she handed Anika the receiver.

'It's wonderful to hear your voice,' Tabilla said, speaking very quickly. 'One of the reasons I'm calling is that I wanted to thank you for that gorgeous present. Mrs Thornton from next door came by this morning. She's been away and got back only yesterday, and she brought it in.'

'I didn't know she was going away or I would have left it with someone else.'

'She didn't know she was going either. A last-minute trip that her children organised. Thank you so much, Anika. The slippers are lovely, just my size.'

'And similar to your others but without the holes.'

Tabilla laughed. 'I'm not nearly so down at heel now.'

Anika told her aunt how good it was to be back in Budapest and how Miklos – it's a shame you've never met him, Tabilla – had come up for the best part of a week, but now he was back at Szeged. It was his girlfriend who was pulling him back, he was besotted with her. 'And what have you been up to, Tabilla?'

'Catching up with the garden. I've been out a bit with friends, and I went away for a few days with Magda and Janos. They rented a cottage at Five Mile Beach. It was lovely to have a break and not do any sewing for a bit. But there's another reason for my call, Anika. Something happened this afternoon that I think you'll be thrilled with.'

Anika's heart skipped a beat. 'Is it news about the painting?'

'Yes, and such an amazing thing! Someone from police headquarters called me. Your portrait has turned up again.'

Stunned, Anika dropped the receiver. It dangled at the end of the cord while Tabilla's voice crackled on and on. Her words were lost to Anika, until she heard her shout, 'Are you there, Anika?'

'Yes, I'm here.' She picked up the receiver. 'Are you sure, Tabilla?' It was an effort to pull herself together. Although initially numb with shock, she could feel joy starting to creep in around the edges of her disbelief.

'Of course I'm sure.'

'Who took it?'

'That's the thing,' Tabilla said, 'I just don't know! All the police said was that it had been returned under *mysterious circumstances*. They wouldn't give me any more details. Just as well you'll be back in a couple of days, Anika.'

'Who returned it?'

'They wouldn't tell me that either. But isn't it marvellous that they've got it? I thought we'd never see it again.'

'Me too. I wonder what *mysterious circumstances* means.' The words sounded ominous to Anika. She hoped the painting wasn't damaged.

'I don't know. Maybe somebody was feeling guilty and wanted to return it, or they discovered they couldn't flog it without a provenance, or they found it in a junk shop. By the way, did that letter I forwarded to you arrive?'

'Yes. It was from Daniel.'

'I thought it might be.'

'Why?'

'His name was on the back of the envelope. Didn't you notice?'

'No. I tore it in half and put it in the garbage bin.'

'You are an unforgiving girl. And I spent good money on posting it to you.'

'I took it out again afterwards and read it.'

'Not completely unforgiving then,' her aunt said, laughing.

* * *

Later that morning Anika bought a stamped postcard from the shop in the National Museum. The assistant, whose extravagant beehive hairstyle belonged to another era, slipped it into a small paper bag. Outside, Anika sat on a bench in the sunshine to compose the message to Daniel. *I'm so sorry*, she wrote on the back of the card, making the letters quite large, and then stopped, wondering what on earth to put next. Maybe she was so sorry for everything. Sorry she misunderstood him. Sorry for taking so long to realise that he was a reserved man, possibly almost as reserved as she. Sorry for what happened to his family and hers, to his country and hers, and to all those countries, in Europe and everywhere else, that were forever warring with one another.

She gazed around for inspiration. There were some people perched on the broad steps leading up to the museum. A man and a woman sitting halfway up were blazing with light as if caught under a spotlight, the sun angling down on their pale hair. All she could see of the man was the back of his head and the length of him as he leaned towards the woman by his side; she reached out a hand to touch his face and it was impossible to miss the tenderness in this gesture. A car on the street behind Anika backfired, a loud popping sound that startled the pigeons on the lawn around her bench, and they flapped around in consternation.

Again she read the words she'd inscribed on the postcard, and she added a full stop after *I'm so sorry*. But a moment later she changed the full stop to a comma. *I'm so sorry, but I will phone you on my return.* This message looked odd, that *but* was not necessary. She crossed it out and inserted *and* above it. Daniel's letter was in her handbag and she pulled it out, though she knew the words off by heart. It was the 'With much love' that she looked at first – his analysis of her character didn't need to be viewed again, it was etched on to her heart – and she copied his address on to the card.

She might have felt happy if it wasn't for the prospect of leaving her beloved family and spending twenty-four hours in the canister, as Nyenye referred to it. That and the fact that a decision had yet to be made about how to sign off the card. Quickly she scrawled the words *With much love* and signed her name, before slipping the postcard into her bag.

On the way back to her parents' apartment, she spotted a postbox on the other side of the road and darted between two Trabants, in her haste nearly tripping over the kerb. She dropped the postcard into the postbox and carried on walking.

* * *

Coming from the kitchen with a tray of tinkling glasses, Anika heard Nyenye and her father in the living room arguing about something, their voices loud but the words indistinct. They rarely quarrelled and Anika hated to hear them do so on her last night in Budapest. The living room door was shut and she put down the tray on the hall runner. Hand on the brass doorknob, about to turn it, she hesitated when she heard the word *provenance.*

'Why didn't you tell me years ago?' her father said, his voice raised so that Anika could now distinguish every word. 'You think I don't worry about you? You're always on my mind. You're too secretive. Think about what's going to happen to us when you pass away, heaven forbid. Let's face it, it looks pretty strange that you've got that huge collection that I'm going to be left to deal with and with no evidence of how the pictures came into the family. Or I assume you're leaving them to me.'

'Of course I am.' Nyenye was almost shouting now. 'Who else would I leave them to with Tomas long gone?'

Though there was a pause in their conversation, Anika judged that now was not a good time to open the door and take in the tray of drinks. Her father said, his voice resigned but carrying, 'There's always the art gallery.'

'I'm leaving the paintings to you,' Nyenye said, crossly. 'Whether you like it or not. And I expect you to look after them well.'

'Of course I will.'

There was another pause before Nyenye spoke. 'You're a good boy, György.' Her voice was soothing now that she had the guarantee she wanted. 'And Anika has reminded me that it is important that you know where the provenances are.'

Her voice dropped and Anika retreated down the hallway. The kitchen door was shut and her mother was clattering around inside with her dinner preparations. A moment later there was a tremendous roar from the living room. Anika's father was shouting and Anika could made out the words, 'That is the stupidest place in the world to keep them, Mama!'

'Don't shout at me, György, you know my nerves can't stand it.'

'I'm not shouting!' he bellowed. 'I never shout.'

Anika moved further away and out of earshot. The seconds ticked by and still there were raised voices from the living room. When she could no longer hear Nyenye and her father yelling at one another, she rattled into the room with the tray of drinks. Nyenye's cheeks were pinker than usual. Even her father's usually sallow face was flushed, and his habitually anxious expression more pronounced.

'What's up?' If the cheerfulness in Anika's voice irritated rather than calmed them, neither gave any indication.

'I'm trying to convince Nyenye that it's OK to own paintings, and that it has been for some time. She mustn't worry any more about getting caught by the AVO. If she wants to worry about anything it should be about getting a burglar alarm installed as soon as possible. And a wall safe for the documents. A few barrel bolts and a door chain are certainly not going to keep a determined thief at bay.'

'And I agreed,' Nyenye said, her voice indignant. 'Surely we don't have to go through it all again, György. We don't want to spoil Anika's last evening with us, no?'

'You call that an agreement? You were just embarking on telling me it was a waste of money.'

'I've changed my mind now, as long as you're willing to organise it all. I don't want to be bothered with great hulking men marching through my home with mud on their boots and superiority on their faces.'

'It's not going to happen like that, Mama. They will be skilled security experts not labourers off a construction site.'

'Yes, yes, yes. I've agreed that it should be done and you will agree to organise it all. Division of labour, no? And what about getting the phone installed at the same time, so you can call me up day and night to see if I've been broken into?'

Rather fortunately, Miklos turned up at this juncture, bursting through the front door in a blast of fresh air. He was carrying a bottle of something in a brown paper bag and a briefcase.

* * *

'I think paintings are like people,' Nyenye said over dinner.

'Why is that?' Anika said, puzzled.

'You can't own a painting for ever, you can only borrow it for a while. Just like having children. They stay with you for a time and then they grow up and go away.'

'It's easy for you to think like that about paintings,' Miklos said. 'You've got a living room crammed full of them, just like an art gallery.'

'It's a bit like memories,' Nyenye continued, as if Miklos hadn't spoken. 'The passage of time means you never possess moments. You have memories of those moments but they won't last for ever.'

'Why not?' Miklos finished his glass of wine and reached for the bottle to refresh everyone's glasses, although his and Nyenye's were the only empty ones.

'Because we don't live for ever,' Mama said. 'And anyway, even within a lifetime, memories are limited by the way our synapses connect. Just think, each time your brain pulls out a memory and then files it away again, that memory is altered.'

'Some memories will just disappear,' Miklos said. 'They'll drift away and never come back. But a picture is a physical thing. A store of value, like money.' Miklos had done a minor in economics and liked to speak like this sometimes. 'Its worth is determined by what you can sell it for.'

'You don't need to tell shopkeepers that,' their father said, grinning. 'But there's emotional value too, don't you forget that, son.'

'Well, I don't want to forget tonight,' Nyenye said. 'The five of us together and darling Anika off tomorrow in the metal canister.'

'But you're getting the phone connected.' Anika patted Nyenye's hand and her grandmother seized hold of her fingers. 'You committed to that with Papa just now. So we'll be able to talk. No more coded messages from anyone. Those clicks have gone.'

Anika glanced at her father, who had a doubting expression on his face. 'We can never be absolutely sure of anything. It's always best to be careful. Remember what we saw on television last night.'

'What was that?' Nyenye said.

'There've been leaked documents from the Internal Security Service,' Mama said. 'Apparently, leaders of the opposition parties are still having their phones tapped and their meetings infiltrated. Old habits die hard.'

'It's illegal now,' Miklos said. 'That's what the Interior Minister said.'

At that moment Anika thought of what Jonno had written in one of his newspaper articles, the one she'd read in the Mitchell Library. That when an old order vanished – together with most of its records – new opportunities arrived for the perpetrators of crimes: they could change their identity as well as their destiny, and escape justice.

'Best to be careful anyway,' Mama said. 'More and more fascists are coming out of the woodwork and who knows where Hungary will end up.'

Nyenye coughed. Her brow was furrowed and her shoulders were hunched over. She might have been modelling suspicion for a life drawing class or changing her mind about having the phone connected.

'It's easy to keep phone conversations simple,' Miklos

said quickly. 'You can talk about the weather and what you're having for dinner. Anyway, Internal Security are only interested in politicians. Once the March elections are over, there'll be no more wiretaps.'

'I love getting your letters,' Anika told Nyenye. 'You write the most wonderful descriptions of shopping and spring cleaning and the seasons changing. That's the sort of stuff I like to hear about. It doesn't have to be politics, just whatever you feel like writing about if you don't want to talk on the phone.'

'I'll be able to talk about domestic things on the phone,' Nyenye said. 'But not about other things. I'm a bit like the Internal Security Service in that regard: my old habits die hard.'

Chapter 32

At the airport Nyenye's expressive face was like the sky on this blustery afternoon, Anika thought. Wind-gusted dark clouds of sadness interspersed with bright rays of vicarious satisfaction that her granddaughter was setting off on new adventures. Anika's father looked anxious but that was the mask he wore most of the time, and who knew what was concealed behind this. Miklos was the only one of the family to appear radiant, but that was because he'd already moved away from them and into the new world he was establishing.

Just before Anika headed through the departure gates, Mama began to weep, fat tears rolling down her cheeks that she swiped away like bothersome flies as she struggled to regain her composure. 'I'm going to come and see you, Anika,' she said. Her voice sounded choked and her eyes were greener than ever against the redness around them. 'Your father and I talked about this last night. Maybe next Christmas holidays. And Nyenye might come too.'

Anika held her close. 'That will be lovely,' she said into her mother's shoulder. Mama smelled of the eau de cologne that she liked to wear for special occasions and that, wherever Anika was, she could never get a whiff of without thinking of home. She hoped she wasn't going to cry herself; there was a prickling in her eyes and sinuses. She needed to get this farewell over, to disappear through the doors that led into passport control, to put behind her this harrowing pain of departure.

At last she was in the departure lounge area with some

twenty minutes to fill in before boarding. There were several other flights departing at much the same time. One to Berlin, one to Rome, and the third was her flight to London. Sadness and regret, excitement and anticipation were spinning about in her head like garments in a washing machine. Sadness at leaving her family behind but happiness at the prospect of returning to work, to her studies, to some warm sunshine.

Ah, the push and the pull. On the plane she would have too much time to reflect. Leaving home but going back home: once you crossed the ocean you were always on the wrong side. That was the lot of the immigrant, belonging everywhere but nowhere. Displaced, and unplaced, and already she was missing her family.

But you had to look forward, not back. And weren't there also advantages in knowing two cultures, in having a foot in the old world and another in the new? Right now, she just wanted to get into that metal canister and fly high above the clouds.

She was unfastening her travel bag to find something to read when a loud voice booming above her made her jump. 'Well, if it isn't Anika Molnar.'

'Jonno Jamison!' In her surprise she let go of her boarding pass and it fell on to the floor. 'Surely you're not on the same flight as me?'

'Where are you going?'

'Sydney, via London and Bahrain and Singapore. And you?' She picked up the boarding pass and dusted off some fluff.

'I'm off to Berlin. I've got a terrific new storyline to follow there. I've done all I can in Budapest.'

'My grandmother has the provenances for all the paintings in her collection.'

'I know that, Anika.'

'How do you know?'

'I met a very interesting man a couple of days ago, the nephew of a Mrs Szabo. Does her name mean anything to you?'

'It does. And what did Mrs Szabo's interesting nephew have to say?'

'He said quite a lot about his aunt and about your grandmother's provenances, once I'd given him a hefty inducement to talk, that is. I dropped around to see your grandmother early this morning to tell her. Did she say anything?'

Anika shook her head. 'She didn't. Now tell me, Jonno, why were you harassing her?'

'It's obvious, isn't it? I was searching for a story. And it would have been a good one.'

'*Looted paintings turn up in Budapest apartment*, is that what you had in mind?'

'You've got it, Anika. That's what I thought. And if your grandmother had been more forthcoming, I could have killed off that idea a week ago. You've got a cagey family, haven't you?'

'I would have thought that you'd understand why, after all your researching and reporting in the Soviet Bloc countries. And that you'd know enough not to mention any *caginess*, if that's what you want to call it.'

'Why shouldn't I mention it? That's all over now.'

'The memories remain. For many as vivid as ever.'

'That's why I became a journalist, Anika. My grandfather was a collaborator in Slovenia, you see. He died in the war but my grandmother and mother ended up in a displaced persons camp and eventually got into Australia.'

'So you write to atone for him?'

'I think of it more as redressing wrongs. But it's also for my mother and all she went through.'

'And what about my grandmother? Didn't you think about how frightened she might feel when you came banging on her door the other day?'

'I'm sorry about that. I hope I didn't scare her too much. Anyway, she kept the chain securely fastened, and she might be small but she managed to shut that door pretty damned fast when she saw me.'

That's because she was terrified, Anika thought, eyes fixed on Jonno. He was now sporting a charmingly rueful smile. It made him look like a schoolboy offering an apology after being bawled out by the headteacher. He might have worked hard over the years at perfecting that air of contrition, or perhaps he was born with it. She said, 'You'll do anything it takes, won't you Jonno, to get your story?'

'I'm only trying to get at the truth.'

A voice came over the tannoy calling the last remaining passengers for the flight to Berlin. Jonno leaned forward as if to plant a kiss on her mouth. Quickly she averted her face and he kissed her cheek rather than her lips. 'Goodbye, Anika. I'm so glad things have worked out for you. It wasn't you I was really after, it was the truth.'

'I knew all along you weren't really after me. The truth is what I've been after too and I've got it now.' *Or most of it at any rate*, she thought. There were still those mysterious circumstances to confront.

Jonno grinned before loping off. She watched him, his easy gait, his broad-shouldered physique. Now it was all over, she felt a reluctant but growing sense of gratitude towards him. Without his irritating presence, she was sure that Nyenye wouldn't have been so quickly forthcoming with information about the provenances.

Jonno turned and raised a hand in farewell before heading towards the doors to the airbridge. Five minutes to go before boarding for her own flight commenced. Delving into her bag for a book, she saw that an envelope had been inserted into it, with her name scrawled across it in Nyenye's hand.

My darling Anika,

Although I'm sad to see you depart again, I am glad for your sake that you're heading off to a new country with new opportunities and a loving aunt for support, for all of us need a crutch to lean on from time to time.

Nyenye's words made Anika feel happy. *A loving aunt for support.* She knew that she hadn't imagined the antipathy between Nyenye and Tabilla but maybe her visit had smoothed some of it out. Their love for Tomas had pushed them apart but their affection for her would bring them together again. It had been over three decades since they'd last seen each other and when they met up again next Christmas – if Nyenye could be induced to travel – they surely couldn't fail to get along. But if they didn't, they'd just have to work at it. That's what families did. Anika read on.

I'm so happy too that you will be an architect, with the opportunity to create beautiful and functional things. What a lovely career choice – and so good to get away from the butchery. God knows, we've seen enough of all of that. I also wanted to say that I value the conversations we had about the past and how they have made me feel more at peace. I think you will understand what I mean.

That man who said he is your friend visited me again just now. Of course, I didn't let him in. I thought it better to tell you this in a quick note rather than talk about it at the airport. So that is why I am sitting down now at my kitchen table composing this brief letter to you. All I told him was that I have the provenances for everything – absolutely everything – that I own. But the strange thing was that he seemed to know this already. He'd tracked down Mrs Szabo's nephew, apparently. And at that moment your father turned up with a contractor for the wall safe I'm getting, and your friend left soon afterwards. He's off to Berlin, he said, so he won't be pestering me any more.

Safe travels, dearest one.

With much love,

Nyenye

Anika folded up the letter again and slipped it into the zip pocket of her handbag, next to her passport. The voice on the tannoy announced that boarding for the flight to London had begun. After picking up her hand luggage, she joined the queue of passengers waiting to show their boarding passes, waiting to climb into the fragile canister that would hurtle them across the world.

* * *

Four hours out of Sydney Anika woke abruptly from a deep sleep. Outside it was still dark but the moon illuminated the cloudscape, long wisps veiling the vast continent of Australia that they were already flying over, though there were still several thousand more kilometres to go.

While she'd been away, her mind had made a seismic shift; it was as if she could now see life from a new perspective. Outside, the darkness was beginning to fade. Soon the streaks of thinning cloud to the east assumed a salmon-pink glow that morphed into a fiery orange before the sun blazed in triumph over the horizon. The air was thinner seven miles high and there was less friction to slow down their progress. Her thoughts floated free. Free of drag, free of resistance, and she felt an expanding sense of detachment. Not only was she seeing the earth from a different vantage point but she was seeing her life in a new way too. Generations of her family had been scarred by upheavals, and their stories were multiplied millions and millions of times all over the globe. Everywhere there were people like them. Damaged people, displaced people. But there were survivors too.

PART VI

Sydney, January 1990

Chapter 33

Early morning. The automated doors beyond Customs and Immigration at Sydney's Kingsford Smith Airport slid open and there was sweet Sally in a bright red dress and dark glasses, smiling and waving. She hugged Anika, hot and sweaty though she was, before grabbing one of her bags and they were off, out into the oblique sunlight that was so bright it hurt Anika's eyes. The smell of aviation fuel diminished as they drove away from the airport. Anika noticed – as if for the first time – the sparkling leaves of the eucalyptus trees as they twisted in the golden light and the gentle breeze, and above them the cerulean blue of a sky that was already brilliant though it was not yet nine o'clock.

'You haven't changed,' Sally said. 'You're a bit paler, that's all.'

'I feel like a different person.'

'So you got what you wanted?'

'Yes, and more.'

'Do you want to talk about it?'

'Not yet. Tell me what's been happening here.'

Though Sally assured her that nothing had been happening, they were able to talk about that nonstop as Sally weaved an intricate path through the back streets of Tempe, Enmore, Annandale, until they got to Victoria Road. Here Sally had to concentrate, here she started swearing at the traffic, swivelling her head as she changed lanes, giving the finger to a driver who cut in front. That was when Anika shut her eyes and opened them again only when they were safely in Rozelle.

Boggabri Street was an oasis, although one with few parking spaces this morning. There was a large 'For Sale' sign in front of Mr and Mrs Opposite's house. Tabilla's front door was open and Anika would have sworn her grevillea had grown another ten centimetres in the few weeks she'd been away. Sally drove slowly by, muttering about parking. Mrs Thornton was already in her yard, leaning on her broom handle and chatting to Tabilla's neighbour from the other side, the white-haired old man who was hard of hearing. Ty Nguyen's ute was parked in its usual spot and was shining in the sunlight, with pools of soapy water on the bitumen around it. Before the dogleg in the road that led to the corner shop, Sally adroitly manoeuvred into a space in front of Penny and Jane's terraced house and switched off the ignition.

In Anika's bag was the little bottle of perfume she'd bought for Sally at Singapore Airport. Sally was enchanted by this, as Anika knew she would be; that enthusiasm and generous spirit were some of the reasons why she loved her. They carried Anika's bags along the street as far as Mrs Thornton's. The old man had moved on towards Victoria Road and Mrs Thornton was able to give Anika her undivided attention.

'How pale you look,' she said, 'and so tired. That reminds me of a friend I used to have...' and off she went, on an adventure into her past.

Sally dumped Anika's bags on Tabilla's front verandah. 'I have to go,' she said. 'I've got a yoga class. I'll call you later.' And she went even before Mrs Thornton noticed her.

While Mrs Thornton was still talking, Anika dived into her hand luggage and pulled out the trinket box covered in red and green embroidery that she'd bought her at Budapest Airport, a last-minute purchase that used up her forint. For once Mrs Thornton was at a loss for words, and her evident pleasure both gratified and embarrassed Anika.

Once inside, Anika felt as if she'd come home. She and Tabilla talked for hours until fatigue hit Anika like a tidal wave and soon after Tabilla said she was starting to spout gibberish and shooed her upstairs to shower and sleep. Anika's bedroom smelled faintly of rose petals; Tabilla had placed a small vase crammed with roses next to the family photograph on the bookcase.

When Anika woke up it was five o'clock the next morning. A band of light defined the edges of the curtains and she felt wide awake and hopeful. Leaping out of bed, she stood in front of the wardrobe mirror to tidy her hair. But it was not her reflection that she saw in the glass. Instead it was Julius Singer's, his face pained as it had been the last time they'd met just before she flew out of Sydney – that sadness in his expression as he spoke about his mother and the woman in the portrait.

After breakfast Anika called Julius Singer's gallery and was relieved that Julius picked up rather than his assistant James.

Julius said, 'I'm so glad you called. I heard you're back.'

'Can I come around tomorrow? I've to go into work today but there's something we need to talk about.'

'The painting's been found.' It was as if Julius were jet-lagged too, his voice was flat and lacking animation.

'I know. I have to visit police headquarters at three o'clock tomorrow. It's near Central, apparently. They wouldn't tell me who took the painting.'

'They want me there too. At the same time.'

Surprised, Anika sat at the bottom of the stairs. Both of them at the same time. This sounded ominous. Certainly, she needed to meet up with him beforehand.

'Would you be able to drop into the gallery beforehand?' he said.

'I'll be there at two o'clock.'

After putting down the phone, Anika glanced out of the window. In this moment of sharp clarity, when the sky was a pale washed-out blue, she knew what she had to do. The Rocheteau was a beautiful thing that had brought her much pleasure before she knew of its history. But once she'd learned that it had belonged to Julius's family, she'd known there could only be one course of action if ever it was restored to her. Hearing Nyenye's heartbreaking account of how Tomas had acquired it had deepened this resolve. Soon she would see Julius Singer and she knew exactly what she had to tell him.

Chapter 34

At the 137 Gallery, Julius was alone apart from the assistant, who was rather ostentatiously ferreting around with wrapping materials at the back of the gallery. Julius immediately ushered Anika into his office and shut the door. After they were seated, him on the business side of the desk and Anika on the other, he said, 'I believe you've met my wife.'

'I don't think so.'

'She isn't well.' He turned away to focus on the courtyard outside.

'I'm sorry to hear that.'

'She used to be an artist, but after her breakdown she gave it up. It was a great shame because she has real talent. And painting helped her keep the nightmares at bay, at least to some degree. But after the breakdown the doctors put her on drugs that changed her in many ways. Some to the good, some not so good.'

His voice had become fainter and Anika had to concentrate hard to pick up what he was saying.

'She did something last year that I've only recently learned about. And it really shocked me, even knowing that she did it out of love. She has a generous heart, in spite of everything. I've been struggling to think of what I should do and how I can go about rectifying what she did without harming her or anyone else who was involved. I've been battling with my conscience and my own feelings. I've got a good many failings and it's taken weeks for me to get this far. But eventually I decided that the best way of moving forward with this was to tell you.'

'To tell me?'

'Do you really have no idea what I'm talking about, Anika?'

'I haven't a clue.'

'I think you have, Anika. My wife's name is Sarah.'

'Sarah?'

'Sarah. She dropped by Tabilla's house one day and you met her. Tabilla was out but you were home.'

With an effort Anika shut her gaping mouth and leaned forward. 'Sarah's your wife?'

'Yes. Didn't she say so?'

'No. It was ages ago, back in autumn last year. I didn't know she was your wife. And she didn't seem ill.'

'Think of it like a depression, Anika. It comes and it goes. Sarah's quite normal a lot of the time. You can probably guess where I'm heading. It's about the painting. The Rocheteau.'

Anika gaped at him, at a loss for words.

'Sarah took it, you see. She took it from you and hid it and gave it to me for my birthday a couple of weeks back. Yes, you may well look puzzled and angry, I can see what you're thinking but just hear me out. Sarah knew how devastated I was by seeing it again when you brought it into the gallery that day. And she's anyway inclined to take the law into her own hands. I'm afraid she has no faith in people, not after all she and her family went through in the war. A lot of us don't, and with good reason.'

Wheels were starting to turn in Anika's fatigued brain. There were a few things Julius needed to understand and now was the time to tell him. Her voice emerged loud and clear as she began to speak. 'I'm glad the painting's been recovered and I'm sorry about your wife. But I want to tell you what I learned in Budapest. My Uncle Tomas didn't steal it from your family, you see. He was given it. I know that for sure now. But anyway, I don't want it.'

Julius looked like misery personified as he leaned forward in his chair and rested his head on his hands. The bald patch on the top of his head was sprinkled with freckles and Anika was moved by the vulnerability of his skull.

'I learned a bit more from my grandmother when I was in Hungary, about what happened after the Russians drove the Nazis out of Budapest. That got me really thinking. The Nazis were very selective in the paintings they collected but maybe a German abandoned it when fleeing the city and it was picked up by one of the Russians. It was a Russian officer who gave it to my Uncle Tomas. He was only a boy at the time.'

Julius remained silent, his head still in his hands, and the freckled pate was all that she could see of his head. She continued, 'I thought when we last met that I had no rights to this painting. But even if I hadn't realised then, once I'd heard how Tomas got hold of it, I became even more convinced that I want nothing to do with it.'

She told him that she couldn't help thinking of what happened in that cellar. Russian soldiers raping her grandmother and other women like her, their officer unable or unwilling to control his troops. Giving the boy of the family a painting as a small compensation for the trauma the family had suffered. No, she didn't want the painting back. Julius's memories were different and he was welcome to have the picture. Not only was he welcome to it, he was entitled to it.

Julius looked up now: his whole face might have been slipping. 'I'm sorry to hear of what your family went through, Anika.' He paused, his lips moving silently, as if they were formulating words that he then rejected as inappropriate. Eventually he said, 'But I also think that Sarah stealing back something that was stolen from someone's family years before was not necessarily the right thing to do.'

Anika asked him how Sarah managed to take the painting

from her bedroom and if she'd had an accomplice.

'She took it on her own. She'd seen it apparently when she dropped by Tabilla's house and you let her in to use the bathroom. She knew Tabilla's sewing room used to be upstairs. She'd been there often for fittings in the past, so she was familiar with the layout of the house. When she went upstairs to the bathroom, she saw that your bedroom was where the workroom used to be, and apparently, she couldn't help noticing the painting, it was hanging where you could see it from the doorway.'

'But how could she have known it was your Rocheteau?'

'She didn't but she popped into your bedroom and had a good look at the signature. Of course, she didn't know then that the painting was my mother's Rocheteau but she thought it looked a lot like what I'd described to her. You know, my memories of my mother's painting.'

'Did she describe it to you when she got home?'

'No. But I told her later that you'd brought in my mother's Rocheteau to be valued. After that she quickly put two and two together. Apparently, she then checked out the lane behind Tabilla's house a few days before she retrieved the painting, and she just upped and took it the night that Tabilla and I went to the concert. That was a Saturday night, so she figured a pretty girl like you would be out somewhere, and she was right. She told me she felt unwell at the last minute and suggested I offer her ticket to Tabilla.'

'And did you know what your wife was doing that night?'

'Of course not, Anika. I had no idea. As soon as the concert ended, I dashed home to see how Sarah was and then I noticed right away that her car had gone. I got a bit worried then, until I saw there was a note for me on the hallstand saying she'd gone for a drive. She got home an hour or so later and seemed fine, in fact calmer than usual. So I thought no more of her absence, though I did ask where she'd been. She said she'd gone to Bondi Beach. She had a craving for a gelato and there's a shop there that sells it, and then she walked along the promenade and watched the waves.'

He stood and began to pace up and down behind his desk like a prisoner in a cell. His brow was furrowed and there were two vertical lines between his eyebrows. Anika wanted to tell him it was going to be all right. She longed to reach out and hug him, to say it would work itself out, although there was no guarantee it would.

Chapter 35

Julius stared out of the side window of the taxi taking them to the police headquarters. His shoulders were hunched over and his exposed neck might have been waiting for the executioner's chop. Anika's fidgeting hands found a hangnail and ripped it off, and she was glad when it hurt. Maybe she was going to be incarcerated, or perhaps it would be Sarah. If Sarah were to be prosecuted, Anika would say that she didn't want to press charges, but what about all that police time this theft had consumed? In her handbag was an envelope containing the photo of Tomas holding the painting, the photo that she and Nyenye had found in the bottom of her box-file, and that Nyenye had given to her. Now she patted the envelope gently. She might need this shortly.

The police headquarters were in a red brick building not far from Central Station. Anika and Julius were directed up to the sixth floor. Here they were greeted by two detectives Anika had never seen before; one was a cadaverous-looking middle-aged man while the other, an older man, was short and as plump as one of the sausages in Molnar's Butchers.

In a small interview room, Anika and Julius settled themselves on hard plastic chairs that might have been designed to make you feel ill at ease. The air conditioning was noisy and ineffective: the room stank of cigarettes overlaid with room deodoriser. Anika put her handbag on the table in front of her but didn't much like the look of it there. It had vertical stitching on its sides and reminded her too much of one of those grilles you saw on television shows separating prisoner from visitor. The plump detective began to talk right away, before Anika had time to transfer her handbag on to the floor, scuffed vinyl tiles in a marbled grey and white finish, and she had to ask him to repeat what he'd said. He wanted to know how the painting came into her possession.

She explained that her father gave it to her to restore to her aunt but her aunt gave it back to her, although it was her husband's, so Anika kept it. Somehow this confused him. Anika had to keep saying it again and again, in a variety of ways, until eventually he understood, and then he wanted to know where her father got it from.

Anika told him the painting belonged to her father's brother – that was her uncle – and he was killed in 1956 in the Hungarian Revolution. Her father was only a boy when his brother died.

'But surely his brother had proof, didn't he, Anika? People are very careful to document works like that, if the works are legitimate that is, and aren't forgeries or stolen.'

'Where is the painting now?' she asked the detective.

'We'll get around to that in a moment. So how did your uncle get hold of it?'

'It was given to him.'

'Given to him?'

She wondered if the man was hard of hearing. 'A Russian soldier gave it to him when he was only ten. In a cellar.'

'That's a very odd place to give someone a painting, Anika. In a cellar. It seems a bit secretive, don't you think? Like someone had something to hide.'

'Everything in their part of town had been bombed. It was early 1945, and they weren't that far from the river. That's where the worst of the bombing occurred. That's what people were living in, cellars under ruined buildings.'

'Bombed? What terrible times you people have lived

through. Though you weren't alive then and so you're going on what people tell you. And you believe them.'

'Where is the painting?' Anika was starting to feel angry and she struggled to keep calm.

'I brought it here, Anika,' Julius said. He looked surprised, as if he'd only realised at this moment that she hadn't been told about this. 'I brought it back a week ago. That's why they wanted me here.'

The plump detective nodded to his colleague who left the room. No one spoke. The only sounds were the wall clock clicking the minutes by and the hum of traffic six floors down. When the cadaverous-looking detective returned he was carrying the painting; gingerly, as if it were a bomb that might explode at any minute. Anika and Julius stood up, and the plump detective clattered his chair back and watched them closely.

Julius was unsteady on his feet and Anika took hold of his arm.

'Is this yours?' the detective asked her.

'This is the painting that was taken from my bedroom.'

The detective holding the picture placed it on the table as if he were displaying it for auction. The glowing young woman with the abundant auburn hair and opalescent skin looked back at them. Leaning forward, Anika saw that those areas that, from a distance, appeared to be of one colour were composed of deft brushstrokes of many hues, each shape borrowing colours from adjacent planes and reflecting back a host of different shades. Nothing about the painting had changed.

But the painting had changed her. 'I don't want it back,' she said. Her words came out loud and overemphatic. 'By rights this belongs to Julius.'

When Julius coughed, she could feel the emotion he was

barely containing. It was as if it were vibrating through his arm and into hers. Neither detective spoke, though they both looked surprised, eyebrows raised, the roly-poly one with his mouth falling open.

The wall clock continued measuring out the seconds. After a good few had gone by Julius said, his voice wavering, 'Anika is a wonderful young woman whom I've been fortunate to get to know a little since we met nearly a year ago. I think she and I would be in full agreement that it would serve the painting best to be given to the state gallery where everyone can see it. And this is what I propose,' he continued, his voice stronger now. 'That we – Anika or me or whichever one of us the police decide the painting should be restored to – donate it to the Art Gallery of New South Wales and that you don't prosecute my wife Sarah.'

'I'll go along with that,' Anika told him. 'With pleasure.' And with great relief too. She could feel her shoulders – and her jaw that she hadn't known until now that she was clenching – start to relax.

Julius began to describe in some detail the various pieces of legislation likely to cover this sort of gift but Anika was finding it impossible to concentrate. Her legs gave way and she collapsed on to a chair. The circumstances in which the painting came into her family were horrible. It was rightfully Julius's. And really it was far, far better that the state art gallery should have the Antoine Rocheteau rather than either Julius or her. There everyone would see it and be able to enjoy it.

She picked up her handbag. It held the envelope containing the photo of Tomas holding the painting. In the envelope was also a picture of Tomas and Tabilla on their wedding day. Anika had thought of these as her insurance, as something that she'd show the police if she had to. She would save them for the Art Gallery of New South Wales, although she would first show them to Julius after they finished with the police. The curators would be able to initiate a provenance search proceeding backwards from this. Somewhere in Vienna there could be art catalogues from the early twentieth century, records that might list the original sale of the painting to the Singer family.

And the provenance of this picture was no longer Anika's concern. She could hand the whole burden of the painting to others. For too long she'd been obsessed by it, and now at last she could move on.

Julius put an arm around her shoulder. 'Are you OK, Anika?'

She smiled at him and he beamed back. He looked years younger. 'Never better,' she said. 'This is the right thing to do.'

Chapter 36

Anika was exhausted that evening when she got home. As she pushed the front door open, she nearly knocked over Tabilla, who must have been standing immediately inside.

'There's someone to see you, Anika.'

'Oh, Tabilla.' Anika's voice came out all cross and that was not what she'd intended at all. It was only that she was so tired and seeing her aunt there was a surprise, and anyway she'd wanted to be able to have a drink with her without having to deal with some visitor first. 'Who is it?'

'They're sitting out on the back terrace. I've just come in to get my cardigan. Why don't you put your things down and go out there and say hello.'

'Why didn't you just say I wasn't at home?'

'Of course, I said you weren't here but then I said you'd be back shortly and offered a cup of tea. I wanted a chat, you see, but now you're home I've got some sewing to do so I'll leave you to it.' She went into the front room and shut the door behind her.

After hanging her handbag from the newel post at the bottom of the staircase, Anika made her way through the kitchen. She felt clammy and uncomfortable. Her dress was damp with sweat, after a nightmare ride in a bus with no spare seats and too much balancing in the crowded aisle with nothing much to hold on to as the bus lurched erratically from one stop to the next. The cool breeze blowing through the kitchen was pleasant after all that heat.

Too quickly she stepped out of the kitchen on to the

brick paving of the terrace. If the man sitting there hadn't jumped up to catch her, she would have been over on her knees and grovelling before him. He held her by her elbows for rather longer than necessary, as if he thought she might collapse again with the shock of seeing him. And it was true that she was completely flummoxed, maw open for so long it was a wonder a fly hadn't settled on her teeth. It was only the dryness of her mouth that made her realise she'd been gawping at him, his face only a few centimetres away from hers, and so close she could see the bristles of his incipient beard and the pores of his skin. She looked down, anything to avoid gazing into those dark eyes. His shoes were brown and scuffed and in need of a good polish, and this seemed somehow out of character. When he bent forward to kiss her lips she was shocked again.

He said, 'Do you remember we almost kissed the night I brought you home after we had fish and chips at Watson's Bay?'

She made a show of struggling to remember but then thought better of it and nodded her head.

'Your neighbour was standing on her front verandah right behind you. As soon as we heard that car backfire, I spotted her watching us. I thought that kissing you passionately under her scrutiny would have been a tad embarrassing for everyone.'

Suddenly conscious of the sweat stains around the armpits of her dress, Anika held her elbows close to her side and took a step back.

'Have a seat,' he said gesturing to one of the canvas directors' chairs, as if he were the host and she the visitor.

She sat next to him. Her dress seemed to have become shorter and her legs were pale and bare. After one quick glance at them he looked away, as if he too were uncomfortable. He transferred his gaze to the garden. Two orange and black butterflies flitted by, their pace leisurely, as if they would live for ever rather than just a few weeks. Above the paling fence at the bottom of the yard, you could make out the wheat silos in the distance, beyond the roofs of the terraced houses stepping down the hill. They sat in a silence that felt like an eternity, although it was probably no more than a few seconds.

'Did you get my letter, Anika?'

'Tabilla forwarded it to me in Budapest. I sent you a postcard but you probably won't get it for another week.'

'What did it say, can you remember?'

'It said that I was sorry and that I'd phone you when I got home.'

The words in Daniel's letter sprang to mind. *I can't help but wonder if, when you get upset about one thing, you immediately start looking for something else you can vent your anger on.* He was right, this *was* a character trait that she had. Together with half of the human species.

'What were you sorry for, Anika?' She could hear emotion block his throat and make the words indistinct.

'Sorry for all that business about your uncle, Jake Rubinstein. Whoops, I mean your Great-uncle Jacob Lacey.'

He smiled and she could tell that he was struggling not to, that he thought she might be annoyed because he was grinning at the apology. His face looked so comical that she couldn't stop herself from laughing.

'I think we might put that behind us, don't you?' Daniel said, beginning to laugh with her.

His face looked even lovelier than she remembered, and suddenly it seemed to her right that he was here by her side on this glorious summer's evening. 'I think it might be a very good idea to do that, Daniel.'

He reached out to take her hand. It was still hot and

sweaty but he didn't seem to mind. Her watchband slipped round her wrist, exposing the scar on her left forearm. Daniel gently raised her hand and kissed the puckered white skin. A kiss that conferred acceptance, or maybe it was a blessing.

Anika began to feel lighter, as if she might float above the terrace, but Daniel's hand was anchoring her, grounding her in this city to which she knew she now belonged. Together they watched the pair of orange and black butterflies fluttering by again, until the clicking of heels on vinyl heralded Tabilla's arrival in the kitchen.

'Don't mind me,' she called through the open doorway. 'Of course, I'd hate to interrupt you, but would either of you like a glass of wine?'

'Do come out and join us,' Anika replied, leaping to her feet. Her aunt was standing in the middle of the kitchen, her expression slightly vulnerable, as if she felt she might be disturbing them. Anika darted inside and threw her arms around Tabilla. 'I'll get the wine,' she said. 'You go outside and sit with Daniel. I'd like to tell you together about what happened to the painting.'

Acknowledgements

Warmest thanks to early readers Alison Arnold, Kerrie Barnett, Heather Boisseau, Clare Christian, Tom Flood, Maggie Hamand, Tim Hatton and Michelle Wildgen. I am very grateful to Alastair McAuley for sharing his expertise on the former Soviet Union and Hungary, although in no way can he be held responsible for my interpretation of the period. Thanks to the team who brought this book into production, and to the many booksellers and librarians who contribute so much to getting a new novel out into the world of readers. Thanks also to Varuna the Writers' House for the opportunity to write with no interruptions when this was most needed. Last but not least, I thank my beloved family for being there.

The Painting is a work of fiction. Names, characters, places either are the product of the author's imagination or are used fictitiously. Any resemblance to actual persons, living or dead, events or locales is entirely coincidental.

Of the many historical books that I read as background for this work, readers might find particularly interesting the following: Judt, Tony, *Postwar: A History of Europe Since 1945*, London: Vintage, 2010; Michener, James A., *The Bridge at Andau*, London: Secker & Warburg, 1957, Sebestyén, Victor, *Revolution 1989: The Fall of the Soviet Empire*, London: Phoenix, 2010; Sebestyén, Victor, *Twelve Days: The Revolution 1956*, London: Weidenfeld & Nicolson, 2007; and Ungváry, Krisztián, *The Siege of Budapest: One Hundred Days in World War II*, New Haven, CT: Yale University Press, 2006.

'Evocative, insightful, thought-provoking'
Karen Viggers

'Booth is superb'
Marion Halligan

THE PHILOSOPHER'S DAUGHTERS

ALISON BOOTH

'Delicately handled historical drama'
Tom Flood

Chapter 1

His Hands Could Span an Octave Easily

'That brings me to my penultimate point.' Dr Bagnall looked up from his lecture notes and peered at Aunt Charlotte, who was sitting next to Sarah in the front row of the packed hall.

At last, Sarah thought. He'd been droning on for a good fifteen minutes and nothing that he'd said was new. Everyone who attended meetings of the Women's Franchise League knew all about the history of the women's suffrage movement. She glanced at her father and Mrs Lydia Buxton. Slumped in their chairs at the back of the platform, waiting their turn at the lectern, their posture could surely not meet with the approval of Aunt Charlotte, who'd nudged Sarah awake only minutes before.

'Get on with it, why don't yer?' shouted a female voice. 'It's about bloody time we 'eard yer last point!'

Sarah felt a thrill of excitement. But alas, Dr Bagnall took no notice of the interruption and continued to develop his second-last point, which seemed indistinguishable from his previous one. *Or perhaps it's all too subtle for me,* Sarah thought, losing the thread of Dr Bagnall's argument as she vanished into the world of her imagination, a landscape whose features were defined by sound. In her mind she was running through the piano suite she'd been practising that afternoon.

She was passing through its valleys and was now uplifted on to a plateau; she was being carried forward towards the peak that was just a few bars ahead when her progress was halted by a harsh sound.

'Give the women a go, why don't yer!' It was the same voice as before. 'We want to 'ear wot Mrs Buxton 'as to say. Get off the stage, yer long-winded burbler!'

Swivelling around, Sarah narrowly avoided bumping hats with Aunt Charlotte. She stood up to see better and – in the instant before the rest of the audience did likewise – saw a tall middle-aged woman in a clinch with two slightly shorter policemen. The woman was still shouting although her words had become muffled, in part by the constabulary embrace, but also by the uproar as fifty or so voices began to talk.

Although Sarah could hear Dr Bagnall continuing with what must now be his last point, no one was listening. All heads were craning towards the performance at the rear of the hall. Surely Dr Bagnall couldn't have failed to notice what was happening to his audience. She turned at the moment a tomato flew towards him. He ducked and it landed on his papers; his shout and the exploding tomato were like a firework on Guy Fawkes Night. Poor Dr Bagnall, how humiliated he must feel. Sarah found a handkerchief and ran up the steps to the platform. While Dr Bagnall wrung his hands, she knelt on the floor and gathered up his notes. She wiped off the tomato pulp as if she were cleaning blood from a wound; her expiation for being pleased, for just an instant, by an act of aggression.

The racket at the back of the hall was becoming louder. People were shouting. Many high shrill voices, mingled with fewer deep male voices, moving towards a resolution of the crisis, as in the final movement of a concerto. Dr Bagnall seemed to have lost all interest in his lecture notes. He leapt down, almost athletically, from the stage and joined Sarah's father and aunt in the side aisle. Sarah absorbed herself in methodically cleaning the pages of the lecture notes. Some of the writing had been washed off with the liquid of the tomato, and her handkerchief was stained with red juice and blue ink.

'That's just not big enough for the job,' said a voice that reverberated like a double bass. Sarah saw a large white handkerchief first, and behind that, a tall figure silhouetted against the harsh lighting. When he squatted next to her, she saw that he had curly blonde hair and a broad, lightly tanned face. 'Such a shame about your handkerchief,' he said.

'Such a shame about the lecture notes. We'll never know Dr Bagnall's last point now,' said Sarah.

'I think we can predict it, don't you?' the man said. 'You have some tomato on your sleeve. Use my handkerchief.'

His hand holding out the handkerchief was large, with long fingers. They could span an octave easily. As she took his offering, her fingers accidentally touched his. She felt a shock as if she had felt something very hot and withdrew her hand so quickly that his handkerchief fell on to the floor. Each of them went to pick it up simultaneously and again she felt that electric touch. She was blushing now and didn't want to look up. As she wiped up the few tomato seeds clinging to the sleeve of her pale-grey jacket, she noticed the monogrammed initials HV on a corner of the handkerchief.

'I'm Henry Vincent,' the double bass man said. 'Delighted to meet you, Miss Sarah Cameron. Charles Barclay told me who you are.'

She wound the handkerchief around her fingers. Sarah, the eighteen-year-old younger daughter of widower James Cameron, that was how Charles might have described her. She wasn't usually shy but she didn't know quite what to do or say next. To offer to return the handkerchief after having it laundered seemed forward, as if she were proposing a future meeting, while to return it covered in tomato seeds seemed inappropriate too. She wished that Aunt Charlotte would join them to offer some guidance but most of all she wished her blushes would subside.

The fuss at the back of the hall was now over and people were resuming their seats. Henry Vincent said, 'Let me take that from you. You've bandaged your left hand expertly. With all those bits of tomato pulp, it looks like a shocking injury.'

She laughed and unwound his handkerchief. His eyes seemed yellow in the artificial lighting, as yellow as the eyes of next door's cat, Lucifer. But people didn't have yellow eyes; they must be hazel or light brown. She forgot her earlier embarrassment and stared at him, almost mesmerised by the yellow. He stared back, unblinking. 'Your eyes are a light brown,' she said at last, as if making a scientific observation, when what she was really expressing was a startling new discovery: that golden blonde hair and light brown eyes were the acme of male beauty.

'And yours are blue,' he said.

She recognised this as a declaration of sorts and not a statement of the obvious. Their eye contact was broken by the appearance of her father, who was puffing slightly after his climb up the stage steps.

'Such an unpleasant incident. This sort of thing should never happen,' he said, nodding to Henry. 'Though Dr Bagnall did go on too long. We'll have to schedule him last next time.'

'Or not at all,' said Sarah.

Henry followed her down the steps. 'There's a lesson to be learned from every incident, our old parson used to say,' he said.

'Let's hope the good doctor has learned his,' Sarah said.

'Up with brevity.'

'And down with repetition.' She stopped and grinned at

292

him. He smiled back. The gap between his two front teeth reminded her of a rodent, of the endearing mole variety. Before she sat down next to Aunt Charlotte, she observed him moving along the line of seats several rows behind, and sitting next to Charles Barclay. Charles, a man of average appearance in every regard, looked slight next to Henry's tall figure.

'I wouldn't have missed this for the world,' she said to Aunt Charlotte, whose hat had become tilted at a jaunty angle in the excitement.

'Nor I. But the most interesting talks are yet to come. Do try to stay awake, Sarah dear!'

There was no chance that Sarah would fall asleep; she had too much to think of, including her father's speech. His words were as carefully reasoned as always, but he dropped the calmness of his usual conversation and adopted the language and cadences of the natural orator. The subjugation of women was political and psychological in origin. It was based on emotion and not reason, on prejudice and not logic, on feelings and not the intellect. And it was prejudice that had led to the creation of institutions and customs that perpetuate this subordination.

After the applause – the standing ovation that her father often received – Sarah couldn't resist turning around, and there was Henry, clapping along with the rest. He caught her eye and smiled. And then the audience sat down to hear what Mrs Buxton had to say. Sarah's father and Mrs Buxton were a double act. Her father roused the audience while Mrs Buxton described how the enfranchisement of women could be achieved.

After the meeting was over and the Camerons were heading into the street, she found that Henry was by her side. He told her he was to dine with Charles at his club. She calculated that, if they walked very slowly, they'd have about ten minutes of conversation before reaching the junction of Wimpole and New Cavendish Streets and the parting of their ways. She was acutely conscious of his presence but the wide brim of her hat, only inches from his shoulder, hid his expression.

'Is this the first time you've attended one of these meetings?' She tilted her head so she could see his face and almost tripped on an uneven paving stone, slippery in the damp. She caught her breath and coughed. The air was smoggy, heavy with soot. He held her elbow until she had righted herself and she was sorry when he let go.

'Yes,' he said. 'Of course, I do think that women should have the vote,' he added hastily, 'But I'm just not a political animal. Never have been.'

'My sister Harriet is a political animal, and so's my father, of course,' Sarah said. 'It's a shame she's at home with a bad cold.' But she was being hypocritical; she was glad Harriet hadn't been there, glad that Harriet wasn't accompanying her as she strolled beside Henry Vincent through the dense fog. 'Tonight wasn't typical,' she added. 'But at least you learned the history of the movement, or did you know that before?'

'I'm afraid I can't remember a word of what Dr Bagnall said. The other talks were different. Your father was downright inspiring. Mrs Buxton was short and to the point. I'll never forget this evening.'

She wondered if he meant their encounter or the riot at the back of the hall or the talks. After a moment's thought she decided he meant all three. 'I'll never forget it either. What brought you here?'

'Charles invited me.' Henry explained that he'd been back in England for only three months and that most of that time had been spent with his people in Suffolk. Indeed, this was only his second trip to London since his return. He was here on business for his father, and what a stroke of luck running into Charles at his club five days ago. He'd been at school with Charles' youngest brother and had often spent part of the school holidays at the Barclays' place in Scotland, so when he'd bumped into Charles it had been almost like meeting a member of his family. School friendships were like that, they lasted, especially for boys who'd been packed off to boarding school from the age of five. It must have been a good three years since he'd last seen Charles, just before he'd gone to Australia. Charles had immediately invited him to dinner but insisted that he first accompany him to the WFL meeting. But he was boring Sarah, he'd been babbling on like a brook in full flow, he really must apologise. He bent to peer under her hat. His face was framed with little tendrils of hair, curling in the damp air.

'Charles can be quite persistent,' she said. 'Father says that's why he's doing so well at the Colonial Office. What were you up to in Australia?'

'I worked at a stock and station agents in Sydney for a bit. That involved a lot of travelling around. Then I spent some time on a sheep station in the High Country of New South Wales.'

'The High Country. How lovely that sounds!' She estimated they were now about thirty seconds away from New Cavendish Street.

'They call the southern tablelands the High Country. Or the Monaro. I loved it there. So much space.' He paused and seemed to be struggling to express his thoughts. 'The light's harsh there. You can't escape it but it clarifies things somehow. It makes you see what matters and what doesn't.' He was speaking so softly that she could barely distinguish the words. 'I've never been good at explaining myself.'

'But you are. That's how I feel about music.' She wanted to continue but there was no time; her father and Charles Barclay had caught up with them.

295

'Charles tells me you've just returned from New South Wales,' Sarah's father said to Henry.

'Queensland too,' said Henry.

'We mustn't forget Queensland,' her father said, smiling. 'Would you like to come to tea next Sunday and tell us all about it?'

'I'd be delighted to.' Henry spoke with such haste that he almost stammered the words.

'Charles can show you where we are.' Sarah's father shook Henry's hand and then gave her his arm. She turned once, when they had gone ten yards, and saw Henry watching them as they walked down New Cavendish Street towards Bloomsbury. She nodded at him and he waved back.

She couldn't wait for next Sunday.

About the Author

Alison is the author of six novels and has contributed short stories to a number of collections. Her debut novel, *Stillwater Creek*, was Highly Commended in the 2011 ACT Book of the Year Award, and *A Perfect Marriage* was Highly Commended in the 2019 ACT Writing and Publishing Awards. Alison was Professor of Economics at the University of Essex until 2013 and is now Emeritus Professor at the Australian National University. For more information visit her fiction website at: https://www.alisonbooth.net/about

Find out more about RedDoor
Press and sign up to our
newsletter to hear about our
latest releases, author events,
exciting **competitions**
and more at

reddoorpress.co.uk

YOU CAN ALSO FOLLOW US:

 @RedDoorBooks

 Facebook.com/RedDoorPress

 @RedDoorBooks